NEVER GO ALONE

A *JAKE RIVETT* THRILLER

by

Denison Hatch

THE JAKE RIVETT SERIES

FLASH CRASH

NEVER GO ALONE

Praise for the first Jake Rivett thriller, *Flash Crash:*

"Dialogue as entertainingly raunchy as that in T*he Wolf of Wall Street* or the Showtime TV series *Billions*."

-Kirkus Reviews

"An absolute bullseye, reinventing the heist thriller for the information age."

-Best Thrillers

"Theft, murder, betrayal, and computer coding come together in *Flash Crash*. Deftly going from the rich world of bankers to the dregs of Chinatown, Hatch's pacing ensures there is never a dull moment."

-IndieReader Approved

"How far would you go to protect your family? The sooner Hatch writes more in this new Jake Rivett series, the better."

-San Francisco Book Review

For more information about Denison Hatch and to sign up for release announcements:

DenisonHatch.com

NEVER GO ALONE is a work of fiction. Names, characters, places, and incidents are the products of the author's imagination and/or are used fictitiously. Any resemblance to actual events, locales, or persons, living or dead, is entirely coincidental.

For more information about Denison Hatch:

DenisonHatch.com

ISBN: 0-9972812-3-5
ISBN-13: 978-0-9972812-3-1

THE FIRST RULE IS:

NEVER GO ALONE.

ONE

TWO FEET HAMMERED THE PAVEMENT. With movement as rapid as it was controlled, the explorer's muscles tensed for what was to come. The target, all twenty stories of unabashedly neo-classical splendor, towered across the street. Infiltrating the building would be easy, but the next step was difficult. And the rest? Brilliant meets impossible.

The explorer was wearing a small camera on his chest, which captured his viewpoint with slightly shaky but high-definition clarity. A parking post stood ahead—cement poured into a strong iron tube. The man sprinted forward and vaulted onto the post. He maintained his momentum, springing off the top of the post onto an enormous industrial air-conditioning unit. Now eight feet in the air, he had only one stride before his next jump. He sailed through the empty air, arms outstretched, fingers tensing—a twelve-foot-high brick wall ahead. Just reaching the wall, the explorer's fingers grasped the edge. His right hand couldn't find traction. His fingernails scraped desperately as he started to fall. But two fingers on his left hand did their job. He hung on, swinging precariously before centering himself and pulling his body up and over the wall.

The explorer dropped down on the other side. His body contracted into a tight ball as he careened toward the construction gravel below. At the last moment, he rotated and achieved a rolling landing—lessening gravity's impact. He came to a stop. Breathing heavily, he took a brief respite from the task at hand. His chest heaved as he peered around the construction site that he'd just infiltrated. He knew that a lone security guard sat in a booth on the other side of the block. But he also knew the guard was engrossed in his cell phone, only stopping occasionally to gaze onto an adjoining street. As long as the explorer was quiet, the guard would be none the wiser. The coast was clear. He reached for a mic attached to the side strap of his backpack.

"All silent. Only one clown in the circus," the explorer whispered into the microphone. Still out of breath, he reached for his hydration tube and took a long sip of water. Then he rotated and watched as three more compatriots covertly slid over the top of the tall brick wall.

They each hit the ground in the same rolling manner, limiting trauma with expert precision. The entire crew was clad in dark outdoor technical clothes, breathable shirts, top-of-the-line Gore-Tex pants and trail runners with all reflective surfaces blocked out by black Sharpie. Their faces were covered by bandanas or ski masks. Respirators, climbing gear, knives, and cameras were both hanging from and strapped to their belts and backpacks.

The crew split in three different directions, acting as lookouts for any errant guard or construction manager onsite in the middle of the night. It was unlikely, but their plans called for extreme caution. That's what had made them so successful—their secret sauce was not daring; it was preparation. After confirming that the others were in position, the explorer focused on the mission at hand.

An enormous tower crane stood against the edge of the construction site. Built like a towering T, the machine's base was a concrete shithouse holding up three hundred feet of crisscrossing steel. The explorer expertly grabbed the side of the crane. Instead of heading for the control booth at the bottom, he simply began to ascend up the latticework that made up the sides—hands followed by legs on an upstream ladder.

Stopping midway to catch his breath, the man couldn't help but look down. Vertigo's tendrils reached out like forbidden fruit. His foot wavered to catch hold of a one-inch bar of the latticework. But he controlled the panic, centered himself, and continued climbing.

A few minutes later, the explorer reached the top of the crane. He pulled himself over the T's edge and gazed along the hundred-and-fifty-foot-length atop the long horizontal span. Instead of traversing in the direction of the construction site from which he'd originated, the explorer headed the opposite way. Careful with the placement of his feet, he headed towards the side of the crane that extended halfway across the street below. It was a slow process. The latticework consisted of both ninety-degree and diagonal pieces of steel, like a series of bars with a crosshatch pattern strung across it. And between the pieces of the crane's structure was nothing—a dark void. One misstep, one hesitation, one dash of grease and the explorer would plummet over twenty stories through thin air and become one with the blacktop of the city. It was not a pleasant thought, making the already difficult process deeply nerve-wracking.

"You will not bust." The man talked himself through the fear as he reached the far end of the crane. He was now extended as far across the street below as the machinery would take him.

The explorer gazed down the gleaming city from the Upper West Side, all the way through Midtown and into Chelsea. It was more than a place now, more than a landscape. By this point at its evolution, Manhattan represented a geospatial-and-social coordinate on the razor's edge of modernity. It was no longer what the future could be. It was the future itself, right now, happening in front of one's eyes and reaching the stage of infinite singularity. As the years had gone on, the surfaces of the metropolis had become smooth, the lights perfect, the façades utterly complete. It no longer beckoned for the masses humbly—*it repelled them.* The construction site the explorer had ascended from would soon consist of glass, marble, and sex. That was all, and that was everything, and if one was rich enough, one could buy it. The new culture didn't care for culture itself. It did not bow to subtlety of argument or freedom of soul. It only knew money—astronomical levels of money. The only people who could afford to live here would be the progeny of sovereign wealth fund managers, tech moonshot winners, and industrial titans. Nothing was free, for anyone—not even the views.

Except for our explorer—right now. It was his, alone. He admired the panorama of New York. Yes, there was the mission, but this was deserving of a photograph. He pulled the camera off his chest harness, activated selfie mode, and turned it towards himself. He lined up, framing the background of the city behind him. *Click.* The camera's flash erupted. He flipped his hand down, as if to form an upside down V slogan. *Click.* Another flash—another selfie—his face shrouded by a hood throughout the entire process.

Having finished memorializing the scene, the man ducked down towards the crane. As he secured something to the crane, he gazed away from the construction site and towards his target.

A sharp contrast to the modern structures popping up like weeds, the limestone apartment building across the street was built during the turn of the century—the last century, not this. Its hulking body did not undulate as it rose. Instead the building consisted of strong vertical bands that ran up to form elaborate choragic arches and support the pointed top of the roof. Four large penthouse balconies graced each corner of the building, easily visible to the explorer who stood above them on the crane. He breathed deeply, then jumped off the crane into the darkness below.

Suspended by a climbing rope, the man careened from the top of the crane and over the street, until he was positioned directly above the penthouse balcony of the old building. The pendulum continued, however, and he swung back.

The second time he was ready. His toes landed lithely on the penthouse's balcony. He paced towards the enclosed glass greenhouse. One of the small windows of the greenhouse was unlatched, exposing a sliver of access.

The explorer carefully maneuvered the window open.

He climbed into the penthouse.

And the city's lights twinkled as if nothing had happened at all . . .

TWO

JAKE EASTON SAT IN THE shotgun seat of an old Honda Civic, ripping through the West Bronx in the utter dead of night. A heavyset Dominican named Jonny Diaz sat behind him, engrossed in a video compilation of backyard brawls and twerkin' chicks. Diaz cackled repeatedly, always reaching a high-pitched crescendo with each guffaw. Also in the backseat was a dark-skinned man of unknown ethnic origin. Jake only knew him by his misnomer of a nickname, "Shrek." Shrek was actually skinny. Almost as thin as Jake himself. And he was always nervous, like a canine lacking socialization. Shrek's knee bounced up and down and he wiped down his nose obsessively as he gazed out the window at the city's neon world. The car was driven by their crew's leader—Hector Trizzo. Mexican-black with tightly curled hair and Polynesian patterns shaved into the sides and back of his hair, the bank job tonight was all part of Hector's grand plan. But what neither Hector, nor Jon or Shrek knew, was that the man they knew as "Eastie" was actually an undercover NYPD detective named Jake Rivett.

"You're gonna let him use that phone, Hec?" Jake inquired, nodding back to Diaz.

"What are you? My stewardess?" Diaz protested. "I need it to relax, homie. Ask Shrek. I get nervous . . ."

"I didn't come here for amateur hour," Jake shook his head angrily. "And I ain't about to get picked up 'cause your fat ass has ADHD and can't stand a minute of silence in his life. Don't you know how the police operate? It won't be less than six hours; they'll be pullin' data from every tower in a couple-mile radius from the bank."

"Oh, and you're a savant when it comes to the 5-0 just 'cause you sell hot parts outta your apartment all day?" Diaz responded.

"Chill out," Hector commanded. "Jonny, turn off your phone. Pull the battery like Jake says."

The bank branch was a recent addition to the neighborhood—the result of an enormous, nationwide, debt-fueled expansion. It stood out like a sore thumb among the densely packed rows of bodegas, thrift shops, and merchants that populated the rest of the neighborhood. The vertical columns that delineated the bank's outline along the street consisted of, no doubt, the same color blue from New York to Mississippi to Alaska. Hector hadn't picked it because of any particular opinion regarding the value—or lack thereof—of the rampant post-recession gentrification that was affecting the city. But the irony was that his decision was informed by the sociological wave nonetheless.

Hector had explained his targeting philosophy in detail to Jake a few days prior. He refused to go after a local community bank or credit union. The reason for that wasn't due to the amount of cash available within, or any sense of right and wrong when it came to denigrating his own community. It was because while a local bank might actually give a crap, Hector knew that this big, national bank wouldn't take the loss personally. The CEO of a credit union actually knew people who lived on these streets. He or she might actually attempt to liaison with the police, hit the streets and locate Hector. But the CEO of their target bank wouldn't even be told that his ATM was jacked the night before. The heist would just become another consolidated line item. The bank's blue was decided on Madison Avenue, credit and debit cards printed in Pennsylvania, ads shot in Culver City, and its insurance came from London. As a whole, the entity that they were about to rob was so strewn out across the globe as to be completely disconnected from itself. It was an octopus that couldn't see its own arms. And although there was a Wells Fargo, a Bank of America, and an M&T Bank all within a twenty-block radius, this was the one. That's because it had a cash machine that nakedly faced the sidewalk. It wasn't protected. No card swipe required, nor bulletproof glass to circumvent. One could step right on up to it.

Hector passed the ATM and parked a block away. All four men pulled masks down across their faces. They stepped out and popped the trunk. Inside were two large pressurized tanks. Similar to scuba tanks in size, one was filled with oxygen and the other with acetylene. Available at most industrial hardware centers, acetylene was a highly flammable gas used most often for industrial welding applications. For example, if one had to ensure that an airplane wing wouldn't disintegrate mid-flight, acetylene was clutch. But in addition to its utilitarian capabilities, acetylene possessed another fascinating feature: When exposed to pure oxygen, it would spontaneously combust.

Oxy-acetylene bombings on cash machines began in Europe in the early two thousands. But they were still very rare. The vast majority of the criminal class still preferred the old techniques; stick up a customer afterwards or crowbar the thing open. The first oxy-acetylene bombing on United States soil had occurred six months ago in New Jersey. That's when Jake Rivett had taken interest. He'd spent the last six months ingratiating himself with Hector's crew. Now Hector trusted Jake more than he did his best friend, Jonny. Hector was the only criminal in the entire country who was using this method to break into ATMs, and Jake—and by extension the entire police force—were extremely curious who had taught him the tactic. Or had he figured it out himself? Jake hadn't gotten that far in the investigation yet, but the odds did not point towards Hector's lone and personal mastery of the subject.

Jake lifted the oxygen out of Hector's trunk, and Jonny picked up the heavier acetylene tank. Hector grabbed a bag holding a series of required accessories. The four of them headed towards the ATM, with Shrek slinking into a shadow to serve as lookout. Jake placed his oxygen tank about fifteen feet away from the machine—to the right. Diaz carefully positioned the acetylene to the left. Hector yanked a screwdriver from his bag. He gently pushed the tool into the cash dispenser slot of the ATM. The plastic slide quickly gave way. Hector jammed a wooden wedge into the slot, permanently holding it open.

"Gimme the tubes!" Hector called out.

Jake unwound a clear plastic tube—the diameter of a pencil—from the side of the oxygen tank. Diaz did the same on his side. Careful not to disengage the tubes from the regulators atop the tanks, Jake and Diaz walked towards one another. They converged near the ATM and passed each of their tubes to Hector. Hector wrapped a small rubber band around the tubes then jammed the open ends of the tubes, together, into the cash dispenser's slot. Hector pulled a quick-acting, gap-filling, expanding foam can from his bag—standard from Home Depot. He stuck the applicator into the dispenser's slot and injected a few square inches of synthetic material all along the crevice. Within seconds, the foam had expanded to form an airtight barrier, essentially sealing off the inside chassis of the cash machine.

"All righty, boys. Time for science class to begin. Acetylene first, Jonny."

Diaz obliged. He turned a dial on the regulator atop the acetylene tank and yelled, "It on!"

Hector glanced at his watch, counting down the seconds as pure acetylene began to pump into the inside of the ATM. "Seven . . . Six . . . Five . . ." As Hector ticked down, he slowly stepped away from the ATM vestibule. At "One," he signaled Jake. Jake turned his own dial, then instantly fell into a crouch, bracing for the epic-ness to come.

At first, there was nothing.

Then—*the supernova.*

A tremendous force rippled from within the interior of the machine —molecular chaos extrapolated to a macro-scale—as a gargantuan explosion erupted. The fireball was next. It was a tongue of red-hot terror, a whirling dervish of insanity, ripping the skin from the machine itself and blasting its screws, plastic sheathing, and metal supports in every direction. The sound followed the light, echoing down the street and unmistakable in its power.

His back still turned, Jake felt a ringing in his ears take hold. Tinnitus —his old friend from the rock clubs—back in action. Or was that screaming? It sounded like a wild, panicked yell. Jake glanced over his shoulder as he shut off the oxygen, past the ATM that was beginning to expel a cloud of black smoke and still flickering with small flames, and across the street.

"What do we do with her?" Shrek yelled.

Shrek was holding a gun to a young woman, nervously clutching her purse across the street. That was what Jake had heard. An eyewitness. She had turned the corner just as the explosive gas erupted.

"Jonny, grab the cash," Hector commanded. He turned to cross the street. Jake followed.

"We gotta take her out, boss." Shrek trembled under the influence of his own weapon and blood zeal.

"What'd you see?" Hector asked her.

"What? . . . Nothing! . . ." she quivered.

"Give her to me. I'll do it clean," Jake said. He held his hand out for Shrek's gun.

"No. I want the bitch," Shrek replied.

"We have four minutes, max. There's no time for anything except a skullshot—you ever killed a person, Shrek?"

"Uh . . . I want to," Shrek said.

Jake reached for Shrek's gun hand while jacking his right elbow up and into Shrek's windpipe. "Get the cash," Jake said.

Shrek reluctantly dropped the pistol into Jake's hand, and ran back across the street towards Jonny Diaz and the cash machine—guts open to the world and filled with crisp bills, half still in the machine and half littering the street.

"I'm good. Don't worry 'bout it. Keep an eye out for fivers," Jake nodded to Hector as he slapped the girl roughly and pulled her into an alley across the street.

He pushed the women against the brick wall, nestling his chin against her neck, centimeters from her ear. She was crying—bawling, actually—a poor soul who had found herself suddenly and accidentally standing on death's doorstep.

"Shut up," Jake addressed her roughly. "You are going to lie down on that ground, and you are not going to move for twenty-five minutes. Do you understand?"

"What . . . are you—"

"It's a yes, or die."

She didn't say another word. She immediately collapsed onto the pavement. Jake placed his gun an inch to the side of her head and pulled the trigger—twice. *Bang. Bang.* The shots echoed out across the street.

"Don't move," Jake said.

Jake turned heel and headed back towards the ATM. He reluctantly took a step onto the street when the sounds of police sirens began to rain through the air. The noise was very faint but sure to increase exponentially in volume within a minute or two. "Hector, we gotta go. Cherry tops are ringin'!" he yelled.

Hector, Jonny, and Shrek raced towards the car, where they met Jake. The four men piled into the vehicle. Hector started the engine and accelerated away from the destruction as the police sirens crescendoed.

And through it all, the blue pillars of the bank's branch shone bright, although the logo above the cash machine flickered on and off. The ATM itself was now nothing more than a gouged-out cave—appearing as if an asteroid had arrived from outer space and dug itself a hole where the machine used to be. Smoking detritus was strewn across the street, and for a few seconds more, the only living thing was the young lady.

But Hector didn't know that.

"You the real deal, Eastie . . . Holy shit! The Iceman cometh. Ice in the veins all the way to 'da heart . . . Exactly the way I like it. My boy! Welcome to the fuckin' crew." Hector grinned wildly at Jake as they fled the scene. Jake grimaced—a passive confirmation of his badassdom. Hector and his crew thought this was living. But Jake was quite sure that it was closer to dying.

▪

The warehouse doubled as a supply depot for Hector's "legitimate" motorcycle-part distribution business, Fireblade Motortech. It was a bare bones and run down spot with just enough shelving and lighting to maintain a small operation. The four men stood around a table and inspected their haul. Jake and Shrek organized the bills, while Jonny— finally back on Wi-Fi—played on his cell phone by the door. Hector placed a cash counting machine on the table. Some of the bills were charred beyond belief, others ripped in shreds. The useable paper had been placed in piles of similar denominations. Hector reached for each stack, ran the cash through the machine, and compiled the corresponding results.

"Twenty-seven," Hector announced.

"Solid haul," Jake said.

"Maybe our definitions of 'solid' are different," Hector chuckled as he continued to count the cash. "Then again, you probably went to school longer than I did. That's a guarantee."

"Military school," Jake said.

"No shit? Sounds posh."

"Sure, if you like getting waterboarded for fun."

"Twenty-nine," Hector continued counting.

"Whatcha think we'll get to?" Jake asked.

Hector gazed out across the table, filled with cash. "Maybe seventy or eighty, tonight," he replied. "Your average ATM holds up to two hundred thousand dollars. But that's rare. We only hit one like that. Remember that place down in Brooklyn, Shrek?"

Shrek only cackled. He didn't talk much, and Jake considered that a beneficial fact in the long run.

"You're pullin' in a lot of dough," Jake said.

"What of it?" Hector asked.

"Nothin'. Just impressive. Hat's off. I been around the block a few times but ain't seen nothin' like this operation."

"Learned from the best."

"Who's that?" Jake asked.

Hector gazed towards Jake, who knew that he stood at a precipitous moment. But Hector wasn't suspicious. He was proud, and he wanted to impress Jake—because Jake had just upped him. Vanity destroys every man and Hector was no different. He lacked the circumspection to put up strong defenses. "Honest-to-goodness truth? I don't even know his name."

"Call him the Leviathan!" Jonny yelled from the door.

"Huh?"

"Truth," Hector said. "There's an organization. I don't know the top guy. No one does. He's the Leviathan. Rest of them are just like us—doing his bidding. That man controls everything. He gets a piece of this cash tonight. That's for sure."

"For serious? You do someone's bidding? I find that hard to believe," Jake said incredulously.

"Musta been a year and a half ago. Back when Jonny and I were just doing strong-arms and takin' down check cashing places. I was down at the Pickle and this Scandinavian bastard—Leviathan's top man—sits down next to me. He's got blond hair like yours. Nah. Actually, it's white as shit. Ain't never seen a man with hair like that. So I'm thinkin', this guy might be in the wrong place. Maybe he's some maggot. Might be a good mark. But then he leans over and he says, 'Hector, you pulled down what? Ten thousand last month bustin' check joints? Want to make ten times that?'

"No way," Jake replied, with a grin. "That sounds like 5-0."

"I put some feelers out. Everybody knows this guy. I mean everybody. Raffaeli's crew. The Belarusians. The Triads. Every single one. Call him the ghost. A week later, he gets in touch again. Like some spy," Hector held up his phone, "always from a different number. Always just a mumble: 'It's me.' I meet up with him. They blindfold me, drive me around all night. Bring me to a warehouse, like this one, and it's got an ATM right in the middle of it. And the ghost spends six hours talking. Teaches me the whole bust, right then and there. But that's not all. He funds it all. The burner phones, the cars. The gas. All I have to do is hit him back with twenty-five percent of the take."

"I had no idea . . ."

"Don't tell you everything. You're still a lil' wet behind the ears."

"Well, let me ask you the obvious question . . . You're a man with larceny in your blood. How would anyone know what twenty-five percent is?" Jake asked.

"You ever heard of a snuff video?"

"Of course," Jake replied.

"Showed me a guy who stole from them. Got the whole family there . . . I can't even tell you what they did to that fool. Sick fucks. Scared me, and you know I got thick skin."

"Crazy, dude. You said he's got a boss . . ."

"Ghost just calls him Leviathan. 'Cause he's huge. He's got fingers everywhere. I know I'm not the only one. They're funding crews all over the city."

"So he's like some sort of . . . kingpin?" Jake said.

"Why don't you be a little less amazed, and do a little more counting."

Jake turned back to the cash at hand. He tossed a charred bill into the trash heap. It landed with a thud. Or at least it sounded something like that to him. Jake whipped his head around. He had heard something.

Jonny did too. He was standing when—

An eight-inch-wide battering ram destroyed the front door. Jonny dove out of the way as four SWAT members piled into the room, screaming bloody murder, "Police, hands up!"

They quickly had Jonny in submission, hands over his head, hair pulled back, eyeballs exposed to burning flashlight rays.

Shrek, however, had different ideas. He reached for a gun sitting on a table. As he rotated towards the assault team with the weapon in hand, the rules of engagement came into play and his destiny was predetermined. Three shots rang out abruptly. A tight circle of holes formed on Shrek's chest. Dead center mass. Shrek collapsed to the ground.

In the back of the room, Jake had already lost sight of Hector, who was sprinting through a door and holding a bag stuffed hastily with cash. With a millisecond to spare, Jake followed Hector as the assault troops crushed decibels. Jake and Hector tore through a supply room and out a back door. Although Jake expected it to all be over in this moment, it wasn't. The police hadn't covered this door, one of a labyrinth of small alleyways and access roads between the cavernous warehouses of the district. They pulled a trash dumpster on wheels until it crossed over the threshold of the door by a few feet and glanced down the alleyway. To the right—a no go. To the left—perhaps. They tore left.

"Who cares about the bag?" Jake screamed, catching up with Hector.

"I can't lose this money."

"Huh?"

"Somebody gonna kill me either way if I don't have the dough. We go HAM. That's the only solution . . ."

They raced through another street and into a long alleyway. Past a fence, there appeared to be a wide-open exit ahead of them. They scaled the chain-link and sprinted towards the opening, dappled lights visible on the other side.

As they reached the opening, Jake discovered that it wasn't an exit at all. They stood atop a concrete bulwark about thirty feet in the air, a massive air gap below them. Down below the three-story open drop was the Cross Bronx expressway. Cars whizzed past with unprejudiced velocity. Hector reached the end a few steps behind Jake.

"Yo!" Hector yelled, trying to get Jake's attention. But Jake seemed to be transfixed by the height. The world was starting to wobble in his head, as if he'd suddenly ingested ten drinks in the timespan of seconds. Vertigo was a hell of a sensation, and its unyielding grasp had locked onto Jake. The feeling was similar to a trance—astonishing and emotionally gripping to the person afflicted yet also rendering them unable to react to the physical world. Hector suddenly pulled Jake out of his reverie. The two of them crashed down to the ground.

"You ain't gonna jump that, homie," Hector whispered.

"We're toast," Jake replied. They could now hear yelling down the corridor. A flashlight beam jostled up and down as it raced towards the chain-link fence separating them from the SWAT team.

"No shit, Sherlock," Hector said.

They stood up. Jake dusted himself off, glancing at the walls around him to see if it was possible to climb up onto the roof. But whoever had constructed these warehouses had done a good job, much to your average criminal's chagrin. The sides of the warehouse were glistening with slippery, high-gloss paint. It would be impossible, especially with only seconds counting down. A second flashlight appeared at the gate, and then the screaming of the black-suited SWAT team.

"Put your hands up! Don't move!" the officers screamed. Jake and Hector could view the dark shape of the first member of the SWAT team climbing over the fence. Then a second. Time was beyond the essence. There were just seconds of personal freedom ticking down inside Hector's brain, before a nice, long, and quaint spell in the pen. Better make the most of it. Jake also stared ahead at four SWAT team members racing towards them, their guns held forward. They were enraged, screaming like bloodhounds. And yet, neither Hector nor Jake moved.

"Get on the ground!" SWAT yelled at them, converging in a semicircle about ten feet from Hector and Jake.

"You thinkin' like me?" Hector asked Jake.

"For sure . . . Ride or die, baby. They try to teach us a lesson? We make it a good one," Jake replied.

"That ain't no question," Hector said.

Jake and Hector slowly raised their hands into the air.

"We have no weapons on us," Hector replied calmly to the approaching monsters.

"On the ground!" SWAT yelled. But the two suspects didn't move. It was a standoff worthy of Sergio Leone ambitions. Two of the four SWAT members lowered their guns and reached to their belts. They pulled out expandable stun batons, nasty contraptions in the shape of large Maglites with an electrical charge running throughout.

Hector channeled an NFL linebacker and dove headfirst at the oncoming SWAT officers. The officers smashed the back of Hector's head and his shoulders with their batons, electricity crackling into the air. Hector quickly succumbed, slumping to the ground in a lump.

Two more SWAT officers approached Jake. They bodyslammed him into the ground as more officers piled on. His eyes wild and wide as saucers, his long and dirty blond hair pulled behind his head, Jake was screaming as loud as he could. "You want me? You're gonna have to earn your pay!" He stuck his ass into the air.

Hector chuckled from his bloody and broken face as he watched Jake's histrionics.

The officers hit Jake repeatedly, finally forcing him into a prone position on the cement. Blood erupted from his nose, a hand jammed hard against his face, his cheek meeting the cement below like sandpaper on driftwood. But there was a maniacal grin on Jake's face the whole time. Almost like he was enjoying this.

And the truth was that . . . *he did.*

Because Jake was an actor in a play. The stage was his life. His circumstances weren't scripted, but they were absolutely predicated. And the other actors in the sphere? Some of them knew who he was behind the mask. And the rest—like his main man, Hector—certainly did not. If this were Broadway, he'd have champagne and air kisses waiting all night in the wings. It wasn't. There was only reality out there, blood dripping from his face, surrounded by the horrible people that operated within it.

The sets changed, but the lights burned hot as ever.

He wanted to scream out loud. He expanded his lungs as much as he could, and he tried to—but then Jake Rivett passed out.

THREE

JAKE'S HEAD SWAYED BACK AND forth groggily in the back of a police cruiser as he came to. He was alone in the backseat. Hector was nowhere to be seen. He could feel the early morning rays of sunshine against his face. He wasn't sure how long he'd been out, but in the meantime, the morning had sprung. As he peered out the window, his blurry vision eventually found focus. It was nature. He saw the bluffs of Rodman Neck and the Pelham Wildlife Sanctuary ripping past the windows. He knew exactly where he was being driven: along Shore Road, about to pass the golf course and enter New Rochelle proper. Although it was a beautiful and serene little town, it was the last place that Jake wanted to be. He avoided the place like the plague because he saw too much of his own self in the little house with the parents who told him what to do. He slammed his hands against the glass partition separating him from the blues in the front seats.

"Don't hurt yourself, Rivett. We're gonna write it all up," the officer in shotgun turned and stared daggers at him.

"Oh, come on . . ." Jake replied, "They pulled me in?"

"Mommy and Daddy are real pissed at you," the cop replied.

∎

The police car slowly maneuvered through the bucolic roads of New Rochelle, where city blocks gave way to tree-lined boulevards and grand homes with a slight fade. They eventually arrived at a perfectly suburban brick colonial at the end of a long cul-de-sac.

The front door to the large house opened, and a man and a woman stepped out, extremely irate looks on their faces. Jake watched them, standing with their arms over their chests like two stern Politburo officials. One of them—the one who looked like a third-grade teacher—he knew very well: Tony Villalon. And the other was Susan. Oh, Susan. How he loathed Susan Herlihy with every thumping beat of his heart.

The world had changed dramatically around Jake in the course of twelve months. It was still moving, actually. As much as he'd tried, he wasn't designed for the system and it felt the same way about him. A year ago—after he'd cracked the Montgomery Noyes gold robbery case—both he and Tony had been rewarded with the pick of the litter when it came to the trajectory of their careers.

Tony had chosen well, leapfrogging managers to become one himself. Jake had chosen in a manner true to himself. He'd stayed in the field. He'd ridden his bike directly into the center of Manhattan—Wall Street—and parked aside the Occupy Wall Street movement. He'd spent four months in Occupy and performed just about as well as everyone thought he would— as the most effective and natural undercover agent that the NYPD had on the streets. He was nothing less than the force's secret weapon, the cop who couldn't be a cop but wouldn't be anything else. His "cover" was hot goods. He had sold stolen cell phones and other electronics to the small percentage of the Occupy set with criminal intentions. A lucrative intel-generating enterprise and rock-solid reputation on the street had developed as a result. Others who needed cheap and untraceable electronics had heard about Jake, Hector Trizzo included. The rest was history.

■

Jake sat on a couch in the living room in New Rochelle. Susan and

Tony sat across from him. He was still having difficulty looking up to Tony, considering that a year ago Villalon had been at his beck and call. But such was the lesson. Politics were critical to ascension, and an aversion thereto could expose one's career to swift mortality. The paradoxical effect of Jake's career decisions, which were largely decided for him by his innate nature, was that Tony had vaulted up the ranks and was perhaps leading now. Jake didn't view his career as dead. It was just that the life he wanted didn't fit within the box. He was guided by black and white—not regulations.

Lieutenant Commander Susan Herlihy, well, she was another story altogether. Susan was a disciple of Tom Marks, the police commissioner. She was highly calculated and driven beyond belief. There was no way she slept. She supposedly had two kids, but Jake couldn't actually believe that. He knew for sure that the children's father was now long gone, and number two was a house husband. The woman was always politically correct, tough as nails, and perpetually done up to the nines. She was perpetually poised. It was very, very difficult to push her onto a back foot. She was a more aesthetically pleasing version of Hillary Clinton, possessing an impervious attitude that rankled Jake inside his soul. It wasn't because she was a woman. It was something else. Maybe he was just jealous. She was similar to him in mental toughness but light years ahead when it came to the strategy of it all. He played headbanger music in his spare time. She didn't have spare time, because she was too busy conducting sociological warfare all over the department. He understood that she was playing the game better than anyone in the entire police department. That's why she was running all of special investigations, including the major crimes division. And that's why whatever Susan Herlihy said, was Jake's law.

She looked fantastic today. She always did. That was her trademark. For a moment, he thought about what she'd be like in bed. She was probably scary. He wondered about her new man. What was he like? Jake presumed that he was one of those bearded fellows who brings the kids to school then goes home and pursues some sort of nascent creative "career." Some households have room for two alphas, but no home had room for Susan Herlihy and another one of her.

Behind him, Jake could hear the hustle and bustle of the house. At one point this mansion in New Rochelle had been a home. But now it was something else—a command center. The second Susan had tasted power, she'd moved the most covert aspects of the special investigations division to the safe house. It was one of the rare decisions that Jake respected. The department was too immense—a wet blanket of loose ends—and information could and did find itself going any which way.

The house in New Rochelle stopped that problem in its tracks. Most of the living room and all of the dining room consisted of long folding tables set up with flatscreens, scanners, printers, and lockboxes. A number of analysts and other plainclothes and undercover detectives worked throughout the home, including the upper floors.

"They said you enjoyed it," Susan began.

Jake cracked back to reality—and then, all could he do was grunt. His response wasn't really an affirmation, nor a denial. But then again Susan hadn't asked a question.

"You're not as mysterious as you think, Rivett. I'm well aware that you're a masochist. But I just don't want to be around on the day you get yourself offed."

"Yeah. That would look bad for you," Jake said.

"You really do think quite low of me, don't you?"

"Sorry. But . . ."

"But?" she asked.

"They're bad guys. What do you expect? Throw my hands up like a saint and prostrate myself on the floor while the rest of them are gearin' up for a battle?"

"I don't even need to ask you about the girl, do I?"

"She'll be fine," Jake said, then to reassure himself, "right?"

"I don't know. Do you care? You gave that poor woman an ear that's never going to work the same again. You're lucky she doesn't know who you are, and she's not going to find out, but I'm not thrilled . . ."

"Again, Suse," Jake started up . . .

"You can call me Susan, or Herlihy, like the rest," she said.

"You either want me to do a job, Herlihy, or you don't. If you don't, don't put me out there."

"Jake, c'mon, let's debrief. Get me in your headspace. Tell us about the scene at the ATM . . ." Tony popped in.

"That guy, the freak. The skinny one. They call him Shrek. He just starts going apeshit on this girl," Jake shrugged. "I had to jump in, frankly, 'cause I thought he was gonna kill her. I figured if I took control, Shrek couldn't take it back from me. But you gotta get it—it's nothing unusual. That's what they do, man—Hector, Jonny Diaz—all of 'em. They take it too far because that's their job description. Otherwise they'd be accountants or bread bakers, not biker thugs."

"Well, Shrek's dead. And Hector's in a cage now," Susan confirmed.

Jake took that in. "So that satisfies the department? Want to know why I really put up a little against the blues? Because the second I heard that megaphone, I got pissed. It was clear. You guys decided to just take the bird in hand. Get the easy caper. Get Hector. Hector ain't a prize. He's an idiot. Runs a crew. You know what's a prize? One word: Leviathan." Jake leaned in towards Tony's and Susan's blank faces. "I was so close. Until you ruined it. Hector opened up to me, man. There's a big boy out there, some huge force, a power we don't have a single bead on. He's above every single organizational crime chart that you'll find on any wall of this house. And yet, for some reason, you two aren't interested. What's up with that?"

"Look. You bring me proof, then maybe there's a conversation," Susan replied.

"My observation isn't proof? Should I write it down?"

"Crime solving is a probability game. It was time to bust Hector. Those guys were violent, horrific criminals."

"You threw the baby out with the bathwater."

"Don't question my decisions. You don't get to do that. That's why I wear heels every day and you wear boots," Susan said. She lifted her leg to flash red Christian Louboutin high heels that only a lady cop with a granite constitution would dare rock. "You really want me to speak to you like a child? The only thing keeping you in SID is me," Susan pointed to herself, "and Tony, who has the godly patience to put up with you."

"Just don't fight cops, Jake. You are a cop," Tony replied.

"Thank you, Tony."

Jake was a special animal and both Susan and Tony knew it. There was no use in arguing. His effectiveness was binary. You either let Jake Rivett go and do what he wanted, or you shut him down. There was no middle ground. Susan collected herself while Tony placed his hand into his pocket.

Jake noticed Tony pull a shiny, metallic blue carabiner out of his pocket—and begin to excitedly drum his fingers against it on the coffee table.

"What?" Jake asked.

"There's a new case . . . It's big," Tony responded.

"You can go ahead and refer to it as a blessing. The only thing standing in between you and the guillotine," Susan injected.

"How poetic," Jake replied.

"Ten robberies in six months," Tony said. "Some sort of master crew. We didn't connect the dots 'til we got the last one on video."

"What are they jacking?" Jake asked.

"Small rocks. Cash. Melt down stuff. Anything that's easy to flip," Susan said.

"But Jake? It isn't what. It's all about how." Tony stood up. He paced down the side of the living room and picked up a remote control. He changed the source of the seventy-inch 4K screen above the fireplace.

Surveillance footage from the crane climbing robbery flickered onto the screen: a view of a penthouse atop a grand limestone apartment building.

"It took us some time to connect it all. Luckily this time around, the construction company had rigged their whole site with hidden cameras. Every single robbery has been conducted with extremely unusual tactics. They're climbing in—like some sort of cat burglars mixed with mountain climbers." Tony pointed to the screen. "Guy lives alone in a fifteen-million-dollar penthouse. Locks the door but never turns on the alarm. Prolly because he's in the clouds and doesn't think bad guys can get up there. Wrong."

Against the side of the frame, Jake could make out a small, darkened figure slowly ascending a giant construction crane next door to the target building.

"This gent climbs the crane on the construction site next door. With no ropes," Tony narrated as the man swung from the crane's jib onto the balcony of the penthouse apartment. "The crane, as you can see, is actually extended across the street by a few feet—which they did not have permits for, incidentally. The person then swings across the street. He goes through an open window in the arboretum. They got more square feet for flowers than I got in my house. Anywho . . . Crew gets out clean with over two hundred large worth of gold and diamonds."

"Crew?" Jake asked.

Tony switched the feeds. Just a few minutes after the robbery, a few blurry figures were briefly visible near the base of the crane. They seemed to be lugging backpacks, ropes, and other gear.

"Wait, do you see that? That's a camera mount. They're filming?" Jake pointed.

"Already on that. They definitely seem equipped to film, but it doesn't look like they did. Not sure why you'd want to memorialize your crime anyways. But check this out. There was one unusual moment. Leads me to believe that we are dealing with younger individuals . . ." Tony clicked on the remote again. The surveillance footage cut back to the top of the crane. The original explorer pulled out his cell phone from his pocket. He turned the camera on himself, took a selfie, and flashed a hand symbol: an upside down V.

"Are you kidding me? He took a selfie?"

"Yes. Which is truly unintelligent," Susan added.

"Maybe," Jake thought for a moment. "It's dumb unless it's all you know. Unless that's your culture. Brag it out. If a tree falls in the forest and no one hears it, did it fall? That sort of thing . . ."

"Now look who's poetic," Susan grinned at Jake.

"They don't disable alarms or cameras," Tony continued. "They wear masks. They move fast. And even weirder, and arguably most importantly, they know how to get away. We haven't been able to pull any footage of them on the streets. They just appear and then they . . . disappear."

Jake noticed that Tony had continued spinning the bright blue carabiner, resembling a figure eight, on the coffee table ahead of him. "Tell me about that thing," Jake asked.

"First piece of gear that they've left behind. A figure-eight rappel. No prints or DNA. They're wearing gloves, of course."

"They're climbers . . ." Susan added.

"What sort of climbers are robbers?" Jake asked.

"That is indeed the question," Susan said. She took a deep breath, something else obviously on her mind. "There's a few more things you should know . . ."

"Always is," Jake grinned.

"Chief Marks has been appraised. But this comes from above him."

"Who's above Marks?" Jake asked, quizzically.

"Berg."

"Ronald Berg? The mayor?"

"You heard me. That entire building is owned by a man named Arthur Metropolis. Know him?"

"No," Jake said, shaking his head.

"Of course not. Metropolis owns a ton of real estate in the city. He's like a Milstein or the Zeckendorfs or Trump. The problem for Metropolis is four of the ten robberies we're investigating were in buildings owned by him. So he's concerned. And that's a problem not just for him—it's a problem for the robbers, and for us. Because Metropolis' best friend is Ronald Berg," Susan said.

"So what you're saying is he gives the mayor a lot of money?"

"I don't know. Don't care. All I know is that Berg is very interested in this case. It's gotta get solved—instantly. He's told Marks to place a whole bunch of resources into play. So you're off Hector, and you're on these . . . climbers." Susan paused. She tilted her eyes at Jake in an oddly menacing way, "Don't embarrass me." Susan stood up and walked away without another word. *Meeting adjourned.*

■

As the evening took hold, raindrops were falling in New Rochelle. Jake and Tony stood underneath the portico of the grand old home. They watched a guy operating a tow truck. He huffed it through the rain and rolled Jake's bike back onto the driveway next to the garage, having towed it from Hector's warehouse.

"I didn't want to say something in front of Susan . . ." Jake said.

"Huh?" Tony asked.

"She wants me to find these climbers, yea? Infiltrate. Ascertain responsibility . . ."

"Exactly," Tony said.

"Ironic."

"Why?"

"I have . . . some problems. With heights."

"Not my issue," Tony chuckled lightly. "You don't have to go, like, up there with them. Just need to be you. Make them think you're the coolest person they know—then rip their hearts out."

"I'm on it."

"Look. Any time you want, you know you can get outta the rain," Tony told Jake.

Jake put his hand on Tony's shoulder. "Nah. Can't do that."

"How come?"

"You all like our arrangement just how it is. You're both afraid of what will happen if I have to sit at a desk."

"Hey. I'm with you. We're solid all the way," Tony protested slightly, although they both knew there was a ton of truth behind Jake's statement.

"She'd crush me in ten seconds if her job depended on it," Jake pointed to the house.

"Susan? She's harmless."

He shook his head. "No. No, she isn't," Jake said. "I'll give her a little credit, though. She would never throw a sucker punch. At least she's the type of person that would stick a knife in my chest while she's staring me dead in the eyes."

"I got your back, Jake. You know that, right?"

"I want to."

"Yeah. I know you do," Tony said after reflection. "Be careful."

"I'm always safe. Check my record," Jake grinned. Tony chuckled.

Jake jumped onto his motorcycle. His headlamps blasted on. He revved the bike and churned out of the gate into the grim world.

FOUR

JAKE'S PAD WAS IN THE Bronx. It wasn't in the safest location on Earth, but it was chosen for multiple reasons that did not include well-being. The place was more than a location where Jake lived. Much more. It was the stage from which he performed his show. Appearances matter in all worlds, the criminal one not excluded. Jake had invested his entire life, 24/7, in the part. And if work-life separation was becoming nonexistent in the business world, it was completely blurred in the land of criminality. The hard truth of the new century was that bad guys no longer took anyone's word for anything—they only did deals with people with whom they'd partied and imbibed, fought against, and slept on the couch next to.

Technically, Jake wasn't supposed to actually be living at the apartment. Susan and the city paid the rent. But he'd begun to spend so much time there that he'd decided to strike his downtown lease and move up there full-time. It was a façade, yes. He'd put the parts of himself that he couldn't expose to the world into storage. But the rest of his reality mixed with the performance. It all swam around him. It was not black and white. His own life was the model for the personality of Jake "Eastie" Easton. Proper undercover tradecraft suggested keeping things simple. That's why Rivett maintained his real first name for each new legend—to protect himself if, for example, he ran into someone from the music club circuit while undercover. But he didn't find it hard to keep his stories straight. He'd always been many Jakes.

Jake entered the apartment. It was an elaborate staged set of a man in the midst of a choking criminal cloud. His shelves were filled with box upon box of stolen motorcycle parts, contraband, and electronics. As a motorcycle enthusiast, Hector Trizzo had proven a perfect target. Bank robberies were just Hector's side job. His bread-and-butter was a motorcycle repair shop a mile away from Jake's apartment. Jake had originally appealed to Hector by offering parts at a steep discount— winking in Hector's direction that there was a less-than-legal explanation behind Jake's ability to sell the stuff. Maybe it was hot. Maybe it wasn't. That was Jake's problem not Hector's. Needless to say, the approach had worked perfectly.

Pictures were pinned to the wall and sitting in haphazard frames. They depicted both Jake's life and his mission: Jake with Hector and the other Dominican bikers. Jake at Palace restaurant with tatted-up gangsters. Jake sitting on the steps of Zuccotti Park, just another Occupy protestor. And finally, a picture of a Jake, his blond hair spiked with gel, standing in front of a microphone—mouth agape and teeth bared as he screamed. That part of Jake's persona wasn't undercover at all. Singing was his hobby, something that had taken his mind off his problems since he was a little kid back in good ol' Albany.

"Screamo" was Jake's specialty, an aggressive genre of rock akin to ordering a vodka shot and chasing it with Everclear. His style was ferocious and completely unapologetic, and that fit well with the rough characters that he brushed shoulders against on a daily basis. At first, maybe a guy like Hector had thought it strange that Jake had microphones and amplifiers in his apartment. And maybe he would have asked a few more questions if Jake had popped up with Dave Matthews Band or—even worse—Coldplay. But when he opened his mouth and the screamo came out? No more questions. Jake was obviously off his rocker. There was no way that a man like that could ever be a pig. *Right?*

As the last year had progressed, Jake had learned that the social life of a criminal could be nothing short of awesome. Jake loved hanging out with the rough-and-tumble types of the world. He wasn't exactly sure why; he just knew how he felt. He felt better. He felt like he fit in. Perhaps that was because he'd grown up Mr. Goody-Two-Shoes and it had done absolutely zero for him. It could be the fact that Jake had spent his later teenage years rejecting convention, and so had Hector and the rest of those boys. Or maybe it was because these people would make his own father quake in his boots—a sensation Jake could never accomplish himself. There was, however, one aspect of Jake's undercover job that he steadily regretted: band time. Every few months, he'd be able to get out of the house and go practice down at the studios in the south end of the city. But it wasn't enough, and it was making the loose collection of musicians and friends that called themselves a band upset. Now that Hector was in jail, maybe he'd have time to go hit the mic hard again. Goddamn it was killing him to let the band down.

Jake passed by the rest of his musical paraphernalia and headed into the second bedroom, which doubled as an office. He flipped open the laptop on his desk. The bright computer screen was the only source of illumination in his apartment. He wasn't sure where to begin with the cat burglars, but he had his suspicions. The selfie, all that photography equipment—it wasn't random. He suspected that while this crew wouldn't be stupid enough to memorialize themselves at the scene of any crime, perhaps they were still out there in the digital sea. Most people, especially the younger ones, liked the Internet to know who they were.

Jake started with Google. He typed in "cat burglar." The only results were videos of actual cats engaging in mischievous deeds, and trailers from movies whose subject matter was fictionalized cat burglary. Jake thought for a moment. The person that he'd seen on the surveillance video looked and acted like a climber. But he hadn't been climbing rocks . . .

He typed in a few more words on YouTube: "crane climbing." The results piled up from all over the world. Jake selected one of the videos and played it. A group of Italian youth ascended the inside of an old rusted crane standing in a long-abandoned construction site. About to click away, Jake became entranced when he saw the kids arrive at the top of the crane. A few hundred feet in the air, they hung from the rusted behemoth with just a hand. One of them did a backflip. The third balanced on one leg. None of them seemed to care that they were one slip, one sweaty palm, one rusty break, away from certain death. Jake couldn't pull his eyes away—the insanity was just too much to comprehend. The video finished and a number of hashtags popped onto the screen.

As Jake browsed through the block of hashtags, he noticed one that the user had repeated three times: #urbanexploration. Jake clicked on the hashtag and was greeted with another long feed filled with urban exploration videos.

"Urban exploration . . . Hell is that?" Jake muttered under his breath. He selected another #urbanexploration video: GoPro footage of a group of German youth in Dusseldorf. They were pacing steadily through a drainage pipe, seemingly underneath the city. The beams from their head-mounted flashlights illuminated an eerie pathway down the drain. As they chattered in German, the growing sound of industrial machinery could be heard, growing steadily until it drowned out their words altogether. The group turned a corner to discover a large gear turning above the water, powered by a huge turbine beneath the surface. All of a sudden, one of the kids in front was swept off his feet—caught by the unseen turbine. The machinery whipped him around in a circle once, then again, as he flailed wildly in an attempt to grab a breath between dunkings. The other members of the crew screamed. One of their braver souls stepped forward —ostensibly a few inches from the radius of the gear—and extended his arm into the dark water. The explorer pulled his friend to safety, and the rest of them ran the other direction down the sewer, yelling and chattering.

"What the—" Jake exclaimed and gasped. He realized he'd been holding his breath the entire time. Jake kept clicking. On videos of various urban explorers around the world. On illegal infiltrations. On skyscraper toppers. On tunnel sledding. He eventually found himself watching another pulse-pounding cut of a climber in Europe, nicknamed "Spiderman," free climbing the side of a glass skyscraper—no rope or harness in sight. As that clip ended, Jake observed the name of the uploader. He'd noticed the same user on a few of the more remarkable videos he'd just witnessed. Another derivation of #urbanexplorer, the username was "NYCUrbex." Jake clicked through to NYCUrbex's profile page.

NYCUrbex's profile was connected to an independent social media site called UrbEx. Jake explored the site. Although fairly haphazard and old-school in construction—not mirroring perfectly formatted sites of the moment like Facebook—UrbEx appeared to be a social hub for urban explorers around the world. This was their digital locus point, the place where they gravitated and discussed locations for exploration, analyzed tactics for infiltration and safe passage, and posted their latest experiences via videos and photos.

In the photos section, Jake was greeted by a number of self-submitted galleries. He found the gallery titled "NYCUrbex"—again mirroring the name that he'd noticed on the YouTube videos. Jake swiped through photos of urban explorers all over Manhattan. Most of the people in the pictures were wearing masks. A few were not, including a red-haired woman in her twenties who consistently appeared within. Something about her face appealed to Jake. Her eyes—they were vital. They spoke to him, ripping all the way from server to server, arriving on his laptop and attacking him from the screen itself. He saw the fanciful sense of adventure associated with a child who has not become numb to the world. He wasn't sure why she struck him so deeply, but perhaps it was because what he saw in her expression he missed in himself. Then again—he shook his head in a wobbly circle—he probably wasn't the only guy in the world who'd seen this woman and liked her. She was magnetic. His charge wasn't unique.

When Jake scrolled to the very last photo in the album, the hairs on the back of his neck flew straight up. The last photo. The same red-haired girl. She was standing on the top of a roof with the skyline of Manhattan behind her. But that wasn't the important part. In the bottom corner of the photo, she held her hand down towards the camera. Her two fingers and hand contorted into an upside down peace sign—*a reverse V.*

"Well, hello there . . ." Jake grinned. He clicked on her profile.

It was private—locked.

Jake spent the next hour creating his own profile on UrbEx. He already possessed a cache of images for this use. For the last year, he'd populated and constantly updated Instagram, Facebook, and Twitter accounts as Eastie. Unfortunately, most of the photos of Jake with Hector and Jonny wouldn't fit naturally on the UrbEx site. But a few would do. Jake yanked a couple clips from Occupy, and even a band photo. He uploaded all of them onto the UrbEx website. He tapped out a brief biography. Even though Jake had never done a lick of "urban exploring" in his life, he purported to be a beginner who'd already done a few runs. He was looking to get more involved in the community. He hated authority. He was down for anything. Hit him up for adventure; he was avail. After Jake finished creating his profile, he attempted to add the red-haired chick again. This time he was allowed to submit the friend request. But her profile was still private. Oh well. Now he'd wait. Anyway, Hector was in the pen, and it was time to celebrate the way he liked it—all by himself.

▪

Jake pulled up to the side of the Silver Pickle, a small bar in the Bronx. A half-illuminated neon sign distinguished the place from the storefronts that surrounded it. The sign didn't say, "Silver Pickle." Instead, it read, "Bar." But only the "B" and half of the "a" were visible. The only way that one would ever know the real name of this watering hole was by sitting at the bar for a few evenings over the course of a few weeks—and hearing it referred to as the Pickle. The Silver Pickle did not advertise. It was not

Web 2.0 savvy. Its only "savvy" was in magically transforming a one-ounce pour into three or four ounces. You went to the Pickle to get sawdust in your shoes and emerge shitfaced.

Jake walked through the long, thin bar filled with smoke and shadows. The Pickle was the type of place where you mind your own business unless you're a regular, and even then, it might be best to not pay too much attention to the guy next to you. Jake sat by himself at the bar. The bartender, Nikki, glanced at his broken-in face with a raised eyebrow, a rail-thin hourglass with tattoos rising up the sides of her neck. She sauntered over in Jake's direction.

"Business?" Nikki asked.

"Pleasure."

Nikki snorted in response. Exactly what she expected out of Jake Easton.

"At least they were cops . . ."

"Bullshit," Nikki flashed a grin at Jake, as if to indicate that she was in on the joke. "See ya never." She jammed her middle finger in the air at Jake, who couldn't help but smirk.

"Ea-Eastie . . ." a voice stammered from behind him. Jake turned and was shocked to discover Jonny Diaz approaching with a cousin, José. They hurriedly rushed towards Jake and sidled up at the bar, nervously glancing in all directions.

"Bro? What up? You seen Hector?" Jonny asked.

"No bail for him, man," Jake leaned in and spoke conspiratorially. "That was some gnar gnar. How'd you get out? You hear about Shrek?"

"Guy's an idiot," Jonny replied.

It takes one to know one. But Jake held his tongue as Diaz continued.

"I got first-timer too, homie. Figured all y'all were goners. Made some plans . . . José and I are gonna jet. You think that's a good idea?"

"A hundred percent," Jake replied.

"Head south till the heat's over. Boca or somethin' . . . You wanna roll with us, homie?"

Jake acted as if he was contemplating the notion. He glanced at Nikki for a moment. "Nah. I gotta stick here and risk it."

Diaz stuck his fist out to Jake, who pounded it.

"You a loner, dawg. I give you shit for that, but I guess it's what a man needs sometimes."

"Thanks."

"All right, we out," Jonny said.

"Wait a minute. You gonna have a burner? Gimme the number."

"No way. Hardcore underground. Till next time, kid."

Jonny and his cousin exited the bar.

Jake glanced around. Nikki hadn't even served him yet. The second bartender was at the far end of the bar, but Jake preferred Nikki. He rotated on his chair to spot her serving a rowdy group of white greasers at a booth across the room. She was flaunting her stuff, leaning down low as she served them beers from a tray. One of the guys slapped her thigh. She didn't stop him. So he grabbed it again, harder this time. This time she twisted out of it with a smile. She shook her finger at the greaser, not quite admonishing him. It was almost a come-on. Jake grimaced as she returned behind the bar.

"Why are you such a tease?" he asked.

"I'm a bartender," she said. She noticed Jake trying to open his mouth to retort. "Everybody has to make their money somehow. Sort of like that face you got on right now. You're not going to preach to me about the merits of good behavior, hunny bunny." Nikki slammed down two shot glasses in front of her and Jake. She poured a shot of 151 into the two glasses.

"One fifty-one?" Jake asked.

"Don't complain. It's on the house."

"In that case, I'll take a beer too."

Nikki grabbed a beer for Jake. She popped it open and slid it across the bar.

"So what's happenin'?" she asked.

"Nothin."

"What happened to you? For real . . ."

"Doesn't matter."

"You don't care about anything. I know that. Mr. Nihil. But you wanna know the truth? I care. I care about you, Jake. Just a little and I would never tell anyone else that. But sorry for asking."

"Got in a fight," Jake shrugged.

"You better drink up then, honey. It'll wipe away the pain."

"Never does."

"At least take a double," she said as she topped off his drink.

"Thanks," Jake grinned. The two of them noticed the greasers motioning for Nikki to come back. "Why don't you go flirt with those pricks a little more?"

"Yeah, I will," Nikki said. Nikki and Jake tapped the shots together and chugged them. She slammed her shot glass down on the bar. "And the whole time I do, I'll be thinking about the gift I'm givin' you after close," she said. Nikki walked away from Jake mock-shaking her butt at him. He couldn't help but grin as he sipped his beer.

▪

A few hours later, the Pickle's neon sign was extinguished. All the clients were gone. But two humans still lingered inside. In the back room, Jake banged Nikki from behind, next to the refrigerator while she held onto a sink.

"You want to come over?" Nikki asked him.

"Uh . . . Nah . . ." Jake said between gasps.

"What about your place?"

"This is fine."

She said nothing.

"Right?" he asked.

"Just shut the fuck up, Jake."

▪

Completely plastered, Jake pulled himself up the stairs to his apartment. He dropped to the floor and passed out.

An hour later, Jake woke from his dead slumber with a panicked shake. What was that? He listened carefully. He could distinctly hear something buzzing.

"Dammit," Jake grumbled. Even in his wasted state, he knew exactly where the noise was coming from. He sighed. He crawled through his apartment, the world still wobbling around him. He crouched down to the right of his desk. He pushed one end of a small piece of hardwood flooring. The wooden unit levered upward—revealing a small safe that had been installed, faceup, in the floor. Jake spun the safe's lock. He opened it. His police badge, two cell phones, a wallet, and a few documents lay in the safe. He pulled out one of the phones, turned it over in his hands. One new voicemail. Jake sighed. His Mom—the real one. He played the message, and the voice of his mother rang out from the speakerphone.

"Hi, honey. It's your mother. Haven't heard your voice in a while, and well, Dad's asleep now. Sorry that I didn't call earlier. We miss you up here. Anyway, you know why I'm calling . . . Happy birthday, Jakey."

Then Jake Rivett collapsed back into unconsciousness.

FIVE

THE MORNING AFTER HIS BIRTHDAY, Jake had even more missed calls to swipe through. But they weren't from friends or family. It was the job. He was required at headquarters.

On his ride into the heart of the city and One Police Plaza, while ripping south on the FDR and obeying no traffic laws at all, Jake thought about his mother. His relationship with her was complicated. With his dad, it was very simple. He hated the moron. His mother was different. He loved her, but he couldn't help but blame her for some of his circumstances. No human can escape the building blocks from which he or she developed. Life is a pyramid in a multitude of ways, and the structure at the bottom of Jake's personal temple had always been shaky. Not that the message he'd received didn't ping somewhere deep down inside heart. It did. It reminded him of how vulnerable his mom was— how alone. The irony was that after all these years of cohabitating with Jake's father, she was still by herself and so was Jake. At the same time, it could have been worse. The best thing that Jake ever did for his family was leave. But that didn't make it less tough. He wanted to call her back. He really did. But he wouldn't.

∎

Jake paced along the familiar corridors of One Police Plaza. He padded across the detective bullpen and past his old office. A clean-shaven man, about his own age, stared back blankly at Jake. Rivett didn't even recognize the guy who now occupied his former workspace. That wasn't the nature of most police departments, but it certainly was in New York. The volume of crime was astronomical and the volume of new detective recruits equally high. In fact, many beat cops spent their entire careers trying to become detectives, only to burn out or transfer out within a handful of years. Jake had once been a boy in blue as well. He'd spent the minimum time required—two years—out in a patrol car. He'd gotten his gold shield ten months after that; primarily due to the sources he'd managed to scrounge up while on patrol in Chinatown. While Jake's ability to measure people was strong, his ability to split them open was legendary. As was his chutzpah. He was like a pit bull when it came to everything, cases not excluded. That was why, during his first few years as a detective, not a single one of his cases went unsolved. But his discipline was another thing altogether. The department was half squares and half circles, but he was four-dimensional. It was a simple as that. Although they appreciated that he was on their side, no one really understood Jake, nor wanted to emulate him.

He was a free spirit, and his ability as a detective went hand in hand with his lifestyle. If a night of watered-down beers with his frenemy and Chinatown contact, Sunny, turned into a weekend bender that ended at a strip club in Long Island with Sunny completely naked and covered in menstrual blood? Fantastic. Jake had a Triad chief on speed dial. What did Tony Villalon and the other grunts have? A worn-in couch from Pottery Barn. No—the other detectives didn't really get him. None of them did, except for one. Jake had recently concluded that although Tony tried his damn best, the only person who had really figured Jake out was that evil bitch—

"How drunk are you on a scale from four to ten?" Susan Herlihy asked.

Susan—standing right in front of him. Speak of the devil.

"Hello, Susan. Always beautiful to see you," Jake said.

"You too, big boy."

"Coming in with us?" Tony stood behind Susan.

"He's here already?" Jake asked.

Tony nodded his head towards a conference room down the hallway.

"Maybe you should just observe," Susan added.

"For once, I agree with you."

"He's a victim. What's it matter?" Tony said.

"Our victim has more power in this building than I do," Susan remarked.

"Exactly. Even better reason to stay out of his eye line," Jake replied.

"Ready, boss?" Tony asked Susan.

"Ever-ready," Susan said.

"Hey. You guys sprang Jonny Diaz already?" Jake asked.

"The Trizzo case has a lot of issues, Jake. Diaz is the least of them," Susan replied.

"Okay. I don't know what that means. But okay."

Jake turned towards a second door, through which he would find an observation room hidden behind a double-sided mirror.

"Rivett . . ." Susan said.

Jake turned.

"Happy birthday. Belated."

"It's your birthday?" Tony asked, oblivious.

Jake shook his head and entered the dark observation room. He really hated her—did that mean he loved her too? That's how it usually went down with Jake.

▪

Arthur Metropolis pranced into the interview a god amongst men. He'd become much better looking as he aged. That phenomenon was not a function of genetics but of money. Arthur's success in the real estate markets of New England and the Mid-Atlantic had allowed for his refined nose jobs, for the skin around his neck to be pulled back and ever-so-gently eliminate his wrinkles. It had permitted the impeccable French tailoring of his shirt and the suit—bespoke—from Italy. Arthur's style wasn't absolutely ostentatious, but it was not refined. Even though his lips now stood still, he wasn't a man with a stiff upper lip. He wanted everyone to look at him when he walked through the door, no matter what door it was. And before he'd even sat down, it was clear: Susan and Tony were the audience members and he was the entertainment.

Perhaps this instinct was a function of his childhood in South Carolina. He was born Arthur Hynes, to a family of farmers who had steadily maneuvered themselves from the middle class into poverty as international agribusiness ate their lunch. Arthur was smart, but not the type of man who aced exams in school. He'd managed to move to Atlanta for college, on scholarship, where he'd studied education. Originally, he'd wanted to become a teacher. But the job market had become difficult in the late eighties, and after his graduation, Arthur hadn't been able to find a job. The best that he could muster was an assistant property manager position at a public school in Philadelphia for misbehaving youth. The Child Pilot School was a grim place, a step away from full juvenile hall admittance. Every single student was on public welfare. Legend had it that Arthur's first assignment, on his first day on the job at Child Pilot, was mopping the floors of the bathroom. It was legend and it was also true. And it was in his autobiography, the one that Arthur had published two years ago with a press tour and plenty of publicity. Publicity—or air, as he only semi-jokingly referred to it—was everything to Arthur Metropolis.

When one door closes, another opens. That's what Arthur had learned by now. Never known for his raw intelligence, Arthur had other tools—like the perfect gift of gab and a very friendly Southern attitude. All of the ladies, including the principal at Child Pilot, loved him. He was a hard worker. He paid attention to details. And that put him way ahead of the pack. After a few years, he had been promoted to the head property manager of the school. In his late twenties by this point, with the nineteen-eighties wrapping up, Arthur's life wasn't anything close to autobiography-worthy. He was happy to be off the farm, but he'd replaced it with an urban landscape only marginally better. He'd go to the movie theater on South Street on the weekends. He loved films. They offered him an escape from real life, beautiful women up close, and men who wielded raw power with the tilt of a head. He loved crime thrillers in particular. *Scarface* was a personal favorite. That was primarily because Arthur saw a bit of himself in Al Pacino's character, Tony Montana. Not the crime and violence, per se. But the urge. The overwhelming desire for something better—and the knowledge, deep down inside, that one's future was destined to be better than the present. And it was while Arthur was sitting in the movie theatre's bathroom that his own future came calling.

"Make Millions in Real Estate with No Money Down" was the title of the small notice that had been taped to the inside door of the bathroom stall. It was one of those "pull this tab" posters with a phone number on each piece. And as Arthur stared up at the poster and the smiling face of "Cash Johnston," he felt something stir inside his soul. He yanked that tag off the door and jammed it into his pocket. The next day, he called the phone number and signed up for a weekend course at the Hilton in downtown Philadelphia. The information wasn't half-bad. Arthur had taken copious notes. Each night, he read over his papers before he went to bed—something he'd never done in college. Beyond the details relating to attracting financing and locating properties on the cheap, the fundamental tenet of Cash's philosophy was "The Edge." The Edge could occur in many different ways and in any industry. But without it, one was fighting an uphill battle against forces larger than one's self. Cash made it clear. Life, business, success—it was all zero sum. Cut a corner, know someone or something, get an edge. Or else.

Arthur had no edges at all. The only organization that he knew intimately was Child Pilot School, and it was a nonprofit. But when Arthur found out that Child Pilot was working on plans to expand their facilities into one of the abandoned warehouses across the street, a lightbulb erupted in his brain. He knew he was looking his edge right in the face. Now was the time to strike. The principal had asked Arthur to estimate the additional upkeep for their budget, and Arthur learned that the school was planning on making an offer on a particular building that suited their needs perfectly. The building had sat completely vacant for years, and had been for sale as long as he could remember—its asking price steadily declining. Arthur took stock of everything that he had in the bank, which was about seventeen thousand dollars. It had been twenty-five, but Cash's seminar had required some real dough. Anyway, Arthur took that seventeen thousand dollars and called in sick to Child Pilot one Thursday before a long weekend. He went to fifteen meetings with hard-money lenders around the city. Pretty much every one of them wanted to know what Arthur's plan for the loan was. But he wouldn't tell them. If he told them his secret, he suspected they would snap the deal right out from under him. Finally, Arthur had found a moneyman who would loan him the cash he needed with no questions asked: a hundred and eighty thousand dollars. The only rub was an annual interest rate of 18 percent and a thinly veiled suggestion that any and all techniques would be utilized to reacquire the money should Arthur fail to make his payments. Arthur readily agreed. The guy who owned the warehouse was much easier. The building was listed at a hundred and eighty thousand dollars. Arthur came in and offered the ask, as long as the owner would close in a day—no inspection contingencies required. By the time the next week rolled around, Arthur Hynes was cleaning windows in the gymnasium of Child Pilot while staring across the street at the warehouse that he now owned.

He had purchased the building under an LLC with a generic name, and found a real estate agent to represent him in negotiations with the school. All the principal knew was that she had purchased the warehouse across the street from Rockford LLC, a real estate investment firm. Unfortunately for the school, the new ownership had raised the price of the building to two hundred and eighty thousand dollars. Take it or leave it. But since it was the perfect building, in the perfect location, and money was already being spent, the principal and Child Pilot's board had no choice. They purchased the warehouse from Arthur and put two times his annual income into his bank account. That money would provide the seed capital for Arthur's burgeoning empire. And twenty-six years later, he owned over a billion dollars' worth of real estate, most of it located in the greatest city on earth: Manhattan.

There was one more lesson that Arthur took from Cash Johnston, and it was the very first thing that Cash told each and every audience he spoke to. Cash was born Josh Johnston. His mom had called him "Joshy John" for thirty years. It was only when he went down to the courthouse and changed his name to Cash that his life changed. Arthur took that advice to heart. A few days after he'd purchased his third building in Philadelphia, Arthur quit his job. He walked himself down to the courthouse on Market Street and changed his last name from Hynes to Metropolis. And on that day, Arthur Metropolis was born.

▪

Jake, listening in on Arthur's origin story from behind the two-sided mirror, could tell the man was used to dazzling people. This was par for the course for Arthur, but was it also a calculated technique? After the grandstanding, Susan finally moved the conversation towards the case at hand. Arthur had inexplicably become the target of a series of daring cat burglaries, all executed by the same team—and all, apparently, quite successful.

▪

"How long have you owned the penthouse, Mr. Metropolis?" Susan dug in.

"For about fifteen years. Actually my wife was the one who wanted it, which is ironic," he said.

"Why's that?"

"Because I hated it back then. My wife, I mean, my ex-wife. We're divorced now. Have been for five years. But it's actually a real impressive place. Go out on a date, come back there, the views are amazing. Know what I mean?"

"Sure," replied Tony cautiously.

"So you use it to entertain?" Susan asked.

"I use it for whatever I want."

"I'd love to know what that means. What I'm really trying to figure out is who's been up there. Let's say in the last year. How many people would know the layout, things like that?" Susan asked.

"Well, the super and all the staff, obviously. And a number of ladies," Arthur responded.

"Like your girlfriend? The model?"

"Oh, no. Not Isabelle. No. My main residence is down in the West Village. An old church, actually. Filled the top floor with floor-to-ceiling crystal. Still have the original stained glass in all the stairwells, though. You've got to see it. Beautiful."

"That's where you sleep at night?"

"Most of the time. I also use my boat. It's at Chelsea Piers."

"So the penthouse is for . . . other women . . . that you're seeing on the side?" Susan asked.

"Listen. Dead end there. I promise you that I wasn't robbed by some broad," Arthur replied.

▪

Jake finally pulled up a chair and sat down. Arthur was a man who liked to hear himself talk. It would be a long interview. Arthur's proclivities with the ladies were almost as well known as his business acumen. Susan was doing an excellent job of biting her lip; Jake knew that must have been very difficult for her. Besides Arthur's presence in the city's social circuit, his relationship with the glamorous model Isabelle Prins, and his book, Arthur was famous for another reason. He was a self-avowed sex addict, who had starred in an ignominious sex tape with yet another model that somehow found itself onto the Internet a few years ago. He was, basically, one of the most self-assured and happy "victims" that Jake had ever crossed paths with.

■

"I'm a problem guy. I solve problems; doesn't matter what tool I use. The problem we have now is that I got robbed. So what are you guys gonna do to help me solve this? Or do I need to do it all by myself?" Arthur asked.

"You don't need to worry about us, sir," Tony said. "If you don't mind, I'd like to run through the manifest."

"Surely."

"According to your staff, we're looking at three bracelets, two rings, a particularly valuable diamond necklace, and approximately forty thousand dollars in cash."

"All very good. Correct. That necklace is really the kicker. Diamonds. They formed an M," Arthur said and then added, "for Metropolis. Gave it to my ex-girlfriend, but she threw it at me when we broke up."

"You gave your girlfriend a necklace with your own initial on it?" Susan asked.

"Diamonds are a girl's best friend, aren't they?"

"All adds up to around two hundred and twenty thousand dollars," Tony narrated.

"Also, do you normally keep that type of cash lying around in your house?" Susan asked, then continued. "You had a safe in the apartment, but it was left undisturbed. The cash was just in a drawer?"

"Yeah. It was out. Pisses me off. But it's a rounding error," Arthur admitted. He was a billionaire—the robbery hurt him like a mosquito bite.

"And why?" Susan asked.

"Groceries for whoever's there," Arthur replied simply. *He wasn't lying.*

"Let's move on . . . If it were just one robbery, we wouldn't be here," Susan said.

Metropolis nodded avidly in agreement. "This is the fourth place that's been hit in the last six months. The first residential. The first one where I've ever rested my head, but . . . Number one was a small office in Brooklyn. Then an apartment building in the Upper West Side. And a warehouse I have in the Bronx that was full of absolutely nothing of value, just industrial supplies."

"Bizarre," Tony replied.

"Do you have any enemies?" Susan asked.

Arthur chuckled heartily. "If my enemies wanted to rob me . . ." he finally said, "they'd use the capital markets."

"We clearly believe you're being targeted. We believe the same crew is responsible. For your buildings—and others. But we don't see any rhyme or reason yet. And it seems that neither do you . . ."

"I'd hope that our esteemed police department could tell me more than that," Arthur said.

"We're working as hard as we possibly can," Susan said.

"Meaning?"

"That means the majority of major crimes is on this. Our very best undercover detective is working it as we speak," Susan nodded . . .

"What's his name? I want to meet him," Arthur demanded.

"That's not going to happen. Not right now. Operational security. But believe me, I understand the importance to you. It's important to the mayor. And you know what? That makes it extremely important to me. We're going to get the bottom of this, Mr. Metropolis. You have my word."

▪

Sensing that the end of the interview was nigh, Jake made a beeline for the door. He didn't want to spend more time in One Police Plaza than necessary. The place gave him the heebie-jeebies. Even when he was a regular detective, he'd spent as little time there as possible. He headed down a back stairwell and emerged inside the truck loading zone in the basement of the facility, where his bike was parked on diagonal yellow lines.

As Jake placed his helmet over his head, he gazed across the loading zone. An imposing black SUV was parked with its lights on. A driver sat in the running car. Another man leaned against the front grille, smoking a long cigarillo-style cigarette and staring out of the bay. He was striking. His features verged on albino. Jake's hair was dirty-blond, but this man was a true platinum. Just then, the elevator door on the other side of the loading zone opened. Arthur Metropolis exited—the car obviously waiting for him. Arthur's aide stubbed his cigarette on the ground and turned to greet Arthur. He opened the back door. Arthur grunted and stepped in.

As the SUV ripped out of One Police Plaza, the aide turned to stare at Jake from shotgun. Jake couldn't make out many details through the tinted windows, but the man's presence haunted him. Besides the guy's blond hair and eyebrows, the fellow had sunken eyes that seemed to stare deeply through Jake's motorcycle mask and directly into his soul. He'd seen people like that before. The man looked like death—like a ghost. But seconds later, thankfully, the apparition was gone.

SIX

JAKE CRUISED ON THE DUCATI while his own voice echoed in his head. He was listening to a recent mix sent by his drummer, Schaub. Schaub and Jake had met back in Rivett's early years in the city—when they were both in City College and Manhattan seemed to stay up later, and be safer, than it was now. Even then, they had been headed in different directions. But they had a deep kinship that divergent lives would never shake. It was called the pursuit of screamo. The mix vibrated between Jake's ears. Schaub had cut it nice and deep, the way Jake liked it, with wall upon wall of cascading sonic beats. Rivett's voice ricocheted through the mix—loud but lulling. For most screamo bands, the lyrics were much less important than the vibe. The vibe was singular. It was anger and resentment boiling over. But this new track did not lack for humanity or eloquence. Titled "Out of the Mist," the song was perhaps a touch poppier than before, with an undercurrent of deep electronic funk coursing throughout. Yeah. Jake was into it. Scratch that—*he absolutely loved it*. His head bobbed up and down as the beats raced through the headphones integrated inside his helmet. Towards the end of the song, it quieted and a loud notification chime played. Jake glanced down at his cell mounted between the handlebars. A prompt read: "UrbEx Friend Request:

Accepted." Jake threw his hands up in celebration, bike expertly balanced between his knees.

■

Back at the apartment, Jake pulled up his browser. Sure enough, the red-haired girl had accepted his friend request. Her name was "Mona," apparently. Jake grinned as he clicked through her profile. She didn't have a huge amount of information listed—but it was a start.

"So what do you do, Mona?" Jake asked as he started through her galleries. "Deep into the urban exploration scene. A real believer, I'm sure . . ." Jake found more of what he was looking for in the albums. He now had access to many more photographs. He zoomed in on one of her images and noticed Mona's hand flung forward at the lens, forming another upside down V. It was striking. The V hand sign was also practically identical to what Tony had picked up on the surveillance tapes from the robbery at Metropolis' penthouse. Jake's grin began to morph into an honest-to-goodness smile. He clicked through to the next photo. Eight explorers. They stood in a line on the top of a building, just below New York's iconic red-glowing "Essex House" sign. The squad was clad in all manner of technical climbing gear, mixed with what could only be described as tactical outfits—gear belts and camo—feet protected by a variety of trail-runners, climbing shoes, and high-ankle boots. Every single face was covered. But what excited Jake the most was that each one of them had their hands turned down to form the V. It wasn't just Mona. It was her entire crew.

"So you got a crew," Jake muttered as he stared at the screen, "but maybe they don't just take photos." Jake clicked back to Mona's profile and scrolled through her main feed. In addition to exploration photos, she would occasionally check in at an art institute. A few of her friends there were tagged. She also seemed fond of posting her own graphic design files —in progress and finished. Pinned to the top of the feed, Jake noticed that she had posted a large advertisement for a party. His pulse quickened while he read the graphic. It was an UrbEx meetup, scheduled to go down that very night: "URBEX MIX N' MEET. WHALE SQUARE IN RED HOOK. DJ NISE & ONE BUCK BEERS."

Jake pushed back from his computer. There wasn't much time before the shindig, and he intended to find the belle of the ball if it killed him. One thing was for sure. The world was expanding in front of him. His case was opening up, just like they always did. He always relished this exact moment in each file. It was the tight-rope walk between darkness and the illumination. He saw the pinprick ahead. The grand solve wasn't anywhere near focus, but at least the light was on. Someone was home. And he was gonna go see who.

Jake stepped to his closet. He pulled out a combination of athletic gear and tactical clothing. Should he go with the collared Under Armour or the black and gray camo tee? About to select the collar, he switched it up and went camo. He paired that with long brown pants that zipped off below the knees and a pair of black Nike trainers. He wrapped a bandana around his neck, emulating a couple of the male explorers he'd noticed in Mona's photos. Something was missing. Jake gazed around the apartment before his eyes rested on a bottle of vodka sitting in his small kitchenette. Jake poured out a large shot for himself. He chugged it. Now he was ready to go to a party.

SEVEN

AFTER CIRCLING FOR FIVE MINUTES, Jake parked his motorcycle on a side street in Greenwood, Brooklyn—just south of Gowanus and Red Hook. A few blocks away from the address listed on Mona's poster, Jake figured it was safer to walk the remainder. It was a lonely area, an old warehouse district along the water of the Upper Bay. The industrial boonies. Dating back to the mid-1850s, this particular quadrant of the city had been formerly dominated by the whale oil industry. The eventual depreciation of the supply of ocean whales and thus their accoutrements— whalers, refiners, and distributors—contributed to the initial decline. But after whale oil, even petroleum had been refined and processed into lubricants and various manufactured oils inside these warehouses. That is until the mid-1960s, when economic and environmental concerns finally pushed the stubborn and aged conglomerates out of the region once and for all. They left behind two hundred years of history and a decrepit Stonehenge of crumbling buildings nicknamed "Whale Square." Whale Square had remained rough for about fifty years. It was only after the Great Recession that real estate developers had become interested in the area again. It was still not a fancy location. Whale Square was on the fringes of trendy, which is saying something. But Red Hook was already too expensive, and the big money was starting to place their bets further and further down the risk line again—now they were focused on these old brick structures to the south with their shattered windows framing gorgeous water views.

As Jake walked down the block, he noticed a banner strung across chain-link construction fence separating the street from one of the old lots. With 3D-rendered text and sky-blue coloring, the banner announced the construction of a "Mixed-Use Masterpiece," chock full of "Reclaimed Wood and European Masonry," from none other than Arthur Metropolis and his firm, MetroVenture. Jake chuckled at the blue. It was apparently the universal color of the future arriving, right now. It was sickeningly fresh, designed to keep the past at bay. As he turned the corner and away from Metropolis' construction site, he saw a bunch of graffiti scribbled over the next advertisement.

The next street was pure old school. The mortar between the bricks of these structures could easily fall out with a finger brush. Some of the buildings had been haphazardly updated for structural safety with the addition of internal steel cabling—the square anchors of the cables like a line of gunshot wounds to the skin of the incredible relics from a bygone era. As Jake paced down the street, he heard laughing ahead. He noticed a young, flashy, olive-skinned man with a girl to each side of him. The ladies were dressed up, and the man wasn't so bad either in tight dark blue jeans and a casual blazer. Suspecting they were headed to the same party, Rivett glanced down at his ensemble and suddenly felt quite underdressed. At least he was headed in the right direction. The trio ducked to the right, into a tight alleyway between two Whale Square buildings, and all went quiet again.

Jake hustled into the alley. But it was a dead end. The people had mysteriously disappeared. Jake had no idea where to go next. Then he noticed that a giant metal door to one of the warehouses was rolled up and open. He stepped inside. The bottom floor of the warehouse was largely barren, brimming with old wooden stalls now filled with trash. Jake heard a girl's laugh splice through the abject darkness. He reeled around but still found nothing. Since there was no illumination in the room, Jake could only resolve details near the door. As he stepped into the darkness, Jake pulled out his cell phone and turned on the flashlight. Another makeshift wooden barrier. A brick wall behind it. He washed the flashlight beam over the wall again before he noticed a peculiarity—a giant white arrow had been spray-painted on the wall. About four feet high by three feet wide, the arrow pointed directly towards the ceiling. Jake guided his flashlight vertical. He could just make out a ledge far, far above him— about forty feet up. Green and purple neon lights danced in an almost imperceptibly thin line along the edge of the outcropping.

"Hey!" Jake shouted desperately.

No one replied.

Jake studied the imposing wall. How was he supposed to climb this damned thing? He put his hands to the bricks, feeling the grooves with his fingers—just a millimeter's span to grip. Perhaps there were expert rock climbers who could rip up this obstacle. He wasn't one of them. Was it a requirement of every party participant to ascend a sheer rock face? Couldn't be. He gave the wall another look and shrugged. Whatever—if that's what they wanted? He'd give it a whirl. Jake placed his right hand into a small, one-centimeter-wide groove and lifted his body. He jammed a foot into another piece of broken mortar and reached up with his left hand. His back muscles ached after about fifteen seconds. Once he'd managed to rise three feet, Jake fell off. Sitting on his butt, Jake heard footsteps behind him.

"Where's your gear?" a voice said.

"Huh?" Jake pushed off the ground and spun around awkwardly. A man of approximately thirty years stood in front of him. He was at least six foot five and on the leaner side. He had dark, chiseled looks and determined green eyes. His hands on his hips, he didn't seem very impressed by what he was witnessing.

"Yeah bro, I'm an idiot," Jake said. "Didn't realize there was going to be a wall . . ."

The mysterious man stared at Jake with slight suspicion, as if he'd answered the question wrong. Then the guy swung his backpack off his shoulders and placed it on the ground. He unzipped the bag and pulled out a racquetball racquet. He unspooled a long rope hanging by a carabiner. The man finally spoke again. "This has been a covert preparation for an overt operation," he said.

A tennis ball was attached to the end of the man's rope. He tossed the ball up into the air, as if serving it. He smacked the ball with the racquet. The ball expertly arced through the air and looped around a pipe on the ceiling, a good ten feet above the platform that Jake had identified earlier. The ball fell back down to the ground, and the man removed it. The guy secured the rope with a noose knot, yanking the rope taut. Jake watched with amazement as the man fashioned a rappel harness using rope alone. Once the harness was ready, the man nodded at Jake and began to slowly climb up the wall. He reached the ledge above and pulled himself over.

"Hey! Will you leave the rope?" Jake yelled as the man disappeared over the ledge. After a second, the rope came slinging down back at Jake like a whip. Jake ducked out of the way then glanced back up. The man stared over the ledge at him. "Thanks," Jake said. "What's your name? I'm Jake."

The man observed Jake silently. Apparently he wasn't a particularly loquacious human. Jake attempted to emulate the guy's knots with the climbing rope. The man watched him fumble.

"Where you rollin' from?" the man finally asked.

"The Bronx," Jake answered.

"No. I mean . . . What crew?"

"I . . . Uh . . ." Unsure how to respond, Jake told the truth. "Don't have a crew."

"I'll see you around, then," the guy said. He dipped into the darkness above, leaving Jake alone again.

But at least Jake now had a rope.

Sweat poured off Jake's brow as he used all his strength to pull himself up the wall. He hadn't figured out how to use the harness in exactly the same manner as the tall man, so his method resembled one long pull-up with rests in between when he placed his legs horizontally against the wall. He finally pulled himself over the ledge, which consisted of wooden planks supported by two steel cantilevered support beams. As his chest heaved in and out, Jake stared ahead. He wasn't anywhere near a party. What he did notice was a long, thin steel beam leading from the ledge towards another side of the warehouse's top floor.

"Unbelievable," Jake muttered. He avoided looking down. His eyes followed the beam to its conclusion: a small hole. Through the hole, Jake could see the neon flashing lights. He could also hear music thumping from a party that obviously was occurring in whatever space was through that hole. Jake steeled himself, and gazed over the edge below. *Shit.* He was a solid four stories in the air. And the steel beam that he was expected to cross? It was three inches wide.

Heights were not Jake's strong suit. They were the opposite—his Achilles heel. He certainly hadn't let Susan in on this fact because Jake was also an expert at reading people. He hadn't wanted to give her any reason to sack him right then and there. The truth was that he liked being a cop—even if he didn't happen to like cops. So his dirty little secret remained. The man assigned to infiltrate a group of building climbers was deathly afraid of heights. Ever since he was a teenager, the sensation of vertigo had affected Jake immensely.

It wasn't purely mental. It began with sweaty palms and ended with blurred vision and reality tilt-a-whirling in front of him. But he had no choice. The beam was the party, and the party was the job. He decided he could shimmy. There was only one direction to go, after all. He slowly worked his way onto the beam. He thought that the relative darkness below would help him, but his pupils had fully expanded by now and he was beginning to resolve the details of the warehouse. He could clearly make out the floor far below him. It was beginning to fade in and out as if his contacts were blurring. But he knew they weren't. It was his brain, trying to stop him from succeeding. Jake closed his eyes tight and began the painstaking process of pushing his body, inch by inch, across the steel beam.

Jake's fingers finally reached the brick ledge on the other side of the warehouse. He crawled across. Now all that was left was the hole. Two large white arrows were spray-painted beside it. It wasn't large, maybe about two and a half feet wide. But compared to the gauntlet that he'd just conquered, it was nothing. Jake contorted his body and slid through.

Jake was immediately greeted by the "uhhhnntss uhhnnts uuhnnts" bass beats of sick electronic dance music—an epic, underground party. The crazed crowd gesticulated in the middle of the room, the bar outside on the roof. Jake stood up and dusted himself off just as a beer flew towards his face. He caught the beer before it nose-smashed him.

"Good work, man. You're only the eighth person to come through that way. Free beer for ya," another urban explorer grinned at Jake.

"Uh, thanks . . ." Jake said, discombobulated.

"Anyone else behind you? I gotta pee."

"No. I don't think so," Jake said and then calculated. "Wait. Did you say the eighth?"

"Yeah. Get a free beer that way. Come in the main entrance and you get nothing," the guy said. He pointed towards the other side of the space. Jake noticed a large stairway easily leading up to the party from the other side of the building.

"You gotta be kidding me," Jake said as the guy filtered back into the crowd. He sipped his hard-earned beverage.

Jake pushed through the crowd and emerged outside on a long balcony overlooking the Upper Bay of the Hudson. The Statue of Liberty was also visible—the size of a small stick figure in the far distance, backlit by New Jersey. Jake drank his beer and observed the crowd. They were a diverse sort. He hadn't yet been able to get a full grip on the urban exploration "scene." The culture seemed to consist of people from almost every income bracket and walk of life. Maybe that was the magic of it, but the concept struck Jake as bizarre. Something had to unify these people. But what was it? As Jake sipped, he noticed the well-dressed, olive-skinned young man from the street. The man grabbed three beers from a cooler on the floor, underneath the makeshift bar.

Noticing the freeloading, the bartender turned. "Three beers. Three bucks."

"Tell Rory I'm good for it," the man sneered with a Dominican accent.

"Emanuel, right?" the bartender asked.

"So what?" Emanuel replied.

The bartender reached towards Emanuel and grabbed his shoulder. "That's messed up, bro. You can't just take stuff. Rory doesn't run this bar . . ."

In one fluid motion, Emanuel snatched the guy's hand off his shoulder. He twisted the bartender's arm practically 360 degrees, forcing the poor guy to his knees. Emanuel held the bartender in a submission hold. "Don't ever touch me, bro," Emanuel said. He dropped his hold and walked off—no remorse.

Jake's body stiffened from the action. But he didn't know what to do. No one else in the crowd seemed particularly surprised at Emanuel's actions. The bartender shook it off and took up his position behind the bar again. Jake began to relax just as a young woman sidled up next to him at the bar.

"I don't know why a guy would want to come to a party when he knows that no one there likes him," the woman said.

Jake did a double take.

Standing right in front of him was the red-haired girl from UrbEx. Mona—in the flesh. She had dark red hair and light brown skin of unidentifiable ethnic origin. He glanced up and down at her, making a reading. Impeccable style. Her tight black jeans were tucked into stomper boots with inch-thick soles and bright red laces. She wore three layers of shirt, the longest one a dark gray that extended almost to her knees. With no makeup, her hair was tied back into an easy ponytail. Something struck a chord inside Jake while he stared, something he hadn't felt in a long time. It wasn't lust. It was understanding. She was a creature who was completely comfortable with herself. He could tell that she knew what she wanted. She conducted life on her own terms. She was the personification of the rainbow-gradient-race-and-culture zeitgeist of the future. She definitely listened to Lorde, Sia, and Lana Del Rey. And she was also about to turn away from Jake, her conversation starter greeted with a gaping open mouth from the quiet blond man standing by himself at the bar.

"That's sort of the problem with putting a party on social media, isn't it?" Jake finally said.

Mona decided to play ball, for just a moment. "What do you mean?" she asked.

"Can't really throw, like, an intimate thing anymore because inevitably someone else who's not there is going to see their friends tagged in a photo and get upset and probably exclude you from their next event, and then you'll get jealous a few weeks later when you see their cool party that you weren't invited to . . . So the next time, you say, I'll just invite everyone. Don't want to leave anyone out." Jake nodded in the direction of Emanuel. "And then a guy you don't like shows up and steals your beer."

Mona chuckled. "You figure that little conundrum out, you'll probably make a billion dollars."

"Nah. I got bigger worries. Like paying rent."

"Damn right," Mona agreed. "Look, it's not the three dollars that I care about. You know that? It's the whole point."

"Which is?" Jake asked.

"Serious? Look," Mona pointed to a small sign atop the bar. Jake read it with interest, "All proceeds go to the Friends of Unincorporated Brooklyn. The only way we fight the developers is together!"

"Developers," Jake said.

"Scum," Mona added.

"Think you're being a little militant about that?"

"Militant?" Mona asked quizzically, "What do you mean?"

"Never mind . . ." Jake realized he'd gone off track.

"If you're going to talk about militant—about tactics taken from war? How about entire blocks of people gettin' kicked out of their houses while the cops protect the bad guys? How about developers paying through the ass to City Hall to change zoning regulations? You know they're altering rent control statutes just to make it easier to raze the past and bring up these monstrosities that look like video game levels. Glass boxes and bullshit everywhere you look. You want New York to look like Dubai? 'Cause they certainly do."

"I was just asking. Sorry."

Mona stared at Jake for a long moment. "Have I met you before?"

"Don't think so . . ."

"You look real familiar."

Jake decided to stop playing coy. "Are you on UrbEx, maybe?" he asked. "I'm Jake."

"Mona."

Jake glanced to the left and right. "Well, the crowd beats my normal spot," he said.

"Where's that?"

"The Silver Pickle."

"Really?"

"You know it?" Jake asked.

"Yeah. The Bronx. The biker joint."

"It's my type of place. Not my type of people," Jake said.

"Sure," Mona laughed, "nobody chills there just 'cause they want to. They go to the Pickle 'cause no one else wants them."

Too close to home. "So, who do you roll with?" Jake finally asked.

"Rory."

"I've been hearing his name a lot. Who's Rory?"

"Rory Visco? Serious?" She realized that Jake was. "He invented this stuff. He started tunnel hacking with his brother when he was getting his

PhD in urban planning from MIT."

"MIT, huh?"

Mona nodded.

"Isn't that, like, a good school?"

"This is a democratic life."

"I'm just sayin', I mean, I just didn't think people that went to MIT would be here . . . I sure wouldn't, man. I'd be like Steve Jobs or something," Jake replied.

"Look, you don't have to tell me. I work at a department store," Mona announced glumly, "but I'm goin' to the Arts Institute too. Graphic design." She pointed to a party poster on the wall. "I made that," she said.

"Yeah? You're talented."

Mona smiled for a second then shut it off. "You're a noob, aren't you?"

"Huh? I . . . I just explore by myself."

"You're a soloist?"

"Yes. A soloer," Jake replied warily.

"That's dangerous."

He tried another tack. "Truth is, I do want to roll with a crew. Will you take me out?"

Mona shook her head. "No."

"How come?"

"I don't know you, Jake."

"I'm a nice guy."

"This," Mona pointed around, "ain't nice guy storage."

"I was lying about that last part then . . ."

"Sorry." Tired of the conversation, she stood up to go. "That's another funny thing about the Internet," Mona said as she glanced back at Jake. "You're never really sure who you're talking to. Maybe you meet a guy at a bar, and he introduces himself to you like it's the first time he's seen you when really he's already spent hours checking out all your pics and memorizing your hometown and the fact that you love yoga and sunsets?"

"Maybe," Jake said.

"Except I was joking about the yoga part."

"I know."

"'Cause I'm not a moron. I don't get my exercise inside a little room that I've paid thirty dollars an hour for permission to enter. I don't get permission." With that, Mona disappeared into the crowd. Jake grinned.

He stared at the dance floor ahead. Fragmentary swathes of light rippled over the crowd, projected from a sophisticated light system. If one was wondering where the most hip and exclusive club in New York was? It was here, tonight, in this place. The hard part wasn't getting in; it was knowing about it in the first place. Looking for Mona, Jake sauntered through the dance floor. Every once in a while, he'd stand on his tiptoes. The crowd was so into the music that the floor beneath them began to vibrate, oscillating up and down by a half inch with each heavy bass vibration. Everyone was in the groove, the beat sucked through their veins and thrusting their heart valves at exactly the same pace. As Jake observed the crowd, he realized what he was looking at. It was a new religion. Dictation was a thing of the past—the future of humanity was feeling the vibe. Millennials were all agnostic or worse. The irony was that they just had a new master: the button pusher. God now dictated their emotions from the controls of a DJ stand towering above. Jake eventually saw Mona's red ponytail whipping around in a wide circle ahead. He moved up behind her and fell into the groove. She danced back, rubbing her body on him. The process was highly choreographed—never obscene but certainly not chaste. After about thirty seconds, she glanced backward to check out who was dancing with her. She suddenly stopped gyrating.

"What do you want, man?" she asked.

"Rory!" Jake yelled over the extreme decibels.

Mona shrugged. She couldn't hear him.

He leaned in, centimeters from her ear. "Which one's Rory?" he yelled.

Mona pointed across the crowded dance floor. On a raised platform next to the DJ table sat a tall, thin man with green eyes. Jake immediately recognized him as the mysterious man, wearing the hoodie, who'd helped him enter the party. It was clear that Rory was held in high esteem amongst the crowd. With a nod to Mona, Jake pushed through the mass. He was heading in Rory's direction. Once Mona realized where he was going, she began to follow quickly.

"Hey!" she yelled, trying in vain to stop Jake.

Finally at the other side of the dance floor, Jake approached Rory.

"Thanks for the hookup!" Jake yelled.

But Rory couldn't hear him.

Jake tried again, "Thanks for the rope back there!"

"Oh yeah," Rory replied nonchalantly, "it's chill." Rory turned back to his friends, not interested in the rando. But Jake tapped him on the shoulder.

"Hey. You asked me who I rolled with, right? I'm a soloist, but I want to roll with you."

"That's not going to happen, bud," Rory said.

Just then, Mona appeared behind both of them. Her eyes displayed just the tiniest flash of fear, as if she felt responsible for Jake bothering Rory.

"Jake! Stop it!" she yelled.

"You know this barn?" Rory asked Mona.

Mona shrugged. "We just met. No . . ."

"Get outta here, dude," Rory addressed Jake. "You're making my girl uncomfortable." Rory leaned in and gave Mona a kiss.

But Jake wasn't done. "Hey. I get it. Nobody gets the keys to the kingdom just handed to them. But are you saying no one helped you along the way? I know that somewhere along the line, you had someone who believed in you. They saw you struggling. They put their hand out for you, and pulled you up the wall, man. I know it in my heart. All I'm asking is for a chance. Let me show you what I got."

"I do what I want," Rory said. "That's it. That's my life. What I want. A hundred percent of the time."

Jake opened his mouth to retort, but a loud commotion behind Rory broke their contact. Jake noticed Emanuel standing below the platform, yelling indistinguishable complaints at two of Rory's crew. Rory's friend Castle was built like a Navy SEAL. Next to Castle was Nik, a dark-garbed hipster with brooding eyebrows and a well-trimmed beard. Emanuel was trying to step onto the platform. Castle was holding him back and jawing right back into his face. It was easy to understand that something was gnawing at Emanuel. Jake tried to get closer. Their words were a few feet from being understandable. Jake crowded onto the top of the platform just as Emanuel pulled a pistol from his blazer jacket. He held it up in the air. Now Jake could hear.

"You gonna hide behind your boys, Ror?" Emanuel screamed.

Another one of Emanuel's friends reared up from behind the Dominican. The guy leaned back and rotated his core in an attempt to roundhouse Castle. Castle ducked out of the way but fell to the ground. Emanuel pointed the weapon towards Castle, who scrambled. Nik was frozen as Rory leaped from behind him towards Emanuel. Emanuel saw Rory coming. He lifted the gun slightly above Castle and pulled the trigger. The bullet ricocheted above the crowd and bounced off the ceiling. Once the sound from the hot lead blasted through the space, the whole place went to riot.

The crowd parted like the Red Sea around Emanuel, who jammed his piece into his pants and turned heel. He pushed through a couple and made his way to the stairs as the panic set in. The crowd's feet formed a stomping herd towards the main exit. Rory pulled Castle off the platform, and the two of them ran back towards the entrance that Jake had used. Jake tried to follow but found himself rebuffed by the crowd—whose desire to vacate the premises was bordering on fanatical at this point. He could only do his best to not get knocked over. The wave took him the other direction. Jake suddenly felt someone grasping for his side flank. He looked down. It was Mona.

"Hey. You want Rory to say yes? You want to roll with our crew?"

"You mean your boyfriend?" Jake asked. He wasn't sure why. It wasn't really his place, and it definitely wasn't in his job description to care.

"What do you think this is, the nineties? I don't DTR." Mona replied, nonplussed.

"DTR?"

"Define the Relationship. Christ," she muttered.

"So you were gonna say. What do I have to do?"

"You want to get him interested? Show him something interesting. Who are you? Why do you matter? How do you fit into the world? What makes you any different? I'd like to see that too. Why should I care? Until then, you're just vapor on the Internet." Her hand gesticulated as if it was flowing through water. "Just another guy, frontin'. Not doin'. Like we do."

Mona quickly faded back into the crowd as if she'd never been there in the first place. And Jake realized he might have a new boss.

One that he liked.

EIGHT

THE PARTY OCCUPIED HIS DREAMS. She was there in every frame. She was always beckoning, but he could never reach her. He woke up the next morning not entirely clear where the rave had ended and his unconscious began. But the events of the evening all came flooding back as Jake padded through his morning routine.

He sat down at the desk in the second bedroom. He leaned to the right, towards the floor. He yanked up the fake flooring, opened the safe, and pulled out his personal cell phone. Nothing. Then the state phone—Susan and Tony's lifeline. Of course, there were multiple messages and four missed calls. Villalon had been trying to reach him for the last two days, but Jake wasn't ready. You can't show all your cards to the desk jockeys too early, even if a gun went off—especially because a gun went off. This one was clearly going to be a tightrope walk, the line slimmer the longer it proceeded, and Jake was only at the very beginning. He didn't want to give them a reason to come down too hard, too early. And he knew he'd find something even more irresistible at the end. Besides, he didn't love their company, so why encourage the behavior? His relationship with Susan was like a night terror. At least it was slightly better with Tony. Jake cleared the alerts, confirmed the device was on silent, and placed it back into the safe. He lowered the floor panel back in like a puzzle piece. He checked the time. It was already close to midday, and he had to find a nice, tall building somewhere in the Bronx—*and climb it.*

■

As he walked through Hunts Point in the South Bronx, Jake quickly absorbed his first lesson about urban exploring: Most buildings did not want anyone climbing them. Now that he cared to look, he realized that the everyday texture of city architecture was much more complex than a bystander might realize. He was looking at the details—and they were formidable. Any number of barriers and systems were utilized to keep people out of the warehouses in this region. Of course, a building owner's desire to not be trespassed upon was completely understandable. That's why some of the warehouses protected their backyards with high fences, others with barbed wire. A few went the extra mile and equipped their buildings with surveillance cameras or horizontal bars to form a ceiling over open areas. Ironically, given the security, not many of the buildings seemed to be used regularly. There was a little deli on the corner, what looked like a web design company in one building, perhaps some sort of textiles business next door. But most of the buildings were empty, including the one with a huge and distinctive sign: "Morton's Eye Drops." The sign—memorializing a long-forgotten brand—would make a great backdrop.

Rivett loitered by the door to the building. Perhaps it wasn't as empty as he thought. But after spending five minutes aligning his department-purchased GoPro camera to a newly acquired tripod-and-selfie stick, no one had entered or exited. Unfortunately, there weren't any alleys on either side of the warehouse. It was completely flush to its neighbors, and all of the first-floor windows were protected by integrated iron bars.

Jake slowly padded around the block. He located an alleyway that provided backdoor access to the buildings on the prior street. Jake spotted a fire escape. The fire escape consisted of wrought iron, and although it didn't extend down to the street, it was only about ten or eleven feet off the surface of the pavement below. Jake glanced around, trying to find a trash can or item that he could use as an impromptu stepping stool. He was careful to be on the lookout for any random passersby. Given his last interaction with the boys in blue, and his steadfast refusal to speak to Tony or Susan until he could prove that he had something solid in his hands, Jake didn't want to bring the home office into his current improv routine. When a group of teenagers walked through the alleyway, Jake pushed a garbage can around as if he were the proprietor.

The garbage can wasn't going to work. Unsteady as a spinning top, even when he was standing on it, he was still a good five feet from the bottom of the wrought-iron fire escape. That's when Jake spotted an old wooden ladder lying next to a garage on the other side of the alley. He sprinted to the ladder and dragged it back towards the fire escape. The ladder was broken. It couldn't expand. But Jake was able to lean it against the wall, underneath the fire escape. When he rose to the second-highest rung, as high as he dared, Jake twisted and saw the bottom level of the fire escape just a few feet above him. Using his legs as pistons, he fired his body towards the fire escape. His hands grasped the rusty metal bar and stuck. As his body twisted below, Jake pulled himself up over the railing of the fire escape. Once he was inside, he was able to quickly dart up five stories along the side of the building.

At the top of the fire escape, his progress was stunted. Jake was now stuck inside an iron cage, a padlock preventing access to the roof; one would escape down, not up, in the case of a raging firestorm. He had to get out of the box. There was a way, but it would expose him to intense danger. The floor below the cage was still open to the air. Jake backtracked and descended. Careful not to look down for too long, he leaned over the edge of the fire escape and stared upwards. Slick vertical bars and no room for error. One wrong move and he'd be a smear on the ground below. Jake fished through his backpack, thinking back to the UrbEx party the night before—he'd kept Rory's rope. He quickly ran up to the box level of the fire escape once more. He secured the rope to the highest point he could reach, allowing it to unfurl outside of the iron bars and hang down against the side of the fire escape. Then Jake returned to the floor below. He grabbed the rope that was hanging in the air, and he fashioned a rope harness for himself. This time around—aided by an hour of YouTube tutorials—his fingers displayed confidence and dexterity. The moves were faster, the knot more secure. Finally, he was ready.

Jake gingerly climbed over the guardrail of the fire escape. He gripped the iron bars above and began to climb up the patchwork. After he'd ascended a few feet, he made the mistake of looking down. The ground below warped in his vision like a funhouse mirror. His brain was sliding reality through a manipulative algorithm of fear and trepidation—and turning to mush in the process. Jake took a few deep breaths. He closed his eyes, reminding himself that the world was not spinning—only his mind. When he opened his eyes again, reality was simply a slow tilting roll. At least it wasn't the massive tsunami of before. Not perfect, but he'd take it. Jake began to climb again. After a painstaking minute or two, he finally reached the top of the cage. He pulled himself across the fire escape and stepped onto the roof of the old Morton's warehouse.

After untying his rope harness, Jake dipped down into a crouch. He only stood when the vertigo had subsided completely. The view was astounding. New York's flat warren of tightly woven city blocks appeared endless. Especially in the Bronx, which was not polluted with intensely high buildings, the top of this structure afforded Jake an incredible viewpoint over the undulating landscape of the city. As he gazed south, his view encompassed a good chunk of Manhattan itself. With the sun beginning to fall, and Morton's Eye Drops casting a long shadow across the top of the roof, Jake knew that now was the time to capture his picture. Or—as he viewed it—his bait.

Jake set up the tripod on top of a ventilation fan and aimed the GoPro towards the sign. He fiddled with the exposure until the device was calibrated to his liking. After commanding the camera to take a photo every five seconds, Rivett turned on the selfie charm. He could be taciturn, but he certainly wasn't shy. If that had been the case, his band mates would never have selected him as their lead singer. But he still wasn't quite sure what to do, or what was expected. When the camera's light blinked red the first time, Jake simply shrugged. The next time he gave a thumbs-up, followed by the middle finger. He hung from the bottom of the Morton's Eye Drops sign for the last.

▪

That evening, Jake sat in front of his computer. He was trolling for likes and not getting the feedback he craved. He'd uploaded the photos from Morton's and he'd gotten only one like—his own. Nothing from Mona, nor Rory. The more he waited, the more Rivett felt like a teenager contemplating his own popularity, or lack thereof. He knew the pictures he'd shot were good. Rooftopping—it was popular. But it wasn't unique. Maybe all of it had been for nothing. After idly clicking through Mona's profile for the fourth time in the last hour, Jake reached a decision. If she wasn't going to contact him, he'd reach out. He composed a message: "Hey, Mona. It's Jake. What do you think? That's just last weekend. There's a lot more where that came from . . . Want to get together sometime?"

Click. He sent the message. Then he read it again and immediately regretted it. Dammit. *Time to step away from the computer, Jakey. You've already done enough damage for one night.*

▪

It was close to midnight. Rivett tried to turn his internal processor off, but he just couldn't do it. He continued to contemplate the utter lack of reaction to his photographs—and to himself—while racing south through the city. At least band practice might take his mind off the case for a luxurious hour or two.

Jake loved screamo because it pushed people outside of their comfort zones—himself included. Screamo wasn't about lyrics; it was jazz for the angry. It's not that Jake was a violent man. He knew what anger problems were and he didn't have them. Or maybe that's just what people with tempers told themselves? Who knows. It was just that there were heavy chips lying on his shoulders. He would never tell anyone about them. Instead, he'd spent his life moving fast and chasing risk in an attempt to knock the past out of his mind. That's why he loved spitting into the microphone and frying his vocal chords. Just like a drug, screamo allowed him to not think. It shut reality down. The music was Jake's form of therapy, the cacophony of noise equivalent to a juice cleanse for a New Ager.

Jake had been listening to screamo for a long time, ever since he'd convinced his mother to buy him a CD player in middle school. To be honest, he'd started out much lighter than screamo, with bands like R.E.M. and Pearl Jam. But he'd been forced to wander—at first musically, then physically—because of his father. His father and namesake, an Albany cop named Jake Rivett Sr., was a consistently loud, angry, and obnoxious drunk. Listening to music that raged harder than his father became Jake Jr.'s therapy. And because upstate New York is a small place, and because the Internet didn't exist and Jake wasn't the most socialized of children, he didn't know how far along the thin branch of musical genres screamo balanced. It was its own subculture inside a culture inside a sliver of an industry pie. By the time his father sent him to boarding school, ostensibly to toughen him up, Jake finally discovered how few people in the world loved what he did. He also found it quite ironic that all the prepsters and military brats at his boarding school liked Dave Matthews Band and Dispatch. Those bands were supposed to be for chill potheads, and those kids were aggressive punks.

After he graduated from boarding school and arrived in New York City, Jake began to discover the world through a new set of eyes. He'd moved into a tiny flat in Chinatown, not far from the studio that he was heading to now. He had thrown himself into the music scene in downtown Manhattan and supported himself by cleaning dishes at a restaurant in Chinatown called Palace. After a few years of attempting to "make it," Jake had learned a few sure facts.

First, overnight success was limited strictly to lottery winners with stunning personal magnetism. Nothing came easy in the music industry, even for those who worked as hard as they possibly could—even for talented guys sanding their fingers off in the back kitchen of a dingy Chinatown restaurant. No one rose to the top without intentionality and Jake had never been oriented towards stardom. Although he wasn't oblivious to his talent, his bandmates—a loosely connected group of barflies from East Village haunts—often had to remind him to be a star. Without trying, he was the most popular guy in their group. His long blond hair and Mick Jagger-skinny body looked the part, but his voice? That was the gold right there. That was the magnet. It attracted fans—women and men alike. It was just that being a front man had never felt perfectly natural for Jake. It still didn't. He just didn't get it. Music was meant to be personal. The audience wasn't Jake's priority. They would always go home and so would he. Was that what life was really all about?

The other lesson Jake learned was the golden rule of Manhattan: *You can make it here.* You can start with nothing and become something. That was the promise and the dream of the place. After a year doing dishes, Jake started helping the proprietor of Palace with supply orders. He quickly mastered Microsoft Word and Excel. He applied to the City University of New York, a small community college that Schaub was already attending. He was accepted. He continued to work at Palace, play in the band, and go to school through his mid-twenties. And when he graduated, he'd applied to approximately one hundred jobs. Ninety-nine of them turned him down, but as he stepped out of interview number one hundred, he'd walked past a police precinct. The posters on the windows made it clear: The NYPD was hiring recent college graduates. Did he want to make a difference?

Jake took a deep breath, he jumped, and he found much more excitement on the streets than on the stage. Unlike the music industry, hard work in the police department was rewarded. Promotions were possible, yes. But his work made the world a better place. What he did took bad guys—bullies and robber barons alike—off the street. Jake Rivett had spent a decade looking for peace. Once he became justice, he'd finally found his home.

▪

It was true. He'd become less mad. So what does a screamo artist do once he can control himself? He writes better songs, apparently. The lyrics that he wrote for Schaub and Mackenzie, his drummer and guitarist respectively, had become softer and much more refined. Tonight, at the studio, was the mastering session for "Out of the Mist"—with its poppy melody running throughout and words that a normal human being might actually discern on the first listen.

"What up, Jakey-boy? You're a little quiet," Schaub asked.

"Just making room for you, buddy," Jake joked.

"Work?"

"Always," Jake said, nodding.

"Want to run it past your pals?"

"Sure, but then I'd have to kill ya."

"A real funny guy."

"What happened with your birthday? We missed you . . ." Mackenzie popped in.

"I would be sorry," Schaub added. "Except for the fact that we were all waiting for you down at Sophie's. But you? Nope."

"Sorry. I was . . ."

"Trust me, I know. Hell if we were gonna go all the way up to the Pickle to pick your sorry ass up," Schaub replied.

"Hey. Can we stop talking about me?" Jake asked.

"Would love that, with a vengeance," Schaub said.

"When's the mix ready?" Jake asked, nodding to the sound engineer on the other side of the window.

"Ten or fifteen," Mackenzie responded.

"Hey. While we got the time, I had an idea," Schaub said.

"Okay . . ." Jake responded warily. Schaub's ideas were never for the faint of heart.

"We should shoot a video. For 'Mist.'"

"Don't have any cash for that," Jake objected.

"I know. But I was thinking . . . Let's do something viral."

"Yeah? You just tell a video to go viral, and it does, right?" Jake replied.

"What if it looks like it's shot randomly, but ain't?"

"What do you mean?"

"That's the technical difficulty. I dunno. Not exactly. But, like, running through a police station . . . While singing? You'd get us permission beforehand. But we'd make the video look like it was random and just, like, berserk."

"Well . . ." Jake pondered Schaub's idea.

"Straight brilliant. I know. I know."

"No way am I asking my boss to shoot a music video."

"How come?"

"'Cause I like my balls, Schaub."

▪

As Jake rode away from the studio that night, he checked his phone. Still nothing on UrbEx. Radio silence. In Internet years, six hours was an eternity. His little stunt at Morton's Eye Drops had done nothing at all except make it clear that he could lose his life at any moment. Maybe Schaub was right. Go big or go home. Make an impact. After all, Rivett had nothing else in the arsenal, no more levers to pull. He only had one more chance to make them care—if that. The only way to demand respect was by becoming irresistible. It needed to be original. It needed to be mind-bogglingly daring. How could he make the most mental urban exploration video the UrbEx community had ever seen? Maybe, just maybe, by stealing Schaub's idea.

NINE

THE HIGH-DEFINITION INTERLACING VIDEO flickered as Jake yanked his GoPro camera along with him down Fifth Street at the edge of the East Village. The video feed bounced forward with each of Jake's steps. Eventually he focused on his target ahead: a beautiful limestone police station. This was the Ninth Precinct, a stunning example of early twentieth-century municipal architecture. With six stacked levels of granite and a beautifully ornate crown towering above the street, the police station could have easily doubled as an embassy building or corporate headquarters. The first floor was highly secured, with cement pylons in front, steel doors for entry, and opaque windows. After using the GoPro to encompass the station ahead, Jake flipped the camera around to himself.

"My boy Mackenzie got drunk tanked last night," Jake said. He was decked out in street garb, with a beanie hat and leather jacket swung over his shoulder. Jake rotated the GoPro back. The image rustled briefly before becoming fixed once again. He'd secured the GoPro to his chest, aiming outwards in an almost-mirror of his own perspective. Jake's hand swung out. He reached for the handle of the police station's front door and pulled it open.

▪

The cop lady at the front desk was ultra bored, but she wouldn't tell you that. The unlocked front door meant that she was protected behind a large, bulletproof cube—like some sort of loan agent. She didn't look up as Jake approached her. He stood above her for a moment, looking for some way to indicate that he wanted to speak. This was bureaucracy at its best, offering the taxpayer no good way of not being rude in order to receive the services that were his or her right. So Jake acted like a normal peasant and knocked on the Plexiglas. The woman finally looked up.

"Hey. Uh . . . My friend was put up here last night . . . I called."

"Name?" she asked.

"Jake . . . Wait, his? Peter, uh, Mackenzie," Jake responded.

"Sign in. Write his name. Have a seat."

"Okey-dokey," Jake said.

Jake signed the guestbook as Jake Easton. He glanced around. A few people were sitting in the waiting area behind him. Jake joined them.

After a few moments, he was feeling antsy. He stood up and approached the desk again. "Hey. Where's the bathroom?" Jake asked.

The cop eyed him over—this time slightly longer than the first. Then without a word, she gestured to a door to the side of the lobby. She pressed a button simultaneously, and the door buzzed. Jake strode towards the door and passed through.

▪

In the bathroom, Jake addressed the mirror while his GoPro captured.

"Ever rooftopped a cop station?" Jake asked himself and then responded in kind. "No? Me either."

He pushed back through the bathroom door but didn't return to the lobby. Instead, Jake marched farther down the hallway into the depths of the police department. Half expecting the lady at the desk to come running in his direction, Jake hustled towards a door marked "Stairwell."

He pushed it open. Then Jake reached for the camera again. He twisted it in his direction and grinned maniacally at the lens.

"Mom and Dad? I'm sorry. But it's better to be a baller than not to live at all, right?"

Jake began to run up the stairs. He flew up one story, then another, rotating around the inside staircase as fast as he possibly could. But when he reached the third landing, a door suddenly opened in front of Jake, who had to duck hurriedly to the left in order to prevent his face from being smashed. None other than Susan Herlihy strode out. She was staring directly at Jake, a decidedly less-than-happy expression on her face.

"Jesus!" Susan screamed. "What the hell are you doing?"

"I thought Tony told ya?" Jake said as he reached for the GoPro on his chest.

"We need to talk . . . Is that a camera?" Susan asked.

Jake's finger flicked the GoPro off.

▪

After ten minutes of justifying himself to Susan and genuflecting heavily, Jake was back in action. The digital video chip inside the GoPro ignited again, and Jake started over. He began to run up the stairs— recording a second take—like nothing had happened. This time around, Susan did not show her face. Even though Jake was positive that she was probably shaking her head with concern right now while placing a call full of vitriol to Tony. But that wasn't his problem. At least not yet.

He reached the fifth landing and kept going. He peered around the corner with his camera, focusing on an ascending set of stairs.

"What's up here?" Jake pondered.

The stairwell door was clearly labeled "Roof."

"Target in sight," Jake announced.

▪

Moments later, the door to the roof swung open. As Jake bounded through, he ran directly into two cops standing in the portico of the doorway. One male and one female. Jake didn't know them, and they didn't know him. They were in uniform, sharing a cigarette. They were quite alarmed, both turning and staring at Jake's camera. One of them reached for his gun.

"Hey! Stop! I'm department, bro!" Jake had to yell. "Damn," Jake continued, "guess I'll have to cut on motion twice. You know what they say about best laid plans . . ."

"Hey, man. Is that thing on? What are you doing?" the female cop inquired.

"Yeah. Yo, what are you using that video for? My wife can't see this."

"Why? The cigarettes?" Jake asked.

"Yeah, Ron. Why?" the female turned towards Ron.

"Listen, she's got problems, you know that . . ." Ron addressed his colleague.

"Right back at her, woman!"

Jake realized that he might have stepped into something deeper than just two colleagues sharing a cigarette. Just his luck. He had to step in to avoid a meltdown. "Hey. Do you guys want to be in my movie?" he asked. They stared at him. So he tried another tact. "Susan Herlihy is in the building. Ask her. Or you could just help me and we'll leave her out of it. Which might be better for all of us."

▪

Serendipity was a powerful thing. While at first Jake was upset by the distractions standing in the way of his plan, he realized that these two blues would add a whole other level of excitement. Back in the stairs, he turned the camera on.

This time, when Jake burst through the door to the roof, no one was there. He continued to orate into the camera's microphone.

"Absolutely incredible. Want to know where I am? I'm currently standing on top of a police station . . . Ninth Precinct to be exact."

Jake guided the GoPro's lens around the entire top of the building. The building itself stood twenty to thirty feet above most the brownstones on the street, affording a fantastic view—specifically to the east where he could make out parts of Brooklyn over the river.

"Might be the most epic rooftopping I've ever done . . ." Jake began. Just then, the camera darted towards a noise behind Jake. Out of the door came two police officers, male and female. They were sprinting across the roof towards Jake, yelling as loudly as they possibly could.

"The hell do you think you're doing!" they screamed.

Jake flipped the camera towards his face. He made a funny look. Then nothing less than a mad dash commenced. He sprinted across the roof, away from the door. Just as the cops were about to overtake him, Jake cut left, cutting them at the knees. He doubled back towards the door and smashed it open with his shoulder.

Inside the stairwell, Jake took the stairs two at a time. Once he reached the bottom floor, Jake stuffed his hat and jacket into one of the trash cans before hustling back out into the waiting room. Breathing hard, Jake sat back down in one of the waiting room doors. He tilted his head downward—winking into the GoPro's ever-recording camera. Then the two cops finally appeared, pushing through the steel door to the exterior and racing outside. They didn't notice Jake. He pulled the GoPro out of his lap and aimed it out the window, taking in the two cops. They were both acting perturbed, like they'd seen a ghost. Then they started yelling at each other before finally making their way back into the building and disappearing into the depths of the place.

Jake flipped the camera around and focused on himself. A look of pure exhilaration raced across him, his face flushed with excitement.

"Explore or die," Jake said into the camera. He lifted his hand up to form the peace symbol. "Peace."

TEN

RIVETT KNEW ENOUGH ABOUT SOCIAL media now that he wanted to make it his bitch. The vigil in front of UrbEx hadn't abated—it had now extended for forty-eight hours. Jake had spent the last two days repeatedly refreshing UrbEx's main feed. But this time around, with the cop house infiltration and rooftopping video, it wasn't all in vain. No, in fact, Jake's new video had over six hundred likes and had been floating atop the feed for a full day now. He'd struck a nerve. Whether it was with the site's users, or the algorithm controlling it all, he couldn't be sure. But he knew the content was damn good.

Rivett sat on a stool at the Pickle, sucking down his third vodka soda of the night and staring directly at UrbEx on his cell phone. He watched with a smile as the views ticked up. With 612 likes and counting, he'd also managed to pull down about nine thousand views. Hey, *viral*—eat your heart out. Not that Mona or Rory, or anyone else from that crew had liked it yet. But maybe they had at least watched it.

Nikki sauntered over, cocking her body in the familiar way. "Where ya been, hunny bunny?" Nikki half smiled, half smirked.

"I've been exploring," Jake replied.

"You're a slippery boy."

"No one's ever accused me of that exact adjective . . ."

"I dunno. Just thought . . ."

"What?" Jake asked.

"Maybe you came by the bar not just for the drinks all the time," Nikki allowed a small smile to escape her lips.

Now was the time to respond in kind. In relationships, you have to strike when the iron is pipin' hot and the other ship's lights are on. He was attracted to her, sure. She was the type of girl that Hector—and most of the guys who hung out at the Silver Pickle—were irresistibly drawn to. It was also a fact that everyone quietly admired Jake because Nikki had picked him. But friendships change and so do operational circumstances. Maybe her boat was throwing down anchors, but Jake wasn't sticking around. It wasn't that he was emotionally unavailable, or that his job explicitly prohibited the relationship. Nikki was on the edge and so was he. Jake wasn't holding out for a Girl Scout. Girl Scouts—like his mother— have their own problems. He loved his mom for everything she did, and hated her for what she didn't. So maybe, like most men, Rivett was looking for someone who was half like his mother, and half not at all. But the real reason that Nikki and he would never work was darker—and more unfortunate. She was too far gone. Jake was an actor on a stage. But for Nikki, the stage was her life. He knew it, she didn't, and therein lay the problem.

"I'm just here for a drink tonight," Jake finally replied.

"It's on me," she said.

"I'll pay."

"With all your gangster money?"

"Funny," Jake allowed himself to grin.

"Now that Hector's on ice, you still workin' with his crew?"

"Nah. But you know me. I'm a hustler. Won't let it get me down. I don't even need a crew." Jake dipped down back to his phone. He didn't look over his shoulder as the door to the thin bar opened and a slice of light from the street spilled into the place. But within seconds, he could feel it. The energy inside the Pickle had changed. A few other men sitting at the bar rotated and splashed out their freshest gazes to someone standing behind Jake. The hair on the back of his neck flung itself upright. He twisted around suddenly—compelled to see who had entered.

Mona. Jake's heart skipped a beat or two and found a new, faster rhythm. She looked slightly awkward—old enough to be there but the youngest in the crowd. She was obviously looking for someone. Once she noticed Jake, she dipped down into an empty booth next to the door. She didn't look up.

"I gotta get, babe," Jake said to Nikki. He laid out a twenty-dollar bill on the bar.

"So I'm just entertainment for you?"

"No. You're always the baddest chick in the room. I love that," Jake said.

"What does that matter?"

"Precisely," Jake said. He headed across the bar, leaving Nikki to process his rejection. Nikki watched him approach the girl, becoming angrier as she connected the dots.

Jake slid into the booth across from Mona.

"For some reason, I think you're here to see me. After all, the only other reason people come here is because no one else wants them," Jake said.

"You're some sorta genius," Mona grinned.

"Right? But you got more going on than that."

"I'm not here for pleasure. Rory wants to show you something."

"So you liked my video?"

"I saw it. So did he."

"What'd you think?"

"Doesn't matter," she said.

"Huh?"

"You wanted to see our world. Maybe you can. You coming?" Mona asked.

"Where are we going?"

Mona took another long look around the dimly lit bar and its denizens. The place was swathed in a nightmarish tint of purple. "Anywhere but here," she finally said as she slid out of the booth. Her fingers hesitated on the edge of the wooden table, tapping lightly. "For the record, I think you're cool. But I don't like what he sees in you," she said.

"What do you mean?" he asked.

"You'll find out. Eventually."

Mona turned heel and walked out the front door without a word. Jake sat in the booth for only about three seconds longer, before compelling himself vertical and scampering after her.

Nikki watched them leave. She reared back and tossed two empty beer bottles into the recycling bin behind her with so much hate that they smashed into a thousand little pieces.

■

As they passed by Jake's motorcycle, double-locked to a gate in the bar's tiny alley, he grabbed a backpack from the secured bin attached to the back of the machine. Mona watched with interest.

"Call it covert preparation for an overt operation . . ."

Mona smirked. "At least some of your words sound right this time, noob."

■

Jake and Mona sat hip to hip on the subway. Neither spoke. They were in a primitive phase. Instant conclusions had already been made—but the rest was at the formation stage. Jake quietly watched through the capsule window, listening to the thundering and clacking of the subway car as connecting tunnels flickered past. Gelled filament lights illuminated each new passage for a brief second, like a heartbeat underneath the place. Jake could feel his own heart beat. He wondered briefly if the pulse would pass through his body and into hers. He felt something whenever his arm brushed against hers. Did she? A sensation of . . . electricity? Or maybe it was just the train, or his cell phone buzzing in his pocket. He pulled the device out. Sure enough, there was a text from an unknown number: "*Call your parents.*"

The message was undoubtedly from Tony, the emissary, sent at the behest of the royal one, Susan. For surrogate parents, they were just about as shitty as his real ones.

"Where do they live?" Mona asked.

Jake realized that she'd been looking over his shoulder. "Upstate. Albany."

"All good with them?" Mona asked.

"Nah."

"That's a shame."

"And yours are perfect?"

"Everyone's different. Mine is mine. We're close," she said. "My sister's everything I got."

"Where do you live?" Jake asked.

"Brooklyn. Closer to Red Hook, actually. Down south. The old part," Mona said.

"Near the party?"

"A few blocks away."

"Cool."

Silence pervaded the space for a few more moments.

"Speaking of the party," Jake started up, "what's with that Dominican guy?"

"Who?"

"Emanuel."

"You got a lot of questions," Mona replied sharply.

"Is that a problem?"

"Not really," she said. "Not for me. But the rest of these guys are paranoid. They're freaks. 'Cause that's what this world is. It's a bunch of people without control looking to scare themselves into it. Get used to it."

"I was just trying to make conversation . . ."

She looked at Jake, verifying his intentions. "Emanuel's an idiot," she said. "He's one of those dudes who goes in and tags up places. Breaks whatever's in there. Destroys stuff. That's definitely not what we do. We don't vandalize. He's not an explorer. He's not what this is about."

"He's always got a gun?"

"He's the type of guy you want to stay away from," Mona nodded. "That enough to satisfy you?"

"Plenty. Forget I asked."

■

Rory Visco was the lone element not moving in the center of the neon spires and commercial artery that was Times Square. Jake strode a step behind Mona as they approached. Rory turned and inspected Jake again, his eyes taking in the newcomer standing in front of him. Much like when Jake met him at the entrance to the UrbEx party, Rory's demeanor gave up nothing. His surface was as still as a lake, but his eyes glistened, making it quite clear that a deep lake of intellect lay beneath.

"I caught your vid," Rory finally said.

Jake allowed himself to beam.

"It was crazy. But it was stupid. A stunt. I would never infiltrate a police station. Because I don't want to give the coppers any reason to ever know my name."

Jake's smile immediately dropped. "Sure. Okay. Then why'd you bring me here?"

"'Cause you were right."

"About . . ." Jake searched, then tossed a dart. "Somebody showed you the ropes."

"Yeah. Someone did. My brother. Will."

"Cool."

"But that just got your foot in the door," Rory said with a grin. "It's what you do now that defines who you are . . . How you fit into the world. And I gotta admit . . . what you did wasn't smart, but it was pretty damn cool. If you have the balls to rooftop a cop shop? Maybe you can roll with us." Rory pointed to Jake's backpack. "What are you packin' there, brother?"

Jake swung the bag off his shoulders and into his hands. Without question, he gave it to Rory. Rory opened it and took a look, his hand quickly dashing around inside the dark corners of the satchel. After a brief moment of inspection, Rory pulled a set of lock picking tools out. Concealed inside a small leather pouch the size of a sunglasses case, the kit included fifteen tempered stainless steel tools, including a selection of hooks, rakes, extractors, and tensioners. They were the one piece of standard NYPD undercover equipment that Jake had figured would make him look golden in Rory's eyes. But Rory shook the lock picking kit in Jake's face, an angry expression on his face.

"You're an explorer, not a thief," Rory said. "Never have anything on you that's going to give the cops a reason to put you in jail."

"Come on," Jake replied incredulously.

"Come on, what?" Mona asked.

"Are you serious? Those could be useful. You guys aren't so clean," Jake said.

"Of course we are. That's how we operate," Rory said. To Jake's disbelief, Rory threw the tools into a nearby trash can. Rory rooted through Jake's bag a bit more. "I guess I need to give this a closer look, don't I?" Rory pulled out a flashlight. "One flashlight?"

"Extra batteries," Jake answered.

"Let me ask you a question. What good are the batteries if the flashlight falls down a drain?"

"Good point."

"How long have you been exploring? And give me the real, for once. Not the bullshit, 'cause I know you're good at that."

Jake took a deep breath. "Listen, ever since I was a little kid I've been exploring the world. Getting out of the house was the only thing that gave me happiness. But it's just recently, like in the last few months, that I've taken it to the next level. I'm a fast learner. I'm not afraid. And I know the city. I hope that's good enough for you."

"Next time? Two flashlights. Minimum. One on your head, one in your hand," Rory zipped the bag up and threw it back to Jake's feet. "Passion isn't enough in this game. I don't care how much you want something. I just need to know that you can do it. You have to know what you're getting into, and pack for it. Otherwise that extra thirty pounds on your body is only good for one thing: To stop you from getting where you want to go."

"I understand. Be prepared. But in the right way," Jake said, "So where we goin' tonight?"

"Where are we going?" Rory repeated Jake's question with a slow-drawl, philosophical tilt. He focused on the masses passing by them. People whizzed past them—left, right, across the street, at a diagonal, every direction possible. "That's not really the right question, is it?" Rory pointed to the crowd. "All the ants marching know where they're going. But they don't know where they are. Come with me, and I'll show you the answer to that."

Jake followed Mona and Rory—ducking out of the way of the panhandlers, topless women body-painted as Uncle Sam, and rappers hawking their latest beats—and down a small street tangential to Times Square. Rory strode down a metal staircase that accessed a couple of businesses located in basement suites. As he did, they passed a large poster for the mayor, Ronald Berg himself. Rory snarled at the poster, gripping it with his hands and ripping it off the wall. Jake watched with interest as Rory scrunched the poster into a ball and tossed it into a trash can at the bottom of the stairs.

"Um . . . Not a big fan of politicians?" Jake asked.

"You got that right," Rory replied.

"Berg?"

"Him and all of 'em."

At the end of the small corridor was a street drain, hidden on the ground behind a wall of stacked wooden pallets. It was protected only by a single steel bar that had clearly been bent upward at some point in the past. There was about a ten-inch gap.

Rory slipped his body under the horizontal guardrail.

Mona was next.

Jake took a deep breath and followed.

▪

Jake splashed directly into a large drainpipe with a wide enough diameter for him to stand up easily. Rory extended his hand and helped Jake out of the water.

"Wow, it's that easy?" Jake asked.

"I know a thousand different ways to get into these tunnels. My favorites are the fake brownstones."

"The . . . what?" Jake asked.

"Manhattan has fake buildings. Façades that look real on the outside but are really just entrances to the sewer system," Rory explained but realized quickly that Jake wasn't comprehending, "Don't worry about it. You'll get there . . ."

The three of them marched in single file through the darkness, their headlamps dancing elegantly and catching a century of moss with each swipe. The faint scent of mildew wafted through Jake's nostrils. The environment was so unfamiliar as to be alien. That's also what made it interesting—not to mention the rhythm of blood pumping ferociously through his heart. He felt alive, vital.

As they walked, Rory shined his flashlight around the entrances to a number of small pipes leading off the main drain they were traversing. Splashing behind, Jake could barely make out Rory's tentative whispering to Mona.

"See any hydras?" Rory murmured.

"Not yet," Mona replied.

"Oh well."

It took ten minutes for the group to arrive at their destination: a circular drain opening located directly at the top of the pipe.

"Crouch down there, noob," Rory ordered, and Jake followed. Rory stood on Jake's shoulders and slid the drain cover to the side. Rory grasped the top of the drain with his fingers and slowly pulled his body into the darkness above. After a few moments a rope dropped down, with large knots tied every foot or so.

■

As Jake climbed out of the circular drain and into a new space, the first thing he noticed was the tile work: Green and white subway tiles graced every single wall, a beautiful and elaborate skin that extended all the way up through vaulted cathedral ceilings. At the top of the room was a stained-glass skylight with dull light passing through. The room curved around a long loop. Rory turned on a battery-powered lantern and led the way. Jake quickly realized that this was some sort of antiquated subway station, obviously no longer in service. It was buried by time, not unlike a pharaoh in his final resting spot: jewels intact, beauty and grace preserved.

"It's . . . insane," Jake finally emoted.

"Where do you think we are?" Rory asked.

Jake glanced around in an attempt to estimate where they'd come from. He couldn't be quite sure. "Um . . . I don't know . . ."

Rory pointed to the ceiling. "We're standing directly underneath where we were fifteen minutes ago. This station was closed in 1945," Rory announced. "Not because it wasn't beautiful. Nope. Logistics were the problem. See how the entire station runs along a curve? The looping design wouldn't work with the longer subway cars that were coming into service. Down those tracks? There's a private entrance to the Waldorf Astoria. It was built for Roosevelt. Bring him right into the hotel and hide his polio from the world. You're looking at history. On pause. Just for us."

Jake took it all in. "How'd you find this place?" Jake finally asked.

"Isn't the real question: Why doesn't everyone know about it?" Rory asked.

"People are too interested in what's right in front of them. Their cell phones. Their jobs. The next appointment . . ." Jake said.

"Right. But I don't buy that. Not completely. Humans are curious. It's in our nature. And we love beauty—that's also inherent. Imagine if you were a little boy and you grew up in a tiny log cabin at the bottom of a mountain. If you lived your whole life next to that mountain, there's a damn good chance that at some point you'd climb that mountain. Probably early. Six or seven. Definitely by the time you were a teen. And you'd get to the top of that mountain and you'd look down at your house and you'd see the world a little differently," Rory said.

"But that doesn't happen in the city," Mona added.

"They take what's in front of them for granted. We don't," Rory said as a ghostly glow cast over his face. "Everyone comes to the city because they think it's the promised land. But once they get here, they're sucked up into it. The landscape reduces your imagination. It sucks away your curiosity. It turns you old—makes you worry about old people stuff. You don't remember that you're living next to mountains anymore. People think that Times Square is about the Disney Store and MTV. They think that a glass building rising into the clouds is a fortress for our modern gods—that the only way in is through the front door and up the gold-plated elevator. They never pull back the layers. They never look under the surface. But we do. We get everything. We get it all. We access all areas." Rory extended his hand out towards Jake. "My question for you is simple," Rory said. "How do you want to experience the world?"

Jake tried to be nonchalant. "The way you do."

"If that's true, you do it my way." Rory took in Mona, as if finally remembering she was there. "Our way. Our rules. It can get dangerous. I've learned that firsthand. First I'll teach you how to not die, then you'll live better than you've ever known. Are you in?"

Jake grabbed Rory's hand in deep agreement.

ELEVEN

"THE FIRST RULE OF URBAN exploration is . . . Never go alone."

Rory spoke to Jake as they walked through the eerie hallways of an old, abandoned insane asylum a few miles up the Hudson from Manhattan. It had been a nervous week since Jake had seen Rory and Mona, but they had finally come through. And now Rivett was observing with wonder a century of wallpaper peeling off the walls of the complex's old cafeteria. The location was not un-similar to a video game, but it existed in real life. The three explorers were also accompanied by two more members of Rory's core crew, both of whom Jake recognized from the party: Jack Castle and Nikolai.

"One partner is good. A crew is better," Rory said. He turned and smiled at Jake. "And hopefully they're a good one. Go ahead." Rory gestured to a steel door in front of them.

Jake pushed through the old steel door and entered a kitchen. As he stepped through, the door shut quickly behind him. Jake rotated and gripped the handle but realized that it was locked. A sensation of deep fear ran through his body. What should he do? He flung his flashlight around the dark room in vain, until he heard the voice of Rory behind the door.

"Brings me to rule number two," Rory shouted loudly. "Never let a door shut unless you've checked the lock from both sides."

A long and full minute passed while Jake stood by. What were they waiting for? When the door finally opened, Rory was grinning. Castle cackled in the back of the group. They'd clearly played this trick on others before.

"Thanks for that," Jake said.

"Learned your lesson, I bet." Mona remarked.

"Ever leave someone behind?" Jake asked.

"Only the ones I didn't like," Rory replied. "Everything's a test."

▪

Later that afternoon, they were back in Manhattan and inside the sewer system, which Jake had now learned was one of Rory's favorite haunts. Rory knew the system underneath Manhattan like the back of his hand. Better, in fact. As the crew trudged through silt at the base of a pipe, Rory began to speak.

"Rule number three. Carbon monoxide will hit you like a sledgehammer. One moment, you'll feel nothing wrong at all. The next? You're out like a light—and you aren't turning back on. Ever." Rory pointed his flashlight down a long underground corridor of arched stone. Blue spray-paint was scrawled on the sides of the wall with "NO O_2," "NO ZONE," and other similar warnings. Jake glanced at Mona as she placed a respirator over her face. Rory handed an extra one to him.

"If a place is a no zone? There's a reason for it. Don't test fate," Rory said. Once they were deep inside the corridor, Rory stopped for a moment. The area they were exploring was old, but Rory shined his flashlight above what appeared to be a downright ancient sewer tunnel entrance. Also spray-painted with "No Zone" graffiti, engraved in the keystone of the tunnel's entrance was a depiction of an ancient beast that vaguely resembled a hydra—the multi-headed serpent of Greek legend.

"What's that?" Jake asked.

"The hydra. It's the city's oldest sewer system. Practically prehistoric. Go in there and you might not come out."

"You were looking for that before. At the subway station, right? How come?"

Rory turned away from the entrance to the hydra.

"You're observant. The hydra snatches lives. But not mine."

▪

It was close to sunset. Rory walked next to Jake along the sidewalk. They had emerged from the sewer and were back in the beating heart of Manhattan. Jake recognized that they were not far from the Times Square location where they'd met.

"It's not really a rule, but the god's honest truth is that these things will save your life," Rory said.

Jake noticed that Rory was holding a pack of moist towelettes. "I get it," Jake grinned. "I'm a noob, right?"

"You are a noob. But no. Not right," Rory said as he pushed the towelettes into Jake's hand. "I'm very serious. Because of rule number four." Rory nodded down the street at a massive construction site. A skyscraper was being built—its interior skeleton arcing into the orange sky above.

"Weren't we underneath that yesterday? That's where the hydra entrance was . . ."

"You learn fast, noob. Knew you would." Rory smiled. Rory and Jake sauntered past the plywood walls that surrounded the construction site. It was a frail wall, painted black and plastered with the ever-present "Post No Bills" command that was only rarely obeyed by the public. Rory nodded through a break in the plywood wall, towards a security booth just off the entrance to the site.

"Rule four. Location hacking is sometimes nothing more than human hacking. What that means is: perception is everything."

The two of them padded around a corner and were quickly joined by the rest of the crew. Jake watched with interest as every single person began to pull out packages of towelettes, including Mona. They wiped their faces clean from the dirt and grime of the sewer below. Mona pulled her hair into a bun. She yanked off her head-mounted light and pulled a yellow hard hat out of her bag. Jake felt someone tapping his shoulder. It was Rory, holding a white hard hat. Jake put it on as he scrubbed his face with the towelette. Within moments, Jake and the crew had been transformed into a group of construction workers, electrical specialists, and in Mona's case, an architect. One by one, they slipped through a large gap in the fence and infiltrated the worksite.

▪

Rory's crew stood confidently in a mesh-enclosed elevator, holding their clipboards tight. There was a nervous pause as an authentic construction worker with a thermos entered the elevator on the second floor. But he didn't pay them any attention. He was too intent upon his cell phone, thinking nothing of the explorers as the elevator flew up towards the top layers of the skyscraper. The view became more monumental as they ascended hundreds of feet into the air, but Jake was having difficulty taking in the scenery.

Mona gazed at the setting sun. When she turned to see how Jake was doing, she immediately noted the grim appearance of his face. Curious, she glanced down and noticed Jake's fingers clenching the elevator's railing as if for dear life—*like a vise*. She said nothing.

Midway through their route, the construction worker who had joined them took his exit. They proceeded towards the top of the building. They quickly exited the elevator a few floors from the top. The sun rested lazily near the horizon, taking its time with the death of the day, and the cement columns of the skyscraper's sub-skeleton cast long shadows across the floor.

"Rule number five. My brother taught me this one," Rory said as he led Jake towards the edge of the concrete floor. About to take another step, Rory flinched and stopped his motion mid-step. "Never go where you can't see. If you don't know what's there? Don't go. Take your time. Survey the scene. Preparation makes all the difference." Rory swung his flashlight towards his feet. It shone on the floor, and Jake could clearly recognize that the concrete was still wet, with dangerous rebar poking out from underneath.

Needless to say, the crew changed direction. They headed towards the opposite edge of the building and took a breather. Castle sat on the floor. Nik strode out along a steel I-beam extending perpendicularly from the skyscraper. Nik then crouched and lay down, closing his eyes for a nap a thousand feet in the air. They all took in the gorgeous sunset from eighty stories up. Magic hour was almost finito and the sky was full of fire. A good fifteen feet from the open edge and standing next to Rory, Jake was able to relax and take in the view. It was truly epic. He found himself reflecting on what Rory had said the night before. Some men and women in this city paid rent the equivalent of Jake's yearly salary—every single month—in order to drink their nightcaps to this view. But Rory was right. Now that Jake had it for free, he couldn't imagine it any other way.

"So where's your brother these days?" Jake asked Rory, "Will, right? He's the one . . ."

"He's what?"

"Who taught you everything."

Rory didn't immediately respond. Instead, he perked up and handed Jake a small camera. "It's click-click time. You asked me yesterday why we do this? The photos—they're our reward. You want to take a squad shot for us? Sorry man, you can't really be in the picture until you pass . . ."

"Pass? Huh?" Jake asked as he reached for the camera.

"Initiation," Rory said.

Ahead of Jake, the group lined up for a photo.

"Everybody ready?" Jake asked. He looked back down at the camera. Pretending to fumble with the autofocus button, he was actually searching through all the photos on the memory card. Unfortunately, his quick scrolling found nothing suspicious.

"What up, man? Take the photo," Rory commanded. "And by the way, that brings us to the last rule. It's a simple one, but it's also the most important: trust your crew."

The group all dropped their upside-down hand symbol at the same time. Now Jake knew what it meant. It was an "A." Access—*the point of it all.* Access was what they desired. They wanted to see a world that no one else could. Not even the rich and famous could have what they had right now. No one could pay for a view like this, unobstructed even by windows. It was free for the taking but impossible to achieve at the same time. And they'd done both.

Click. A brief freeze frame on the camera as the picture came through. Jake looked up at Rory. "I think it's great. Want one on your phone too?"

"Nah. That's good enough," Rory said.

Jake handed the camera back to Rory, who was busy gazing vertical.

Up a flight of stairs to the very tip-top level of the building, an angled crane on a rotating jib extended another two hundred feet into the sky. The crane was like a groom's hand waving out from the top of a ten-tier wedding cake. Once Rory noticed the crane, it was clear that he had to conquer it. Rory glanced at his watch.

"Twenty more minutes 'til nautical sunset. Plenty of time. Right?"

"Sure," Mona said. "You could call it that."

"Hey, Nik!" Rory yelled. "Get the Phantom out!"

Jake watched curiously as Nikolai opened his backpack and pulled out the pieces of a four-rotor Phantom drone. Nik's hands moved deftly, like a watchmaker who's seen the parts a thousand times before. Within a minute or two, Nik had assembled the drone. Another GoPro camera was attached to the bottom of the drone, and it was secured to a rotating gimbal, controllable from a remote tablet. As Rory started towards the crane, Nik launched the drone into the air like a falcon.

The crew slowly followed Rory up the crane, climbing up the runway, a solid piece of steel that held the skeletal arm of the crane like a massive geometric elbow. As Rory reached the steel gridwork that composed the crane's limb itself, he looked back. He noticed that Jake had stopped moving, just a few feet onto the runway.

"You all right, bud?" Rory asked.

"I think . . . I . . . Uh. Not feeling too good all of a sudden."

Rory noticed Jake's foot anxiously tapping the side of the crane, slipping every few seconds while he attempted to stabilize his core.

"No one's forcing you to do anything. Exploring's about you. Can you take control? Ultimately you're the only guy who can answer that question."

"I know," Jake nodded. "But like, all it takes is . . . A little bit of grease . . ."

Rory shrugged. He continued up the crane. Mona reached Jake on the runway.

"Don't be scared," she said from behind him. "Are you afraid of heights?"

The answer was clear, but Jake didn't dare expose himself completely. He simply wasn't moving. He looked ahead. Rory, Castle, and Nikolai had moved much farther up. Jake gazed at them. "Nah. I don't feel good . . . I think I just ate something bad . . ." Jake said. He began to slide back down the runway towards the relative safety of the top of the building. Mona held onto a rail as he passed. Rivett was almost in a trance at this point. Mona exhaled a deep breath and followed him down. Jake sat down on the top of the building, his head hanging between his knees. Simply trying to regain his bearings, the entire world was spinning around him. It wasn't until Mona sat down next to him that he felt better. Her presence grounded him. Her shoulder was a solid waystation within the ocean of vertigo.

"You're okay. You'll be fine. Breathe deep," she said.

He did, and after a bit, his cranium began to revive itself. He didn't want to look down, so he ran his eyes up the crane that he hadn't been able to conquer—all the way to Rory, Castle, and Nikolai.

▪

The drone circled above the three men on the final homestretch. They methodically climbed up the inside of the crane, its angle rising from 45 to 55 degrees, and eventually steeper. It was patently insane—the wind whipped their clothing like Tibetan prayer flags. Unable to hear each other due to the gusting wind, they relied on hand signals. Eventually the crane's internal angle was such that it turned into a vertical ladder. They continued to ascend with no ropes. Finally reaching the highest point of the crane, Rory found himself on the top of the world. As the three of them gazed around, their natural perspective began to resemble a fish-eye lens—they were up so high that the horizon was slightly rounded.

Nik hung onto a rung below Rory, one arm and one leg connected, the other two hanging free and clear like a monkey from the canopy. He screamed with delight, pointing at the drone flying above.

Castle glanced down and noticed Jake back on the ground with Mona. Waving to achieve Rory's attention, Castle pointed down to Jake with a questionable expression on his face. Whether it was Jake and Mona sitting like two peas in a pod, or the fact that Jake hadn't followed them up the crane, it was clear that Castle didn't like what he saw.

Rory only shrugged.

▪

Down below, Jake watched Mona's phone stream the video from the Phantom. After Mona confirmed that the three men were back on the way down, she turned off the feed. She gazed at Jake.

"It's okay to ask for it . . ." she said.

"What?"

"Help."

"With?"

"Whatever it is that scares you . . . about looking down at where you came from."

"Will you help me?" he finally asked.

"With what?"

"Heights."

Mona smiled brightly. "Thought you'd never ask."

TWELVE

IT WAS A SLEEPY MORNING on the High Line park. Sprinkled tourists and joggers strolled along the trendy, renovated greenway that was spreading across Manhattan—a modern punctuation mark denoting the city's "coolness." Jake sat on a bench composed of aesthetically pleasing poured cement. Tony Villalon was next to him, smoking a cigarette nervously.

"It's been a week. I feel like a girl who's getting stood up. Why aren't you calling me back?"

"I'm working the case a little too hard to play phone tag," Jake replied.

"If you don't follow protocol, I can't protect you," Tony said.

"Sometimes I think I'll have a bigger problem if I do."

Tony sighed. "So, what's up?"

"Everyone thinks this place is so fresh. But did you know the park was inspired by one in Paris? Promenade Plantée. Built twenty years ago."

"Great." Tony chugged his cigarette. "I've never been here before."

"That doesn't surprise me. You've only lived in New York your whole life."

"I don't have a lot of time for history lessons," Tony answered. "Talk to me, Rivett. Can you finger them yet?"

"Don't think so." Jake shook his head negatively.

"Why not? What have you been doing?"

"I'm getting in there. Slowly, but it's working. Went to a party. Met a bunch of them. Went out with them the last couple nights. But there's a problem—it's not small. They're like Boy Scouts, Tony. They made me feel like a bad guy for bringing a pick set with me."

"For real?"

"I don't know what to say. I pushed back, but they literally made me throw the thing out."

"But they're the ones with that stupid hand symbol . . ." Tony replied.

"I still can't confirm if it's just the Rory Visco crew, or if everyone does that."

"Why don't you ask?"

"They don't take kindly to questions. Not yet," Jake replied. "Did you and Fong make the electronic pulls?"

"Yeah," Tony said. "Truly zilch. No selfie. Nothing else incriminating on their phones or computers."

"I might have one thing. A lead. Name's Emanuel Vipa."

"Who's that?"

"Some guy in the scene. Just see if he has a record, okay?"

"That's all you're going to give me?" Tony asked. "You gotta learn how to take some help here and there."

"That's funny. Someone else said that to me yesterday."

"What I don't get is . . . Why do you like doing it all yourself?"

"It's like you and the cancer sticks, Tony," Jake said. "You're smoking that right now because Jon and the kid are at home, and this is a great excuse to get you out of the house. You can't smoke at home, which is what you really want to do." Jake grabbed the cigarette from Tony's fingers and took a long drag. He exhaled the smoke lazily into the air, luxuriously—no care in the world. "Only difference between you and me is that I'm honest with myself. That's what no one ever gets. I live the way I want to because I like it. It's all my choice."

"I guess . . . I knew all that," Tony said.

"You and I aren't really that different, you know. Both of us wanted something different from our lives. And we were gonna get it—come hell or high water."

"That's why I protect you, Jake," Tony said, his eyes locked on the cement pathway below him. "Something else I gotta brief you on . . ." he finally said.

"What?"

"Hector," Tony answered.

"What about him?"

"DA's not going to prosecute," Tony shook his head lightly. "Whole thing was messy to begin with, and . . . Whatever. They didn't like what you did to that girl. They're calling it entrapment, even though it's obviously not. We don't want to expose you, especially not right now. So we can't get you deposed or on the stand to take him down. It's all bull in my opinion, but he's going to skate."

"What the hell?" Jake's dumbfounded.

"Sorry. Keep the cig. You're right. I gotta get home," Tony said.

Tony stood up and paced away from Jake on the top of the High Line.

When Jake was by himself, he reflected. The whole system was such a goddamned circus. Problem was that he was the lion tamer. He was the guy standing in the cage with all the motorcycles spinning around him. Nah. If Susan was the ringmaster and Tony her assistant, maybe Jake was just a clown.

▪

Later that night, Jake hung from the iron sides of the Brooklyn Bridge with a single hand. Suspended and staring down into the depths of the water below, he couldn't help but wonder how he'd gotten himself into this state of affairs. The case. But was it? He'd always flown a little closer to the sun than necessary. Jake was the guy who would always say one more thing to his dad. He was liable to smash through that last desk with his crowbar during a search. And he was certainly inclined to say yes to a girl.

He stopped philosophizing as the height took hold—its transcendental power whispering to him. No. That was a person. Someone yelling. But the words were modulated by the wavelengths of his own brain into a mushy echo. He couldn't quite figure it out.

"Jake!"

Jake broke out of his reverie. He jerked. The source of the sound: Mona. There she was, standing above him, already having ascended the side of the bridge's base. She was holding out her hand. He grabbed it. Jake climbed up on top of the giant concrete abutment that held the cable spans in place. They crouched down on the concrete pad as a heavy mass of traffic whizzed past below.

"Are you insane?" Jake asked.

"What?"

"Guess I didn't take you for one of those people that believes you can just toss a baby in a pool to teach it to swim."

"There's a better way?"

"Thought you said you were going to help . . ."

"I'm going to help you help yourself," Mona announced. She gazed up the bridge's suspension cable ahead of them. "Now's the easy part. You're going to walk right up that span to the top of this bridge."

Jake gazed at the incredibly thick suspension cable as it arced parabolically into the night sky towards the iconic elevated brick towers of the bridge.

"Christ," was all he could emote.

"It does become tricky at the end. Let's worry about that when we get there. Don't worry. Keep your core aligned. Head straight ahead. I'll be there."

"What the hell. It's only my life," he exclaimed.

"And aren't you happy that you're living it?"

At first, the ascent was fairly easy, like the beginning stages of a long, swooping mountain pass. But once they were halfway up, Jake's pace slowed. When he glanced down to make sure his feet were in position, he couldn't avoid noticing the distance between himself and the bridge surface. His equilibrium was further altered by the blackness of the water below, like a mass of infinity ready to eat him up in the event of any minor error. He stopped moving. As he took a series of deep breaths, Jake realized that his hands had turned clammy—a cold and paralyzing sensation spreading to the center of his chest.

"Proceed!" Mona yelled from above, having turned around to check on him. She extended her arm out, attempting to help him climb up past the next divider.

"I'm going to puke."

"No. Grab my hand," she said.

But he didn't. Jake suddenly collapsed over the parapet guide wire. His eyes were drawn to the water below—transfixed—a panic attack taking hold.

Mona backed down towards Jake. She grabbed his face.

"Jake!" she yelled.

Jake's eyes finally cleared up. "Wh-what?"

"We're halfway."

"I'm . . . I'm fine."

"You got this far. You can do this. Your body is more than capable. The only thing pulling you back is your head. Who's in charge? Take control."

Jake looked up. The ascent began to pitch sharply up, turning from a mountain path to scaling K2 with a ladder. He wasn't sure what to do, until the beam of a strong flashlight flowed over both him and Mona.

Jake gazed down. A Port Authority worker had parked his official pickup truck on the side of the road. With the blinkers on, he was interrupting the flow of traffic and causing quite a commotion. Actually, Jake reflected, *they* were the cause of the commotion.

"Get down from there! Right now! I called the police on you already!" the worker was screaming.

Mona nodded at Jake, a worried look in her eyes. They slowly traced their way down. His heart pounding deeply out of his chest, Jake led. He did his best not to look down. For some bizarre reason, the adrenaline of the trouble awaiting them kept him focused. They finally reached the cement pad where the cable met the end of the bridge. Jake twisted over his shoulder. The Port Authority supervisor was backing up along the bridge, still in pursuit. The vehicle beeped as it did so, yellow flashers going wild. But due to the flow of traffic, it wasn't going very quickly. They had just a few more seconds to escape. Jake dropped off the side of the abutment and onto the street below. He reached up for Mona and helped her down.

As they sprinted away from the bridge, Jake noticed a large park across the street, the Brooklyn Heights Promenade.

"Over there, the park . . ."

They scurried across the street and into the relative darkness of the park. As they walked through a grove of trees surrounded by a stone wall, Mona pulled her backpack off. Out with the towelettes.

"Think they're going to chase us?" Jake asked.

"Abso-hella-lutely," Mona said. "Rory's going to be pissed."

"Why?"

"Let's just say that if we get nailed, he's going to disappear into the ether . . ."

"Come on, you guys are family. He wouldn't do that."

"Stuff changes. You gotta know that," Mona said. "Come on. Quick, quick, clean me up too."

She wiped off Jake's face. He did the same to her. Now they could hear shouting coming from the side of the park closest to the bridge. Two police cars converged, their lights on.

"Should we leave our stuff?" Jake asked.

She began looking through the grove of trees for an adequate hiding spot.

"Ever heard of a bear bag? One of the only good things I learned upstate," Jake said. He scanned the trees above while he pulled a rope out of the back of his bag. He flung the rope over a knot of branches in a tree. After it flopped back down, he secured both of their bags and quickly ratcheted them vertical until they were well secured—about twenty feet off the ground.

"Pretty impressive," Mona said. "Albany, right? How'd you get down here?"

"Rather not talk about it. It's not like you tell me a lot either . . ."

"You haven't asked," she said.

"Want me to?"

"Don't care. But you do."

"What?" he asked.

"Let me put it this way. Between the two of us? You're the closed book."

The vibrating sound of helicopter rotors ricocheted through the park. Jake angled up and spotted an NYPD helicopter flying above, scanning for them.

"Instead of standing around and talking out our family histories, maybe we should get out of here," he said.

"Superb idea," she responded.

"Want a drink?"

▪

A few blocks from the back of the park, it finally seemed as though they'd escaped unscathed from the police presence. Jake spotted a dive bar across the street. They crossed towards the bar, striding past another couple smoking cigarettes. As they were about to hand the bouncer their IDs, Jake noticed a police car roll down the street. He pulled back and put his arm around Mona's waist. As the officers drove past and shined their high-powered, car-mounted spotlight at the bar's entrance, Jake pulled Mona in.

They kissed. The moment was brief. At least it should have been. But then they didn't find themselves stopping. Even when the spotlight had passed. After thirty seconds, they broke.

"A drink?" Jake asked.

"That's probably enough lessons for one day."

"Well, you're the only teacher I ever got to make out with at the end of the class."

Mona smiled coyly.

"Is that a problem?" Jake asked.

"What do you mean?"

"With Rory?"

"Rory's not a problem. I live my own life. I make my own decisions."

"Me too," Jake replied. "So should we try again tomorrow night?"

"Don't think I can. The crew's going out . . . It's been in the works for a while."

"Let me come? Come on."

"Not my call."

"You're going to hold out on me? Thought you trusted me . . ."

"He invites you," Mona shook her head, "not the other way around."

"When do I get to not feel like a second-class citizen?"

"Initiation."

"When's that, Mona?"

"I'd tell you, but I don't know."

"So what can you tell me?"

"Listen, Rory is more observant than you'd guess. He goes right for the gut, Jake. Rory goes for your Achilles' heel and he knows what it is."

For once, Jake didn't have an easy quip.

"It's late. I'm going home," Mona said. She turned and walked down the street.

"Hey . . ." Jake yelled after her. "Thank you!"

She didn't look back. She never did. Maybe that's what he liked so much about her.

▪

Rivett ripped the motorcycle north along the west side of Manhattan, on his way back home to the Bronx. Passing an ancient retaining wall he'd probably seen a thousand times before, Jake noticed something new. The embankment had been built over an old sewer entrance, iron bars preventing access. He slowed. He noticed the keystone of the arch above the entrance was imprinted with a hydra. The hydra. A recurring piece of the city that formed a texture in and of itself—and largely for itself. The hydra was a map to a landscape that Rivett had never noticed before. He had never even known it existed. Now he couldn't avoid it.

Ring. Ring. Jake's phone was blowing up as he rode. He could hear the Bluetooth-enabled speakers inside his helmet blaring. He answered.

"A little late for you, Tony? Why aren't you resting your little head?" Jake said.

"Let's talk Emanuel Vipa . . ."

"What'd you get?"

"His rap sheet's long enough that you and I are pulling cable guy duty."

"When?"

"All day, every day," Tony said.

THIRTEEN

JACK CASTLE CONSIDERED HIMSELF SOMETHING of a chameleon. Castle had originally met the Visco brothers—Rory *and* Will—in the halcyon days. That was long before websites and social networks had proliferated with detailed instructions and play-by-play routines for urban exploration. Nowadays anyone with a cell phone could find the most coveted locations across the globe. It certainly hadn't always been that way. Times had changed. For a long while, it had just been the three of them out there in the urban wilderness. They had no proof that anyone else was doing what they were. When they'd started out, there were no rules for urban exploration. The culture didn't even have a name. Rory invented one when it became too distasteful to mention in casual conversation that he'd spent all weekend "trespassing." Rory had coined most of the jargon of the scene too: rooftopping, drainsledding, sewering, geotagging, and many more.

But Castle had been there the whole time next to him.

They were a good combination. Castle taught Rory about the streets, and Rory imprinted the power of behavior on Castle. Castle didn't go to MIT like Rory. He was barely educated. He'd actually dropped out of high school in eleventh grade and begun working at a tattoo shop as an assistant, where he'd later met Will Visco. That's also the place Castle perfected the small details of his chic greaser look: the shaved sides of his head, hair up high and Brylcreem slickback applied every morning without fail, the tight dark jeans with an inch of roll up. That was Castle's natural appearance, his preferred style. What Castle had learned from Rory, over the years, was that appearances could be very deceiving. Castle dressed the way he did because it offered a glimpse into the emo bravado that pervaded his soul. But you could also dress in a way that you were not. You could also offer an artificial façade to the world. The devil was in the details. A man could be perceived as a banker if he dressed in a blue Brooks Brothers suit with a lightly patterned silk tie, but a poseur if it was double breasted or if his shoes had the cheap stitching of Chinese leather goods. You might be let into a club if you wore a simple Alexander Wang T-shirt, but the velvet rope wouldn't budge if you were wearing Hanes. Yes, they were the same color and style of shirt. But they signified diametrically opposed arenas of life. No one had taught Castle this lesson more completely than Rory. Upon meeting, Castle did not guess that Rory had scored a 1600 on his SATs, that his mind could render engineering diagrams faster than a CAD program, or that he made tens of thousands of dollars a year self-publishing urban exploration books online. Rory didn't advertise his past, present, or future. He just *did*.

By taking his life lessons from Rory, Castle was able to transcend the tattoo shop. He had wanted to experience the world and occupy a larger sphere than his own. He had wanted to be around people who would show him an interesting viewpoint upon reality. He worked as a backstage manager at music venue for a year, and followed that up by bouncing the hottest nightclubs in town. He'd moved to the private crew of a Russian-owned yacht, memorized every working detail of the boat, before jumping into the hospitality business. Of course, there was an ulterior motive to the jobs Castle picked. He wanted to know what these worlds were like—and learn how to act like the people who occupied them. And he wanted more than that. He wanted nothing less than to become the people he idolized.

Rory didn't know what Castle was doing tonight. Castle felt it was his job to protect and insulate his boss, his buddy—*his best friend*. It was something about the brash attitude. Jake Easton rankled Castle. It went beyond the fact that Castle was the tough guy, the one who'd try anything. Jake wasn't gonna take that spot from him, ever. No fucking way. But it wasn't only that. It was something about the man himself, about the way he observed the world, about his essence. Maybe a sycophant can recognize himself in another. Castle had spent his life trying to become someone other than who he was, and by most measures he'd succeeded. And now someone else had entered his realm and he knew that person was doing the same thing he had. He didn't like it.

He'd listened to Mona intently when she described her conversation with the new guy. He knew where to find Easton, or at least people that knew him. And if his mission came up with nil? At least he'd done the dirty work. Someone had to keep them safe. Someone had to turn over each and every stone. Rory would be so proud of him. That's why Castle was pounding down the pavement deep into the Bronx. He was dressed as a lower-key version of himself, or perhaps an earlier iteration. It was back to the tattoo shop, back to piss in alleyways and two or three knives on the body. That's what the Silver Pickle called for and he wasn't going to be fucked with. He'd fit right in. They wouldn't glance over him twice.

▪

Nikki was struck by the new guy's protruding, angular cheekbones. She'd been working the Pickle for three years. She'd bonded with all the regulars. Not only that, but she could spot semi-regulars and even people who'd been in just a few times. It didn't take much. A few trips around the block and she knew ya. That was part of her charm, because most men and women alike appreciate being remembered. The feeling was universal —no matter who or where one was. For a person at the end of the long barrel of life, there was nothing more special than the brief feeling that his or her existence had a purpose. But this one? She couldn't place him.

Jack Castle idled up to the bar, only occupied by an elderly gentleman at a corner and two construction workers in the middle. Castle sat one stool away from the older man whose presence seemed permanent. The man was glued to the television, his personal belongings strewn in a circular fashion around the bar as if a workspace. An ashtray with multiple cigarette butts sat ahead.

Nikki approached the newcomer, "What can I get ya?"

"A beer. A lighter one."

"Coors? Heineken?" she asked.

"Sure."

"Which?"

"I'll take the Coors, thanks."

"Don't need to ID you, right?" Nikki asked.

"You can do whatever you want," he grinned.

"Wasn't a compliment," Nikki said. "I know you're over twenty-one. But most men know exactly what they want to drink." *Zing*. Nikki was always memorable.

While she rummaged around a cooler in search of a Coors, Castle turned his attention to the elderly gent sitting next to him.

"Here a lot?"

"My favorite place. Favorite girl, too . . ." The old man yelled, "Right, Nikki!"

"In your dreams, Pastor!"

"You're a pastor?" Castle asked the man.

"Without a congregation. But I still write my sermons," the man gestured to the work in front of him.

"You ever seen a guy named Jake Easton here? He's a thinner guy. Skinnier than me. Wears leather. Blond hair, like a vampire?"

The pastor pondered Castle's question. "I dunno . . . Maybe. Now that you mention it, I think I have, in fact."

"What's that guy do?" Castle asked.

"What's he do?" the pastor started to cackle, which turned into a cough. He took a sip of beer, calming his throat. He followed that up with a puff from his cigarette, which only exacerbated the situation.

Castle waited patiently until the man had regained control of himself.

"What's he do? He drinks!" the pastor said. He began laughing again.

"You know who I'm talking about?" Castle asked.

"John. Yeah. John!"

Castle sighed as Nikki approached him with the beer in hand.

"Why do you want to know about Jake?" Nikki asked.

"You know him?" Castle said.

"What's it to you?"

"I just want to know what he's about. He's been rolling with one of my friends lately."

"That girl?" Nikki said.

"Mona."

"I don't know . . ." Nikki shook her head

"Her name's Mona. I just want to make sure he's the real deal. Not going to mess her life up."

"If you care about that girl, you're real lucky you came here." Nikki smiled coyly. "'Cause I can guarantee you he'll turn her heart to mush. Then right when she's in the palm of his hand, he'll close it and crush her."

"He have a job?" Castle asked.

"Don't think so. Not a real one anyway. He was rolling with a bunch of bikers that were slingin' out of this place called Fireblade. That's all I know. He likes to sing."

"Sing?"

"Yeah. He's in a band. What's up with the questions?"

"I'm just lookin' out for my girl."

"So they're dating?" Nikki asked.

"I wouldn't call it that," Castle said.

"I don't think that he'd be thrilled I'm talking to you. Jake's a . . . He keeps to himself," she said. "That's . . ." she trailed off.

"What?"

"Never mind."

"Listen, Mona and I go way back. She never picks the right ones. So if this cat does anything you don't like? You think she should know about it? Call me, babe," Castle said as he stood up from the bar. He'd only taken a tiny sip of the Coors. He slipped a piece of paper with his cell phone number across the bar.

"Funny way to give a girl your number."

"Text me—anytime," Castle said with a grin.

"Don't bet on it, bucko," Nikki replied. But she swiped the paper anyway and jammed it into her hip pocket.

FOURTEEN

EMANUEL VIPA PREFERRED VIDEO GAMES over babes. Although a couple of well-dressed ladies sat in the back of Vipa's living room, he was focused on digital murder. He and his buddies were playing Call of Duty on a massive screen at the end of the room. This was a party if you wanted to call it that. But in reality, it was a few male Homo sapiens sipping on medication-enhanced juice and glued to the giant rock in front of them, while their ladies sat in the back of the room on their phones.

"This dude's gotta be using cheat codes!" Vipa's buddy, Sammy, yelled at their digital opponent across the globe.

"You are such a pussy," Emanuel laughed, "I guarantee you homie's a twelve-year-old kid with his eyes closed and he's still crushing you, bro." After his character died in a bloody flux of pixels, Emanuel put aside the controller. He picked up a huge bong, sparked a lighter, and hit it as hard as he could. A huge plume of smoke erupted from Emanuel's mouth. He giggled. He was quite stoned. There was nothing more pleasurable to Emanuel than a sudden burst of tetrahydrocannabinol directly into his brain. It also had the added effect of making the 4K resolution of his television screen particularly vibrant. Of course, deep down inside he knew that Valeria might be pissed later tonight when he couldn't get it up.

The drug made his video games better and his sex life worse. But there was a time and place for them both, and he was celebrating tonight. She'd stick around. Because underneath the bong, there was a huge stack of cash sitting on the coffee table. The easiest money Emanuel had ever made. And his new friends were more than willing to pay for what seemed like no work at all. It made Emanuel feel good. He wasn't a thug, he was an information worker now. He was working his way up the food chain, shoulder to shoulder with big hitters. Heavies—like he'd always wanted to be. *No.* Like he could be. Like he was.

■

Electronic wavelengths zipped and ricocheted through the ether surrounding Emanuel's apartment. Somewhere between the Wi-Fi, cell phone, radio and infinite other frequencies on the spectrum, close attention was being paid to Vipa. The watchers were police officers, and they were stuffed like sardines into a cable van across the street.

Inside the vehicle, a flatscreen flickered as it displayed a heat-sensing "FLIR" system. The forward-looking infrared radiometer screen portrayed a mirror image of what was occurring in Emanuel's apartment, but displayed as a heat map. Bodies burned the brightest red, and the corners of the room faded from green to blue. Tony Villalon sat on the chair closest to the monitor, his elbows leaning against the counter in front of the unit. His wrists ached. He'd been listening to the banal conversation of Emanuel and his crew for the last three hours—the sound ferried into the van through another contraption, a volume-penetrating mic system the CIA had recently unloaded on them. Vipa, Sammy, and the others seemed to occupy a space somewhere between your average urban pothead and low-level drug dealer. But neither of those classifications deserved the utilization of an advanced rig like the cops were rocking.

Jake sat behind Tony, paying slightly less attention. While he listened to Emanuel's conversation filtering through the cheap speakers on each side of the FLIR monitor, he also had a headphone earbud in one ear. He was surreptitiously vibing to the mastered cut of "Out of the Mist." He liked what he heard a helluva lot. Music had always drowned out reality for Jake. He used to muffle the loud diatribes of his father, but now he was avoiding the cynical cacklings of lowlives. The application was different but the effect identical. It was utterly cathartic.

Next to Jake were two more undercover agents who worked out of the safe house in New Rochelle: Markle and Fonger. Markle was a compact, 0-percent-body-fat warrior from Texas who spent all his off-time watching reality television. He was on loan from SWAT and had worked with Jake many times in the past—one of the most intelligent and kinetic operators in the department, bar none. No one called Dennis Fong by his first name, if they even remembered it. He was a big guy with a past in the special forces who for all intents and purposes should have been a bruiser like Markle. But Fong was actually a technical expert. He'd worked in Afghanistan but couldn't talk about it. Nor could he tell you about his time in Libya, or Syria, or Yemen. He was held in particularly high regard by Tony and Susan because of his unflagging work ethic and dedication to the job. Ironically, given Fong's refrigerator-like build, he was as stealthy as a mouse and could be counted on to break through a window or drop himself down an air-conditioning vent in pursuit of an ethernet router, with more proficiency than practically anyone else on the force. By this point in the night, even the zen-like Fong was getting antsy. It was cold in the van, and they weren't able to run the engine. They had a small heater on the floor, but these four men had been stuck in a room the size of a closet for hours, and they were straight miserable.

"I'm getting a lot of high school flashbacks right now," Fong said.

"You smoked weed?" Tony asked.

"Yeah, till my Mom found out and I went out and drove around the park and smashed my bowl into a million pieces and sent myself to the military."

"For real?" Jake asked.

Fong nodded. "I felt guilty."

"So you joined the military because you felt guilty about smoking weed? That's a pretty big swing the other direction . . ."

"Still feel the guilt?" Markle added.

"Nah. Now I'm just waiting till I don't work for the government," Fong grinned. "I do want to bust this punk and get it over with, though."

"I just don't see it," Jake said, shaking his head.

"What do you mean?" Tony said.

"Maybe Vipa's the type of guy who'd want to do a primo heist. But come on," Jake gestured to the screens. "These bozos don't have the chops for that."

"That's not a good enough hunch for me. You said he's got a gun. He's a hothead, and he's shown aggressive tendencies in the past. He's considered a talented explorer. He's either our guy or he's part of the puzzle," Tony announced.

"It's really a grand irony, isn't it? This dorknut. Breaking New York State laws. But because they're not bad enough laws, I get to sit here and watch my skin crack," Jake said.

Tony shrugged. "All of us are on Vipa now. That means you too, Jake. This man," Tony leaned back and pointed to the FLIR machine, "is our primary target."

"Wish he weren't," Jake said.

"And if you're cold? Smoking heats the body up." Tony pulled a blue e-cigarette vape from his pocket. "Tell me if the smell bothers you. It shouldn't. It's raspberry. Uses oil droplets—or something. Whatever. It said on the back of the box that it's much safer than cigs. Johnathan still hasn't figured out where the smell comes from, which is also nice."

Fonger patted Tony on the back. "You're my type of man, Tony."

"Don't know if you mean that exactly," Jake grinned.

"I like people who do what they want . . . and just don't talk about it."

"Me too," Jake replied.

▪

Fifteen miles south, blue and gray glass spilled down the side of the SoHo Modern building like an undulating river. The exactingly perfect building was one of the phalanxes of nouveau architectural projects that had sprung up in the city post-recession. It was an artistic movement that didn't even have a proper name yet. With the fall of the financial titans, the modernist and postmodernist styles which had dominated the city from the sixties until the early two thousands had fallen out of style. What emerged from the rubble was just as 2.0 as everything else; it was completely computer powered and idealistic and utterly individualistic. Frank Gehry personified the new wave of architecture, but even he was a senior within the new realm. The SoHo Modern could never have been erected ten years earlier, because disruption had not occurred. It was disruption that had created the numerous new material compounds necessary for a building like the Modern to go up. But now that the Modern was a few years old, a few hundred other projects like it were emerging. They were slick. They looked like a dream. The glass bent, the metal warped, and yet the whole thing stood like bedrock. The Modern wasn't for the public. It was a boutique residence with forty ultra-expensive units. The cheapest apartment in the building was a one-bedroom that recently traded for north of three million dollars. The most expensive? Who knows? New records were being set every day.

▪

Across the street from the SoHo Modern, a night watchman switched the lights off inside a bank's office building. He was about to leave when he stared across the street and towards the shaded glass of the Modern. He had noticed a Sprinter utility van stopped in an alleyway next to the Modern a few minutes earlier. As he gazed out the window, it was still there. Now the back doors were open. Three men jumped out of the van. But none of that was what stopped the night watchman in his tracks. It was what they had in their hands. Each man was holding a long ladder—with large hooks welded to the ends. Their tops curving around, the ladders now resembled giant fishhooks.

"What the . . ." the watchman muttered under his breath. It wasn't his job to protect the building across the street—only to admire it. But he reached for a phone in any event. They were too close for comfort, and he'd heard some things in the news recently.

■

The first person in the crew leaned his ladder against a cement wall that supported the bottom of the Modern. The second man, still holding his own ladder, raced up the leaner. Once his feet were at the second-to-highest rung, the second man extended the ladder he was holding. He reached upwards and locked the J-hook of his ladder onto one of the rippling glass surfaces of the SoHo Modern's façade above. The curved end of each J-hook had been wrapped with dense tape for grippage. Once the ladder was secured, the second man climbed it. He moved up the undulating side of the building and pulled himself onto a tiny ledge. He balanced then pulled the ladder up from below him. The man glanced to his side. About four feet right—and eight feet vertical—was another ripple in the surface of the building. The man took a deep breath, sidestepped, and careened into blank space. Holding his ladder like an extension of his own arms, the man flew laterally and latched the J-hooks onto the ridge above him. He slowly moved up the side of the building; hooking the ladder, climbing, pulling it up, and repeating. Below him, the first and third men followed his lead with this "salmon ladder" move, like contestants on *American Ninja Warrior*. Within a minute, the three dark figures were forty feet in the air and ascending quickly.

■

Back inside the bank, the night watchman's jaw was open. Dumbfounded, he finally came to his senses. The office phone was in his hands. He quickly dialed 9-1-1. Those weren't residents—that much was clear. They were robbers.

■

Jake Rivett was still stuck in the back of the van—running surveillance on Emanuel. Vipa hadn't moved off the couch for the last two hours except to take a bathroom break and gesture for beers from one of the girls.

Tony sucked instinctively on his e-cigarette, which no longer lit blue. After many hours of constant use, it was out of charge. But that didn't stop him. Like chomping on a cigar, he would do anything for the hit. The FLIR radar inside their van displayed the same image it had for hours: Emanuel and his buddies crowded around the television. Just another Friday evening. Then Tony noticed his phone vibrating on a small ledge in front of the monitors. The name: Susan. Tony tapped speaker.

"What the hell are you doing? A crew of climbers are hitting a penthouse in SoHo as we speak!" Susan screamed.

Tony didn't even have to glance at Fonger—he was already on the move. Fong hopped out of the side of the van and raced around to the driver's seat.

A few seconds later, the previously sleepy cable van accelerated out of its parking spot like a bat out of hell.

▪

The cavalry had already arrived. Two police cars and a SWAT truck were parked in front of the SoHo Modern as the surveillance van sped up to the entrance.

▪

In the hallway outside the penthouse, SWAT prepared to breach entry. One member of the team crept towards the penthouse's door and waved a keycard past a sensor embedded in the door. The lock mechanism disengaged, making a clunk inside the door. But when the point man tried the door's handle, it wouldn't budge.

"We sure about this?" Jake asked as he joined the back of the column of assault team members.

"Silent alarm was triggered five minutes ago," Markle replied. "Van's still in the loading zone. There's a window that got jacked open with some sort of hydraulic up on this level, and last report from a security guard across the street had them entering the penthouse."

A hulking SWAT member ran alongside the column of specialists, holding a steel doorbuster. He swung the battering ram towards the penthouse door with all his might, crashing through the handle with one blow. The doorjamb splintered. After another two violent thrusts into the door, the door suddenly swung open. SWAT burst into the penthouse, checking angles and screaming loudly. As they canvassed the apartment, all was still. No one was there.

Jake followed behind, his gun at attention. He took in the apartment's posh surroundings. It had the uniformly exquisite look of the alien class. At this price point, it didn't matter where in the world you were—everything looked the same. The residence dripped with money. The walls were adorned with velour-textured damask wallpaper, and crystal chandeliers tumbled from the ceilings of every room. The colors were never too obvious or in your face. They were calming, like the interior of a spa, accented with modern art and silver tables and floor-to-ceiling glass and white marbled walls.

Jake padded through the kitchen. He admired the multiple sinks, the waterspout above the massive Viking stove, and the glass skylight above. But nothing seemed amiss. As he worked his way into the master bedroom, Jake carefully checked windows. These windows weren't supposed to open, but he had noticed a draft drifting throughout the unit. He couldn't find its source.

Jake bounded into the walk-in closet aside the master. A jewelry case was open, along with desk drawers. The pieces were all in disarray. At the bottom of the jewelry island, a cabinet door had been ripped off its hinges. It looked like something large had been removed. Jake scanned. His eyes were instantly drawn to the lone window in the closet. One corner of the molding was splintered. The window had been shattered—levered open. He peered around the edges of the opening. Then his foot tapped something lightly. Jake looked down.

A yellow tennis ball rolled on the ground—a rope had been secured through a hole in the tennis ball. The rope was sheared. Jake took in the window again. His vision was complicated by the reflective sheen of the glass surface dancing off the city lights. They weren't in here. They were out there. Jake pushed his head through the opening.

Jake carefully maneuvered his body through the cracked window. The undulating glass flowed like a series of waterfalls towards the ground below. His eyes to the side, he gazed along a single tier of the building like a treasure map. There was a channel—only eight inches wide—that ran at an angle from his window towards the roof of the building. Jake held onto the window as he steadied himself. The grooves of the façade above him formed a perfect rail for his hands to find balance. He scooted along the side of the building. He timed each shuffle with a breath, careful not to look down. It didn't take him but a minute.

As Rivett's feet hit the gravel on the top of the building, he spotted a dark figure sprinting along the roofline away from him—and holding a large black object the size of a briefcase. Jake pulled his weapon.

"Stop! Police!" he yelled to no avail.

The figure turned for a brief moment and stared directly at Jake, but it was too dark for Rivett to make out any of his features. The robber was about 150 feet away from Jake and heading farther. Jake kept the figure in his sights as he rushed along the roof. The roof's highest level was a flat platform that snaked along the top of the building like a river, sometimes as narrow as a foot across and at other times much wider. Ahead of Jake, the robber reached the end of the building. The robber crouched down with the object, then picked it up with both hands and flung it off the top of the Modern.

Before Jake arrived, the robber stood. He was holding a J-hook ladder. The robber took a running leap off the edge of the roof and flew across a small alleyway. Miraculously, the J-hooks on top of his ladder were extended in the air and caught onto a fire escape across the street.

Jake neared the edge. He glanced over. He saw the robber acrobatically twirl around the J-hook ladder, yank it down, then step backwards off the fire escape. The robber dropped through the air, twenty feet in milliseconds, before catching the fire escape again with the J-hooks. Jake saw one more of the dark-clad robbers standing on the street below the fire escape, watching his brethren descend.

"I'll shoot!" Jake screamed.

The robber didn't seem inclined to stop. He fell another twelve feet to the ground. The two dark figures crowded around the heavy box below them. Jake steadied his gun. He pulled the trigger. *Bang. Bang.* Two quick shots. Both missed, but they caused the two men to scatter quickly. They raced around the corner and into the night.

Tony blasted through the exit door on the roof of the building as Jake turned.

"You okay?" Tony asked in a panic.

"It was them."

"Who? Where? How many?"

"Two," Jake said. "You know who . . ."

Tony jumped onto his radio, updating SWAT with the last known positions of the subjects.

"Markle's not going to be able to find them . . ." Jake said.

▪

"According to the property manager, the penthouse is still owned by the LLC that built the SoHo Modern. So he doesn't actually know who was living in there—says he could describe him, though. Developer's name is Appian Trust LLC. You were right, by the way," Tony said to Jake as a large mass of police, representatives of the building, and others congregated in the lobby of the Modern.

"Didn't find 'em?"

"Nope."

"Just like the last one, right?" Jake asked.

"Indeed."

"They're in the sewers."

"Well, at least we know who they aren't," Tony said.

"Vipa," Jake concluded.

"Exactly."

"I'm convinced this was Rory Visco and Jack Castle. Maybe more of them. The tennis ball. I told you about the tennis ball . . ."

"Get me some hard evidence, pal," Tony said.

▪

Rivett strolled along the outside perimeter of the Modern. He was searching for the box he'd seen the perps toss. There was nothing underneath the fire escape across the street. He pushed a dumpster a few feet away from a wall, and he saw a dark mass on the ground. Jake reached down and dragged the box out from behind the dumpster. Once it was in the light, he was surprised to find it was a small safe—heavy at sixty pounds but still mobile. Jake scanned the edges of the safe. The front panel had become loose from ground impact. Jake tried the safe's door. It rotated open easily. Jake reached inside but found no fine jewelry or cash. Instead, he pulled out a handful of SD cards.

"Tony!" Jake yelled. But Villalon was too far around the corner to hear. Jake hustled back towards the entrance. As he did, a dark SUV pulled up in front of the Modern. And when Arthur Metropolis stepped out from the shotgun side of the car, Jake decided that now might not be the best time to tell everyone what he'd just found.

▪

Metropolis stomped through the police in the lobby like an elephant marking territory, his own large coterie hyena-ing behind

"The hell happened here, detective?" Arthur asked Tony.

"Uh . . . Mr. Metropolis? Can I help you?"

"I got robbed. I own this building.

Jake passed by Metropolis' head of security, Stian Ziros, as he entered the lobby. Ziros was smoking a cigarette and staring at the ground. There was definitely something off about the man, and now that Jake had a chance to see him closer up, he could tell what it was. Ziros dressed like he was in his twenties. He was very fit. His clothes were ultra-trendy. But the lines on his face belied a much longer life. He was well into his fifties, the same age as Metropolis—older actually.

"Appian. That's my LLC. It's a subsidiary of MetroVenture," Arthur told Tony. "Just got the message."

"That's insane," Jake popped in.

"Who are you?" Arthur turned.

Tony jumped. "One of our guys."

"Why are they targeting you, man? Why don't you just tell us and get it all over with?"

"Jake, will you please let me talk to Mr. Metropolis by himself?"

"You're Jake?" Arthur asked. "I always like to know who I'm talking to. What's your last name? Are you one of the undercovers workin' for me? For us, I mean?"

"I'll take care of this," Tony pushed Jake out of the way. "The penthouse. Your manager told me it was the developer's apartment. So that was yours?"

"I have lot of places," Arthur said.

"Sure. But this is the second time they've gone after a place where you actually lay your head," Tony said.

"I know. I'm not blind. There's a lot of people that don't like me out there. I'm the new breed. The Modern isn't exactly affordable. Pushes people out. I make enemies that way. But I also get rich. It's a trade-off," Arthur said. "But I don't sleep here. Sometimes my security does." Arthur nodded to Ziros at the door. "What was taken?"

"More jewelry," Tony said.

"I'm going up. Stian! Let's go!" Arthur yelled.

Jake watched as Arthur whispered into Ziros' ear while they entered the elevator to the penthouse unit. Arthur stared out of the elevator doors and through the glass, directly at Jake. He didn't drop his gaze until he rose.

Jake shook his head, palming the SD cards he'd found on the street. The cards would stay with him while he figured this out. Two of Arthur's buildings getting hit in a row might be a coincidence. Sure. But it was a damned good one. The only thing that did make some sense was Arthur Metropolis. This was the first crime scene that Metropolis had bothered to show up at personally—and quickly. It was perfectly obvious. There was a reason for Arthur's actions. Arthur knew something was up there. Something that he didn't want anyone to have—maybe not even the police. And perhaps that thing was sitting in Jake's pocket at that very moment.

▪

Up in the penthouse, Metropolis looked around while nodding at Ziros. "So what are we looking for?" Arthur asked him.

"I don't keep valuables," Ziros said.

"Please have a look, anyway," Tony requested.

Ziros nodded and began to take a mental inventory. Tony watched as Ziros walked towards the master.

"Nice place," Tony said to Metropolis. "All your employees get free rent?"

"Stian's my best man," Arthur said. "But I'm good to my people. It's my policy. And I gotta tell ya, Tony, I'm always looking for top-notch security staff."

Ziros returned to the living room. He didn't seem particularly concerned.

"They took three of my gold chains and one watch. A nice one. Cortébert."

"That's it?" Tony asked.

"I loved that watch," Ziros replied. "But—yes."

FIFTEEN

RIVETT WAS RAGGED. HE YANKED his badge and lanyard off his neck. It fell to the ground—he'd put it in the vault later. His entire body ached. His brain hummed with the adrenaline of the evening. He tried to replay the events on the Modern's rooftop over in his head, but he had to contend with the annoying fact that the human brain was not perfect. He knew the robber had turned towards him, but Jake hadn't been able to make out a face. It was too dark. What about the other way around? Could that person have identified him? Rivett didn't think so. But he didn't want to allow an assumption to be the reason he ended his life in a shallow ditch. And then there were the SD cards . . .

The cards. Against his body's every wish, Jake pulled himself off the bed. He sat at the computer. The SD cards were burning a hole in his pocket. He pulled the small pieces of plastic and microchip out. He had seven SD cards in all—none were labeled. He inserted the first one at random. There was a single folder inside, labeled "videos." Jake clicked on the folder and found a long column of video files. Most had random numbers for names, such as "382311229799.mov," making them largely indistinguishable from one another. There were over two hundred videos on that card alone. Jake clicked on the top of the data size column, sorting the files by file size. He opened the largest file.

A video began to play. It didn't take long for Jake to realize what it was: professionally produced and scripted porn. The nineties variety of pornography. Jake stopped the video and moved down the list. Someone had broken into the SoHo Modern just for a porn stash? As Rivett began to open video after video, they all returned the same sort of content. It seemed as though the robbers had indeed made off with Metropolis' or his henchman's personal collection—nothing more. Jake inspected the file names again. He discovered that fifteen of the videos had a different naming convention. These files obeyed a format similar to the first one, but with "MOV_" starting out their name. He clicked on "MOV_23488.mov," and found that he was looking at something quite different. It was still sexual, but taken from a fixed position—a camera set up above a bed. A completely naked woman, lithe and fit, stepped into the frame and turned towards someone operating the camera. She smiled and beckoned with her finger.

"Come on, Arthur," she said.

"I'm just making sure it's recording, honeybun," Arthur Metropolis' unmistakable voice orated back.

Then Arthur's large, muscular, and hairy frame blocked the view as he moved to the bed. Jake kept watching, although he didn't need to. He was truly amazed at what he was seeing. Arthur Metropolis and his girlfriend, Isabelle Prins, had decided to make a sex tape. Fifteen of them, actually. She was a world-famous model, the type of woman that the paparazzi hunted across the city. And Metropolis was certainly newsworthy in his own right. No wonder they'd kept this thing locked up tight. But this small answer pointed towards larger questions. Did Metropolis know that *Ziros* had these tapes? Likely, but unknown. And why did Arthur shoot them in the first place? And more importantly, how did the people who'd robbed Arthur know about them?

As Jake pondered these thoughts and their infinite hall of mirrors, he began to hear a repeating echo in his head. No—the apartment.

Downstairs. It was a knocking. On his front door.

"Who is it!" Jake yelled.

The knocking abated. Then Jake heard another loud cacophony at the door. He yanked the SD card from his computer and dropped all seven of them into his safe. He closed and secured the safe, then warily headed down the stairs. He gazed through the peephole, then pulled away. Clearly unhappy about what he'd seen, Jake took a number of sharp breaths. The safe house wasn't a secret location. It was part of the act—always had been. But now he regretted his lack of self-control. She was the last thing he needed. He collected himself and opened the door for . . . Nikki. She stood with one hand on her waist, hip cocked sassily out to the side, a lascivious smile on her face.

"Where ya been, hunny bunny? It's been a few and I ain't seen you at the bar," Nikki said. She was drunk. She tried to push through the door, but Jake stepped in her way. He put his arm across the threshold, preventing her from entering.

"Come on. Take care of me . . ."

"It's too late for that," Jake said.

Nikki pulled down the front of her shirt seductively. "You're a night owl. You been out all evening. I know how you operate. You and me, we're like the same person. That's why we get along so well. You know I'm right," she said.

"I'm serious, Nikki."

Nikki's demeanor suddenly flashed and twisted on a dime. Her intent went from seduction to destruction as she became more and more upset.

"So where you been? You been out with that chick? Mona?"

"How do you know her?"

"You're gonna get yourself in trouble . . ."

"I asked you a question." Jake started at Nikki suddenly, his fist raised for . . . something. But she was giggling. She liked the aggression. He clenched his hand in front of her face and slowly let it drop. "Let me worry about myself," he finally said.

"Just tryin' to help. But if you don't want to hear it? That's fine too."

"Nikki. What does it matter to you?"

"So that's your game? Just run through chicks? I don't know why those bitches are attracted to you . . ."

"That's crap. I always shot you straight."

Nikki shook her finger at Jake. "You're a jerk," she said.

"And so are you. And you knew that about me from the very get-go. I'm going to bed. Go home," Jake said.

"You're just going to leave me out here?"

"How'd you get here?"

"I drove."

"Then I'd suggest that you get in your car and drive yourself back where you came from," Jake replied sharply.

He shut the door and watched through the peephole as Nikki stumbled back to her car, which was parked across the street. *Jesus*—what an evening, with a decaying cherry on top. Jake made sure the door was highly secured, double checking all three locks. Then he stumbled back upstairs and fell asleep to delirious visions of Arthur Metropolis and the model whose body and face had sold a million magazine covers.

▪

Emanuel Vipa was sound asleep with Valeria when his cell phone blew up. He didn't wake on the first ring, but his lady stirred. After a few more rings, she was up and wondering hard. She rolled over Emanuel and looked at the screen. The phone simply read "Blondie."

"Emanuel, you got some explainin' to do!" she yelled into his ear.

Emanuel was stuck in the depths of a video-games-and-weed-imposed REM cycle.

"Blondie? If that's a *cuero* on the line, she ain't gonna see straight . . ."

Emanuel finally stirred. As he gained consciousness, he pulled the cell phone from her hand. He accepted the call. "Hey," he said groggily. Emanuel listened for a moment, then hung up and pulled himself out of bed.

"Where are you going?"

"I'll be right back," he said.

"I swear to God this place is going to be on fire unless you tell me that is not some *juera* you sidelinin."

"You like all your shit I get you? That Louis I bought last weekend? That's all 'cause of this guy. I gotta go meet him. So you'll stay right there, and I told you, I'll be fuckin' back," Emanuel said as he tugged a sweatshirt over his body.

"Why his name 'Blondie' then?"

"'Cause he looks like a ghost."

"What's that mean?"

"He scares the shit out of me," Emanuel said.

▪

It was the middle of the night. No one was awake in the city that never sleeps. Emanuel padded down the block and around a corner— where a giant black SUV was idling against the sidewalk. The back door opened, and Emanuel hopped inside.

▪

"Do you know a guy named Jake?" Stian Ziros asked Emanuel.

"Jake?"

"Yeah. With Visco and them . . ."

Emanuel thought for a moment. "Nah, don't think so," he finally said.

"Blond. Skinny. A little bit punk rock—wears leather."

"Oh. I think I've seen him on the site, maybe."

"Confirm that?" Ziros asked.

Emanuel loaded the UrbEx app. He brought up Rory's profile and scrolled down the page to a recent mobile upload. There was a shot of the side profile of Jake, standing atop an under-construction skyscraper.

"That's him," Ziros announced.

"That's who?" Emanuel said.

"Jake."

"I don't know his name . . ."

"I'm telling you," Ziros said.

"So what do you want?"

"Any idea how much money they raised for Unincorporated Brooklyn?"

"At the party? A few thousand dollars, tops."

"What's the pot at? What are they funding?"

"I'm working on it," Emanuel said.

"Work harder. Stay on the opposition. But now, we need to know more about this Jake guy too . . ."

"What do you mean?"

"I want to know how often he's with Rory. I want to know where he lives, who he's fucking. I want to know if he's boxers or briefs, cereal or goddamned yogurt, man. We need to know everything."

"Same day rate?"

"If you find out where this cat lives, there's a big bonus for you. I don't know what it is, exactly, but I haven't let you down. Have I? You know my money's good—and it's endless."

"You got it, boss. I'm right on it," Emanuel said.

"Don't call me boss," Ziros said.

"Okay, you're right."

"As far as you know, I don't exist."

"Perfect," Emanuel confirmed.

SIXTEEN

JAKE WAS IN DEEP SLUMBER as the sun rose through the windows of his apartment. It was bright and early when he heard a loud knocking at the front door. *Nikki.* Again? Jake groaned. He pulled himself out of bed after about six hours of less-than-superior shut-eye. He padded down the stairs and gazed through the peephole again—and his eyes blew wide.

"Rory," Jake said as he opened the door.

"Morning sunshine," Rory said. Rory had a big smile on his face. Extending a coffee for Jake, he took in Jake's demeanor. "Late night?" he asked.

"Nah," Jake deflected. "Just catching up on my beauty winks."

Jake grabbed the coffee and extended his other hand to shake Rory's. Rory grimaced.

"What's wrong?" Jake asked.

Rory rubbed his wrists. "Just a little sore," he said.

"From the evening?"

"What?"

"Oh . . . Mona told me you guys were going out," Jake said.

Rory nodded. "And how about you?"

"I was just chillin.'"

"Never know," Rory grinned. "I feel like I look over my shoulder, maybe I'll see you one day."

Jake gave Rory a once-over. He grinned. "Don't think I'm sneaking up on you. Not yet, at least. So what's up, dude? How'd you find me?"

"Think I wouldn't check up on a guy I might want in my crew?" Rory asked.

"You said 'want.' I'll take that as a positive."

"Sure," Rory shrugged. "Gonna invite me up?"

"My place is a mess," Jake said.

"Whatever. Let's roll," Rory said.

"Uh . . . I wasn't . . ." Jake stuttered, trying to figure out what Rory was getting at. "Now? I just woke up."

"Today's a big day. We gotta get."

"Where?"

"You'll see."

"All right, hold on," Jake said. "Just gotta get my stuff together."

"No problem," Rory smiled.

Jake tried to shut the door, but Rory stepped into the small area at the base of the stairs.

"I got a go-bag packed already. Just gimme a sec!" Jake yelled as he raced up the stairs, two at a time.

He knew that Rory would be right behind him, and he didn't have time to make sure that there was nothing visible in the apartment. Beyond the shock of seeing Rory at his doorstep, there was definitely something else going on. He could sense it. It was like when he was in boarding school, just about to go to bed, and knew the hall prefect was up to something. He'd have to brace for anything and everything. No matter how much a man changes himself, he can't fully run away from the person that he used to be. Jake hated feeling powerless—not knowing. He chafed against it because he felt better when he was in charge, even if the only person he controlled was himself. Jake grabbed the bag with all of his exploring gear and pivoted.

Rory was right there, as expected, gazing around the apartment.

"Nice place," Rory admired the stacks of counterfeit equipment on racks in the room. "This is what you sell?"

"Yeah. Some of it," Jake replied. "Ready?" Jake stepped in front of Rory and headed down the stairs, hoping that Rory would follow. He did.

▪

There was one more human who was very awake on Jake's street at seven in the morning: Nikki. Her nose was running and it wasn't from a cold. By all appearances, she had been up all night. All sorts of insane in the membrane, she was sitting inside her car on the other side of the street. The problem with Jake was that he didn't know what she did. She was certain they were meant to be. It was obvious to her, and it was probably obvious to him too—but maybe it was just in a place he couldn't access. Yet. That's why he was fighting so hard to keep her away. They were too similar. They were people of the hardscrabble. They'd both had to pull themselves up from nothing. And they'd both survived, in their own way. But they could be more powerful together. And if that wouldn't work? Well at least she'd make sure that Jake knew damn well what he was missing. He wasn't going to be able to just stomp on her and trade her in for that cute little chica. Not without a fight. Not without a *statement*.

After Jake and Rory walked away from the apartment, Nikki stumbled out of her car. She crossed the street. Smoking a cigarette by the entrance to Jake's building, she nonchalantly dropped a butt. As she crouched by the lock, she dug into her purse and pulled out a credit card. She slipped the card into the door crack and fiddled with the lock and handle to Jake's apartment. The handle rotated slightly, and she felt a small bit of tension release on the lock, but she wasn't able to jostle it enough. The door remained locked.

"Crap."

She eyed the edges of the door. The door and its frame were both made of wood. She glanced left and right. No one was around. Nikki reared back and slammed the door with her knee. Once. Twice. Again while jamming the card and—the lock didn't give. But the center panel of the door did. She looked down at her skinned knee, having bashed a small square out of the bottom quadrant of the door. Just enough to push herself through . . .

Once she was up the stairs, she didn't dilly-dally. She pulled out a can of spray-paint from her purse and she used that thing like a fire extinguisher at a burning orphanage. Bright orange spray-paint flew through the air like a plume, exploding all over the surfaces of Jake's apartment and his possessions. She gave new meaning to the expression, "the writing's on the wall." It was. Like "Die Scumbag" and "Asshole!" Nikki wasn't happy and she made it clear. After turning the screens of his television and laptop completely orange, she moved to the bedroom. She treated Jake's comforter to a new color hue. As she stepped around the bed, she looked down.

Jake's gleaming NYPD badge stared back at her from the floor, and a gun sat on the night table next to his bed. Nikki was stunned. She was supposed to be the predator today. But now she was a deer in the headlights.

"Oh my god . . ." she said.

And then she dropped the can of spray-paint on the floor and began to think.

▪

In the south Bronx, Jake and Rory walked off the subway and down the stairs from the raised tracks of the 167th Street Station. Once they were on the ground, Rory put his hand on Jake's shoulder.

"Today's about me," Rory said. "I know you have a lot of questions. I'm going to tell you why I am the way I am. It all started here." He pointed four blocks down the street towards the bustling activity around Yankee Stadium.

▪

Once they were closer to the stadium, Rory glanced up into a shadowy area underneath the train tracks.

"This is the place," Rory said. It appeared to be home to a thousand varieties of bird.

"What about the animals?"

"If birds are gonna stop you, you got a world of problems ahead of ya, buddy."

"Nothing's going to stop me," Jake said.

"That's what I like about you."

"What?"

"You believe what you say. Even if it's all a front."

"Thanks."

"There's a lot of winners who are like that," Rory said. "And a lot of dead people."

"I'll take my chances," Jake replied.

Jake and Rory slowly climbed up the latticework of the train track's structure. They pulled themselves onto a horizontal platform, designed for servicing, just underneath the tracks. Hearing a cacophonous rumbling behind them, Jake held on for dear life as hundreds of tons of metal vibrated above. Once the train had passed, Rory and Jake continued working their way along the largely invisible sub-layer of the raised track.

A hundred feet later, they finally reached a position directly across from Yankee Stadium. A piece of slanted steel about five feet wide angled down from the subway structure and towards the stadium. Rory shimmied onto the steel surface. It was precarious. They were about thirty feet above the ground. The only feature that prevented Rory from slipping off the bridge was a small beam at the base of the slanted steel support. Rory lay back, his spine resting on the steel and the balls of his feet anchored against the beam. Once he was in position next to Rory, Jake realized that it wasn't all that bad. It was like a metal sun lounger, at a slightly higher angle than one might be accustomed. But the best part was the view that their free seats afforded them. They were able to stare directly between an outfield scoreboard and a brick wall that supported the stands inside—into the field itself. Rory and Jake sat back on their urban explorer-style vantage point and watched the Yanks take on the Phillies.

"Pretty good," Jake said.

"Sorry there's no popcorn, man. When me and Will grew up, we didn't have any money. This is what we did for fun. We figured out how to see the games for free. I've probably seen two hundred innings from right here, and not one time in my life has anyone noticed." They both watched the game proceed. During a brief lull, Rory spoke again. "We figured out how to do everything for free. Not just baseball. Whatever you could imagine, Will and I figured it out. Getting into concerts, Coney Island, anything. We did it."

"I've been meaning to ask you," Jake said. "If Will taught you everything . . . why doesn't he explore anymore?" Jake glanced towards Rory.

"Will's dead," Rory finally said.

"Oh, dude . . . I didn't know. I'm sorry."

"He always wanted to drainsled the hydra from the top of the city to the bottom. One day he started at the Cloisters up in Washington Heights . . . but he never came out."

"That's horrible, man. I'm so sorry."

Rory shook his head. "It never made any sense. You know the rules. Will created those. He kept to them. The hydra's dangerous. He knew that more than anyone. He wouldn't have gone in without spotting it."

"So what do you think happened? He just made a mistake?"

Rory didn't reply. He stared out over the baseball field.

"Let me tell you about Will. He wasn't just an explorer. First and foremost, the man was a humanitarian. He cared about people—all people —because he knew they were what made a place special. Nothing about New York matters when it's just a bunch of glass boxes. Even here. When we were kids, walking up River to the old stadium? It used to be filled with little vendors' shops, one-of-a-kind restaurants. All sorts of entrepreneurs selling handmade bats, shirts they'd manufactured in the garment district. You name it, and it was there. Now all that's gone. It's been replaced with bricks that try to make the place look old but were put up in 2009. You know? It's one chain restaurant after the other, owned by conglomerates who spent a thousand dollars on décor, bought some old Yankee jersey off eBay and put it inside a Plexiglas box so that their customers can think they're still in the past. That's the future. The future offers no hope for someone from the bottom because there's nothing that you can touch and feel anymore. Will knew that. He saw it coming."

"Did he go to MIT, too?" Jake asked.

"No," Rory shook his head. "But he made sure I went to college while he worked in the community. He's the guy who started the Friends of Unincorporated Brooklyn. He put his life on the line for the people, for vibrant places that were being starved for life by the big money that started flowing in the eighties. He stood for something, and he taught me that's the most important thing you can do. We don't climb up to the tops of buildings just to say we can. We don't even go into sewers for the pictures. We want to understand our world. We want to know how it's changing. Otherwise we'll all turn around one day, and there will be nothing left."

"I gotta tell you . . ."

"What?" Rory asked.

"I'm on board with that, Rory. I couldn't agree any more," Jake replied.

"It's not all glamor," Rory said. "I want to make sure you're prepared. You might have to get your hands dirty."

"That's my favorite thing to do," Jake grinned.

"There are heavy interests against us. Arthur Metropolis? You know him?"

"Uh . . ." Jake stalled. "He's a developer, right? He's building that complex down by Whale Square."

"That guy hated Will. He hates us now too. But we're not as good as Will was. At organizing. We try, but we're just not. So once he passed,

Metropolis had less friction. Less problems . . ."

"Wait. You think Metropolis had something to do with your brother?"

"I don't know," Rory said. "There's a lot of mysteries below the depths —once you peel back the surface."

"But that's outrageous."

"Is it? City wouldn't even look for his body at first. Berg said it was too dangerous."

"The mayor?"

"Used to be city superintendent . . . He's the man who shook my hand and told me that I'd never see my brother again. Guess who his number-one supporter is?"

"Metropolis."

"Bingo," Rory said.

All of a sudden, Jake was much less worried that Rory had made him last night. But that didn't end his anxiety. Instead, his heart was pounding out of his chest. Jake had been waiting for this moment for what seemed like an eternity, waiting for the small door to open at the end of the hallway. But what he'd heard was nothing like what he was expecting. It was worse. It was a rabbit hole, and unfortunately Jake knew that he'd have to jump in and stay on the trip—all the way to the bitter end.

"Will was urban exploring before there were even words for it," Rory continued. "Whatever your biggest fear was, Will would make you tackle it head on. You weren't allowed to have any weak links if you were in his crew. It was scary as hell, but he was right in the end, and I took that to heart. That's why today's your day."

"My initiation?"

"Tonight I'm gonna find out if you're just puttin' in the paces, or if you've actually learned something . . ." Rory trailed off. He gazed at Jake, his eyes flickering with a delicate balance of friendliness and malice. "And you know how I'm going to know?"

Jake didn't. "No," he shook his head.

"If you don't die."

SEVENTEEN

WIND WHIPPED THROUGH JAKE'S CLOTHES on the ferry's observation deck. They had just departed from Battery Park in the southern tip of Manhattan and were heading down the bay. Jack Castle stood next to Jake, wearing what looked like a hotel uniform.

"Just get off work?" Jake asked.

"Gotta make my bones somehow, cowboy," Castle shrugged.

"How long you been doin' that?"

"I go through them pretty quickly. My jobs and my hobbies don't really gel."

But before Jake could respond, Rory jumped in and put his arm around Jake.

"So, figure it out yet? You're looking at it. At her, actually. Lady Liberty," Rory pointed over Jake's shoulder. Jake turned and took in the oxidized copper of the Statue of Liberty looming over Liberty Island.

"Seriously?"

"Of course," Rory replied.

"Impossible," Jake said.

"No, no. I've done it."

"So you're going to show me how?"

"You'll lead this one. You and Mona. That's it," Rory answered.

"How come?"

"Can't get that many bodies up there. Don't worry, man. When have I let you down?" Rory paused for a second. "And the crown doesn't count. I need a picture of you on the top of the torch. Unfortunately, you can't just walk right up. Torch level was closed a hundred years ago after the Black Tom explosion. Nineteen-sixteen. I guess terrorism is age-old. Anyway, it never reopened. Some improvisation will be required."

His marching orders having been delivered, Jake glanced up at the imposing figure of Lady Liberty, rising over three hundred feet into the air. He took a deep breath, but it felt more like a gasp.

■

The biker stood upright on his whip—two feet on the seat. He slowly surfed the motorcycle down the street. Directly in front of a rowdy bike shop, Fireblade Motortech, the man jumped off his bike and engaged in a controlled, burning spin. He jumped down and rotated the bike in a circle, two hands holding the handlebars but his feet on the ground. A vast quantity of smoke rose into the air. His boys, sitting on chairs and on the pavement outside of Fireblade, clapped and laughed as the man stuck his tongue out. Almost losing control, but wrenching it back at the last moment, the controlled burn finally came to an end with a cacophony of approving hoots and hollers from the shop. Then all of the men's necks snapped abruptly, their attention suddenly drawn to a newcomer standing at the end of the street: Nikki.

As she walked resolutely towards the bike shop, she was immediately eyed up by men with teardrop tattoos hanging from their eyes. Overall, they gave an impression of not wanting to be fucked with, and their impression held up quite well. It wasn't that she was in the wrong place. It was just that few women believed Fireblade was the right place to be.

"Wassup, bonita?" a fat biker yelled. It was Jonny Diaz.

"Hector around?"

"Hec? I dunno. What's he want you for?"

"I got a good idea 'bout that," another with a mohawk yelled.

Nikki cocked her hips at the two bikers. She was used to guys like this. They were her bread and butter. "He doesn't know it yet," she said. "But I'm going to blow his mind."

All of the bikers grinned, parting like security behind the velvet rope, to allow her into the back of the bike shop. She stepped into the darkness.

▪

Hector Trizzo towered over Nikki in his depraved den. He had just listened to the most fantastic story he'd ever heard in his entire young adult life—complete with pictures that Nikki had taken on her cell phone.

"So what do you get outta all this?

Nikki eyed some drugs on a table near Hector.

"I don't care. Maybe a little pick-me-up . . . ?"

"Revenge is a cruel mistress, ain't it?" Hector grinned.

"I wasn't his mistress."

"Right. You were less. And it pissed you off."

"Coulda' been more if he had any smarts about him. But it's clear he don't. 'Cause if he did, he wouldn'ta treated me like this," Nikki said. "So what are you gonna do to him?"

"That's the easy part. But first I gotta find the guy."

"There's the apartment . . ." Nikki said.

"Let me guess. You left it like that, with all the spray-paint."

"Uh . . ."

"That will never work. He'll be outta there insta-like, and he'll be on guard the whole time. Jake's a slippery shit. He was one of the best. Always so responsible to his own version of criminality. Now I know why."

"I got another way."

"What?"

"Some guy that Jake's rolling with now. He left me a number," she said.

"Why'd he do that?"

"He was just checkin' up on Jake. He's one of us—not a normie. Could be he's Jake's new mark."

"What's his name?"

"Castle, I think he goes by."

"Well, maybe Castle and I should have a little chat about our mutual friend," Hector said. He observed Nikki staring at the tray of cocaine on the table in the middle of the office. "Help yourself," he said with resignation.

▪

Jake and Mona pushed through the crowds of tourists in Flagpole Plaza on Liberty Island, but Mona stopped him before they reached the queue to the statue proper.

"I want to be one of the last groups up. 'Cause we'll start with the lemmings. But we're not going to end with them . . ."

"So what do we do until then?" Jake asked.

"Be tourists?" Mona shrugged. She held up her camera. "Smile," she said.

Jake grinned goofily. *Click.* Mona took the shot. Then she rotated around while still holding the camera, moving into the frame herself. *Click.* Jake started making funny faces—like he's a shy guy, then a sly guy, then maybe not even a guy at all. Mona loved it, chuckling the entire time. Jake started laughing too.

"Want to know something funny?" Jake asked.

"What?"

"I've never been here."

"You've never gone up the Statue of Liberty?"

"Nope," Jake said.

"Wow. I used to come here all the time with my mom."

"Right."

"Well, anyway," Mona said, "your first time is gonna be a doozy."

They spent the last two hours of daylight gallivanting around the grounds of the statue like true tourists. It was the most relaxed Jake had been in months. At first he'd thought it was just this assignment, and these people, that made him feel at ease. And it was true. They were nothing like

Hector, dissimilar to any criminals that he'd investigated in the past. They didn't seem to have much evil intent, even if they were responsible for some incredibly daring and profitable robberies throughout the city. That made them bad guys, yes—but not particularly bad humans. But it wasn't just that, and Jake knew it. The reason today didn't feel like work, that he was enjoying his time way out in the field, was because of the woman next to him. Mona. It wasn't because she happily talked back to him. It wasn't due to the fact that she was in charge. It was her view of the world. She believed in the ethos of exploring, perhaps even more than Rory. She didn't write books, run a commercial Instagram account, or reveal herself publicly for acclaim. She didn't worry about her standing in the scene. She was the purest of them all. She just wanted to see a world that wasn't available to anyone else—and she'd found a way to do it.

▪

As the sun set over the river, Mona and Jake trailed behind the very last tour group of the evening. They entered the statue's structure and began the 354-foot ascent up the thin steps inside her chassis. They lingered at every possible moment, until they were the last two tourists trudging up the steps. It wasn't easy to be so tardy and make it look natural. And what would happen if one of the tourists fainted or pulled a muscle and emergency rescuers had to be called? Their whole plan would be thrown off. But there wasn't much time for Jake to think about negative outcomes. Not in this moment. Just before they reached the crown, Mona slowed even further to allow a full vertical story's worth of space between them and the guide and visitors above. She glanced around.

"Now," she said.

"Are we high enough?"

"We have sixty seconds, Jake."

Jake and Mona launched into premeditated action. They'd spent some of their time lounging on the grass outside of the statue practicing, so now the motions were temporarily engrained into their muscle memory. They whipped their backpacks off, readjusted clasps, straps, and carabiners to turn the backpacks themselves into makeshift harnesses. Mona ducked down. She reached underneath the small steel landing and attached a carabiner to an opening in the bars holding up the stairs. Jake did the same on his end.

They glanced at one other. Jake held out his closed fist for her to pound. But instead of reciprocating, she stepped backwards and jumped over the edge of the landing. Jake followed in his own direction. They both fell into the dark recess of the interior of the Statue of Liberty.

Their descent was abruptly cut off with a loud clank. Both Jake and Mona were suspended, in a dark crevice, just a few feet underneath the serpentine stairs. They'd picked this location specifically. Based on the gyrations of the stairs below and above, there was no way for Jake and Mona to be visible to anyone walking up or down. They hung in the air, not uttering a word, as their own tour group worked their way down the stairs. As Jake and Mona swung around, the loud stomping above caused the staircase to creak loudly. Mona and Jake had to hold hands to stop the oscillation. Mona put her finger to her lips.

"Shhhh . . ."

All Jake could see were angled steel girders and industrial rivets. Jake tried to listen for the last round of security in the proverbial belly of the statue. But his ears picked up only echoing noises from below mixed with the groaning of the steel in the wind. Finally, loud footsteps clanked above Jake and Mona. The beating of a single set of feet continued for a while, before descending far below them.

"I think that was it," Jake said.

"Hopefully," Mona whispered. After a few more minutes, most of the lights that lined the stairway suddenly extinguished. Jake grinned. Mona checked her watch.

"Time," she said.

She contorted her body through the air, reaching for one of the steel girders that supported the inside flank of the statue. She began to swing like a pendulum, until she finally gripped the girder with her hands. But her fingers slipped away, and she came sailing back towards Jake. The second time, Mona swung towards the girder with an open carabiner in hand. She wasn't aiming for the support beam itself this time, but the metal mesh that the formed the inside layer of the statue's cladding. This time around, she successfully attached the carabiner to the meshing and held on. Using her other hand, Mona quickly fed a rope through the carabiner and connected it to her harness. She gave Jake a nod, and he unclasped her from underneath the stairs. Jake used Mona's method to reach the side of the statue as well. Now the two of them were hooked into the statue's meshing on its inside layer, hundreds of feet in the air.

They slowly and carefully climbed up the mesh. The inside wall was vertical where they began, but soon the slope began to lessen until they were able to stand without attachment. Jake illuminated the path with his headlamp. They slowly walked across the steel mesh, making efforts to stay quiet. Jake noticed the exterior copper cladding of the statue narrowing around them.

"This must be the shoulder . . ."

Mona nodded. They were in the right shoulder of the Statue of Liberty, an area originally designed to be traversed by visitors in a manner similar to the crown. But it hadn't been open to the public for a hundred years now, and rarely saw maintenance. Jake's headlight beam captured old construction materials strewn about the bottom of the shoulder. Leaning down, he noticed an ancient *New York Times*—a collector's item in its own right. The price? One full US cent. He also kicked over a turn-of-the-century construction helmet.

"Don't you think that's weird?" Jake asked.

"What?"

"All this stuff was just left here? You'd think someone would have picked it up."

"Exactly. 'You'd think.' But you wouldn't know. Isn't it better to see it for yourself? See what's behind the curtain?"

"It's cool," Jake agreed. He was surprised that the detritus of the past had been left behind. But she was right. Her theory mirrored what he knew about crime solving. The only way to truly find something out was to do the work and see it with one's own eyes.

Jake and Mona finally reached a ladder. This would ostensibly lead them to a platform near the top of the flame, where Jake could take some photos to prove to Rory that he'd really been there. *Mission accomplished.* Mona began to climb the ladder while Jake kept aim with the lamp. But as she reached the top, about fifty feet vertically from where Jake was standing, she found the entrance to the old platform had been blocked by steel bars. Mona tried to pull the steel door open, but she realized it wasn't just locked. It didn't even have hinges. The bars had been welded together.

"It's welded shut!" she yelled down to Jake. "We're kicked, man."

Jake looked around. Besides the ladder, Jake shined his light on a small portal door built flush into the side of the copper tunnel.

"We're never kicked," Jake answered.

Jake examined the door. It was chained shut, but the padlock appeared to be one hundred years old—like everything else in this corridor. The chain itself was completely rusted through. Jake lifted his leg and jacked it against the lock. The chain simply disintegrated in front of him. But although he pulled on the handle of the door, he couldn't open it. It wouldn't budge. Jake took out a pocketknife and went after the rust, gouging out a small line of detritus around the edge of the door as if it was old caulk. He tried the portal again. The door slowly scraped open. Jake was greeted by a massive gust of wind that almost knocked him off balance. He was about to fall, but Mona steadied him. She had worked her way down the ladder just in time. Jake pulled himself through the small door.

▪

Jake hung onto the exterior cladding of the Statue of Liberty's right arm. Wind accelerated around him, rippling through his skin. His fingers were dug into tiny, quarter-inch recesses of copper plating. The higher he climbed up, the riskier of a proposition this ascent would become. It was basically impossible—the cracks in the surface weren't wide enough for him to jam a spring-loaded cam in and reattach his rope. But Jake had another idea. He'd come this far and he wasn't going to give up. Mona peered out from the doorway entrance at Jake, who had yanked his head up in an attempt not to look down.

"You don't have to do it," Mona said. "There's no shame in living."

"Sometimes? There is," he replied.

They both stared at the arm and torch above. Mona grinned at Jake. "Explore or die, babe," she said.

Jake tied two of their ropes together and then attached the cord to a tennis ball. He slowly stood up and hurled the ball with all of his might towards the railing of the torch above. The ball missed and bounced off. Jake wound the rope back and tried again. This time the ball looped the railing of the torch and slid towards Jake. He secured the rope. Where there's a will, there's a way.

The only foot and handholds available were the rivets and edges on the side of the statue. Each rivet was about the size of a quarter, and extended off the flanking of the statue by less than a quarter-inch. Jake began to climb up the side of the Statue of Liberty's extended vertical right arm. It was tough going—like rock climbing a sheer glass wall. Halfway up, Jake caught a view of the water below.

He froze.

Then he heard Mona—*erupting*.

"Don't! Don't stop!" she was screaming. It took a while for Jake to resolve the words, but when he did, he finally regained a sense of control. He suddenly clicked out of his height-induced ordeal. He reached up with his fingers and pulled painstakingly. Once he had made legitimate progress on his ascent, Mona attached herself to the rope as well. She began the climb. Jake was now directly below the flame, where the statue's hand tilted back against him. He was essentially climbing upside down as if bouldering in Arizona. But this was far from any rock climber's environment, and there was no thick blue pad underneath. Jake finally reached the railing. He pulled himself up and over, collapsing on the tiny platform. After a few moments, Mona arrived as well.

They gazed over the most amazing and exclusive 360-degree view that New York had to offer. The city flickered in front of them, but it felt like a dream to Jake. It wasn't just the view itself; it was the endorphins that were rushing through his being. It was the way the rippling water below them reflected off the city. It was the joy that permeated through every line on Mona's face. It was a perspective that he'd never seen before—something so sublime that he couldn't even have imagined it. It was a one-time feeling. It would never be so good. Sure, they could take a photograph. But no one else would know how it felt.

Mona took a few shots of Jake, then a selfie, the gold flame of the statue burning behind them.

"Now you can rock it. For sure."

Jake flashed the upside down V at the camera. *Click.* Mona put the camera down. They stood close to one another.

"That was pretty impressive," she said.

"I came this far. Wasn't going to give up without a fight."

Mona looked up at Jake. There was something more in her facial expression now. He'd been waiting for this moment. He leaned in closer, focused on her eyes at first, but then her lips.

"I don't know what you're waiting for," she said.

Jake kissed her. Hard. She kissed back. And for a second, he didn't even know where he was. The city wasn't behind him. He wasn't standing on the torch of the Statue of Liberty. He simply *was*.

But their kiss was abruptly interrupted by a spotlight washing across them. Jake glanced over Mona's shoulder. A US Coast Guard helicopter was racing through the bay and seemingly headed directly for the Statue of Liberty.

EIGHTEEN

THE YACHT WAS A SLEEK black iceberg. It rose from the dark water like a razor blade tilted slightly upwards, befitting its name: *Razor*. *Razor* was less the rounded horizons and gilded surfaces of old and more angular —like a piece of extreme Scandinavian architecture that also happened to float. It was the pride and joy of its owner, an owner who enjoyed his high seas fiefdom immensely. Especially when the boat was in international waters, it was a fortress of solitude, wealth, and privilege. The boat's owner had found the urban environment less and less safe recently. To call his current living situation a retreat would be unkind—but it might not be far from the truth. He resided on the boat now, bobbing around on the side of the island that ought to be his home. A bunch of pests had made it a tough place for him to live. The world was still on his side and working hard for him. But he knew deep down inside that he alone was responsible for the Damocles' sword that swung above.

Due to *Razor's* recent birth, the ship was equipped with all manner of security instruments to defend against a professional thief. But the ship had an Achilles's heel, and that was technology itself. The whole craft, from its Internet-connected cameras and locks down to the pressure-sensitive pads built into each hallway, was controlled by a computer in the engine room of the ship. There was only one way to own the soul of this boat without one's name on the title. If a particularly creative thief could get into the engine room, possessed a specific piece of cracked encryption software, and had experience with yachts? *Razor* might be theirs for the taking.

The key to the subterfuge was simple: *speed.* Any conspiracy breaks down over time and the thieves knew their operation depended on an accelerated timeline. The man in the Chelsea Piers polo, purchased for $29.97 from an Internet printer, only had a few minutes before the curtain would be drawn on his act. He had a large pack of pencils and pens in his pocket. A tape measure, an electric meter, and a current tester hung from his belt. He traipsed down the boardwalk, holding a clipboard like he owned the place, which he would for about five minutes. He spent the first few seconds aside the boat, searching for the shore power hookup and increasingly cursing. Eventually his vitriol grew to the level that the crew noticed him.

"Hey! Can I help ya?" one of the deckhands yelled from twenty feet above.

"We're getting funky measurements from your current. Have you checked the continuity on a Transcat recently?"

"Uh . . . I'm not sure . . ."

"Well, I don't know if you want me to take a look at it. But the computer up in systems is giving you a crazy-high electric load right now. I think it's an error. Gonna cost you a pretty penny if you guys don't get on it soon!"

"You can check it?" the deckhand asked.

"Sure," the man said.

Three minutes later, Mr. Clipboard stood inside the engine room. The deckhand was watching him, but deckhands are very low on the intellectual totem pole. The thief would just have to use a bit of slight of hand. While he checked the fuse box with one hand, his fingers puttered around the back of the boat's central nervous system with the other. He found the manual power switch to the computer and thumbed it off.

This thief was not one of your sophisticated hacker types. He did not have encryption software pre-loaded into a soldered microchip. He engaged strictly in location hacking, not the digital variety. But now his mission was complete. It had nothing to do with checking electrical circuits. That was a task that he was barely prepared to do. But Mr. Clipboard was well versed—an expert, in fact—in making people like this deckhand bend to his bidding.

▪

The instant the computer turned off, a second thief in a black wetsuit emerged from underneath the dock aside which *Razor* was floating. All was quiet—for the time being. It was impossible to walk directly onto the boat because the ramp had been retracted by the deckhand. The swimmer floated towards the giant inflated balloons that formed the boat fenders for the yacht. He crawled onto one of the bumpers, quickly stabilizing himself. Then the swimmer grabbed the thick cable that secured the yacht to one of the dock's bollards. Hanging from the cable, he put one hand over the other and pulled himself up. Still about ten feet from the main deck, with the cable angling upwards until it became almost vertical, the swimmer pulled out a climbing ascender. It latched onto the cable and could be pushed vertically but would not retract without being specifically unlocked. He attached the device and then flung his two feet around the cable like an upside down cat. He began to slowly pull himself up the rope, using his feet to retain balance and the ascender's latching mechanism to avoid slipping back down. Within forty-five seconds, he was on *Razor's* main deck.

▪

While the deckhand hadn't realized that anything had happened to *Razor's* computer, it was another story altogether in the security room— built into a series of cabins behind the captain's wheelhouse. The yacht's security chief was a hard man named Avi. While boats in general were a soft target, they were not often in the crosshairs. If he had been in the French Riviera and hosting a phalanx of drunk supermodels decked out in millions of dollars of jewelry, the entire yacht's security team would be at a much higher level of alert. But New York was generally safe, and the last three weeks had been a snoozer. He liked working for the boat's owner. The organization paid well and on time—always. Both were important, and rarely were both so consistent in the yachting world. Avi was paid over two hundred thousand dollars a year to ensure that no hiccups ever occurred. He was paid well because a snoozer could turn into a shitstorm on a dime.

And then it did. While Avi sat at his desk, legs kicked up and reading a maritime safety brief from Stratfor, he noticed all of the security cameras go black on one side of his dual screen. The application was still running, but he was getting no feed at all. He jumped onto the radio while he clicked through the application.

"Deck, Engineering. Report," Avi commanded into his radio.

▪

Mr. Clipboard heard the radio call from inside the engine room. He watched as the young deckhand brought the radio to his face.

"I'm almost done. Just need to check out the conduits in the hallway," he said.

"Okay," the deckhand responded, then spoke into his radio. "I'm in the engine room with the Chelsea Piers maintenance guy."

"Don't move," Avi said. "And don't lose him."

Mr. Clipboard had already scooted out. The deckhand raced outside into the hallway, where the man was standing fifty feet down the hallway, staring up at electrical conduits.

"Hey! Our security guy wants to talk to you."

"You got it," the man replied. Then he broke into a sprint. The deckhand was shocked for one moment. Mr. Clipboard took a set of stairs at the end of the hallway, rising through the bottom level of the boat, into the second sub-basement and finally reaching the poop deck in the back of the boat. The deckhand followed, yelling into his radio.

"This guy's running! He's out the poop deck, by the engines."

▪

Avi raced out the back of his security room, onto a balcony that overlooked the boat's stern. In the darkness, he could barely make out the deckhand shaking his head in confusion.

Mr. Clipboard was gone.

▪

In the meantime, the swimmer was scaling *Razor's* bow, climbing up the glass windows of the first floor towards the forward balcony that made up the main stateroom's window. The swimmer reached the balcony and tried the door. It was locked. He pulled out a throttle—a piece of titanium about as thin as paper, but unyielding. He wasn't going to pick the lock. There wasn't time. He simply placed the throttle into the doorjamb and used the power of leverage. The swimmer plied and then rotated the shiv. Within a second, a small, one-inch space appeared between the double-paned glass layers of the door and the frame. He pulled the door with all his might, and the glass shattered.

▪

About ten seconds later, *Razor's* computer began to reboot automatically. Lights blasted on all around the yacht, accompanied by loud sirens. The whole place woke up in a hurry, with dozens of staff members rushing to the surface.

Avi held a pistol on the top deck. He could see a wet and black-clad intruder running towards the bow, now illuminated by extremely strong spotlights.

"Stop!" Avi screamed.

But the swimmer did none of the above. He didn't stop as Avi lifted the gun. Instead, he turned to view the yacht in all of its beauty. He had just conquered this beast, and all of its denizens were running around with their heads cut off. He could vaguely hear the yelling and commotion around him as he placed his hands behind his head—as if he was actually conceding. He saw the security man holding the pistol and charging towards him. And just when they were a few feet away, the swimmer stepped back. He lifted his feet to the sky and flipped over the yacht's front railing. Within seconds, he was enveloped by the murky black hole of the water below.

Once the swimmer was underwater, he held his breath. He paddled as hard as he could. He was looking for a light and finally found it, blinking far ahead. He strove for the light, which was submerged into the water and seeking only him. He finally breached the surface just as his body was quaking with the necessity of air. He looked up at the small Zodiac boat there to pick him up. A few sets of arms reached into the water and yanked the swimmer out of the cold.

"It was a covert preparation," Mr. Clipboard said.

"For an overt operation . . ." the lanky swimmer said while he pulled his six-foot-four body into the small Zodiac boat.

NINETEEN

MONA AND JAKE COVERED THEIR faces with their hands as they sprang through the empty visitor's center. The front doors were locked, but a fire exit to the side of the ticket booths led outside. Of course, it would also cause an alarm to go off. But that was a small price to pay considering they had a helicopter on their tail—their second in a week. Mona pushed through the door, and the alarm blasted in loud, shrill decibels that reminded Jake of his music.

·

They stole across the grass. Jake glanced over his shoulder. The copter was much closer now, about thirty seconds from the island and searching high and low for them.

They reached the far end of the flat island. Mona jumped over a railing and began to climb down the large stone bulwarks.

"We're dead meat, Mona."

"Have a little faith."

Below the bulwarks were large, piled boulders that led into the Hudson itself. They were the final line of preservation that protected the island from the elements. Jake ducked into the shadowed protection of one of the immense boulders as the helicopter's light washed directly over where he was just standing.

"Easier said than done," Jake said.

"Relax," Mona said. She pulled out a small flashlight and aimed it into the darkness. She pressed the button on the side of the light three times in quick succession then waited. After a long pause, a small flashlight returned the illuminated call. One time—then off.

"Told ya!"

Jake continued to crouch behind the boulder. He could make out the hum of a small engine motor. After a while, the murmur grew louder. Out of the murky darkness, he began to resolve a small micro-Zodiac boat being steered towards them. Rory was at the helm. Jake scampered towards the water. He helped Mona onto the boat and then jumped on himself. They ducked down for cover as Rory ripped the Zodiac away from the rough edges of Liberty Island.

Just a few seconds after they departed, the helicopter flew over the edge of the island again, its large spotlight washing over the location that the Zodiac had just occupied. But there was no Zodiac. It was now a blip, barely visible in radar, moving farther away from the island with every passing second. A large Coast Guard cutter's sirens filled the bay behind them and arrived too late, its loudspeaker straining in vain for the urban explorers: "This is the United States government. You do not have the right to access this site. Turn yourself in immediately. You are trespassing!" the speaker blared.

▪

Once he'd found a spot in the boat to cool down for a moment, Jake looked up. Rory was skipping. He had a large, thick fleece blanket wrapped around him and seemed to be soaking wet. Jake was slightly surprised to see Castle and Nik on the boat as well. But unlike most interactions, Castle had a huge grin on his face.

"Maybe you ain't so bad," Castle nodded.

"The boy did good. That statue? That's the tip-top, that's the elite, that's infiltration at its finest," Rory yelled.

Jake glanced at Mona. She was pumped too. She raised her palm.

"Yes!" she yelled.

Rory gestured to Jake. "Come 'ere." Rory wrapped Jake into a big bear hug with one of his arms. "How does it feel to finally be alive?" Rory asked.

"Good," Jake said. "Really good."

"Yeah?" Rory said. "You've just scratched the surface, kiddo."

Jake noticed a lump near Rory's feet: an all-black waterproof bag lay on the floor near the wheel. It was relatively inconspicuous. Except that a padlock secured its zipper shut. *Weird.*

■

Rory's home was a jarringly trendy mash-up of the roughly industrial and smoothly posh. The ceilings were open, revealing electrical conduits and the raw beams holding the place up. But the kitchen cabinets were slickly metallic with pure white marble countertops and pricey appliances. For a man who seemed to support himself by means of alchemy, not appearing to hold a regular job at all, Rory was living large. His loft was in the prime of Williamsburg, a far cry from the shithole where Jake resided. The pad even had a garage. Rory had just given Jake the combination to said garage and announced that he was welcome to park his bike there at any time. It made Jake feel good. There was a friend somewhere inside Rory—just waiting to break out. Jake had a job to do and he knew it. But it had also been a long time since Jake had a damn good time, especially with a lovely lady by his side.

The whole crew relaxed in Rory's living room, punctuated at one end by large windows overlooking Manhattan. They quickly made themselves comfortable, and Jake realized that this was the final puzzle piece. This was the beating heart. Rory's house was their clubhouse, their base of operations—*everything.* Jake was in the belly of the beast and he felt at home. Rory pulled a bottle of champagne out of the refrigerator and popped it open. He tipped the champagne into Jake's mouth. Jake chugged. Mona was next, and then she passed it around to the rest of the group. Jake glanced around the room slowly, taking in the details. He noticed that one wall of Rory's apartment was plastered entirely with maps and building schematics. Jake ambled towards the wall.

"Like what you see?" Rory asked from behind Jake. "Some places I want to go. Every unit you see just happens to be owned by Arthur Metropolis."

Jake checked them out. "Trump Tower, Time Warner Center, Eighteen Gramercy Park, The Millennium, and Fifteen Central Park West," Jake said. "They're all residential. High end. High security. Those would be really tough."

"I like to challenge myself," Rory nodded, "Come on . . . I'll tell you a little bit more about what I'm thinking later. We could use a guy with your skills in our crew."

"A climber?"

"No, no," Rory said. "A guy who doesn't piss himself when the cops show up."

While Jake sat back down and sipped his drink, he noticed Castle pick up the waterproof bag he'd seen on the boat. Castle positioned himself behind a desk at the other end of Rory's living room. He unlocked the bag and pulled out a laptop. Nikolai joined Castle. Jake could hear them quietly murmuring to each other as the laptop started up. He couldn't make out the words at first, something about a "BIOS hack," but then he distinctly heard Castle mutter, "Tell me if you find the video."

Jake stared at Rory across from him.

"Are you gonna rob those places?" Jake said.

"What?" Rory turned suddenly.

"Come on, man. It's obvious. I'm not an idiot. But I thought that was the whole point of initiation—I'd finally get the truth. Didn't I show you how real I am?"

"It doesn't concern you."

"Yeah, it does. I'm part of this crew now. But it's not just that. I want to knock that guy just as much as you do. Metropolis? I hate what he's doing to our city. I just want to be part of it, part of taking him down. If that's what you're doing . . ."

"Look, you came in late to the game," Rory said. "If I choose to get you involved, I'll let you know. It's a one-way street. But we're nearing the end."

"The end of what?"

"The investigation."

"Huh?" Jake said, suddenly alarmed.

"Nothin'. Why don't you get yourself another drink."

▪

Rory's place was expansive, and the cherry on top was the patio outside the large windows that overlooked Manhattan. Later that evening, Mona and Jake sat on a bench on the patio, gazing over the dappled lights of the Brooklyn Bridge in the distance.

"Got a nice view, doesn't he?" Jake said. "I gotta get a gig like Rory's."

"Some people are luckier than others. Rory's an enigma," she said.

"Where's all his money come from?" Jake asked.

"Honestly? I don't know." Mona pondered for a second. "I think he inherited it. Family money. Just like half the people in Gotham."

"You know, a lot of what I was doing dried up . . ."

"And what was that?" she asked.

"Selling electronics and bike parts. Buy 'em down in Chinatown, whoever will give them to me cheap. Sell them on auction sites or to some of the dealers."

"Why can't you keep on doin' it?"

"My competition wants to kill me," Jake chuckled.

"Do me a favor. Don't worry about money tonight. Think about the good stuff. Like the fact that I cured you."

"Of what?"

"You have to admit. You didn't panic up there," she said.

"The vertigo," Jake said. "I knew you'd help me."

"No, you didn't," Mona laughed, "But I proved you wrong. I told you . . . Believe in me, and it will all work out."

"So are you done for the night?"

"That depends. You?"

"Not if you're with me."

"So where we rollin'?"

"Maybe we should finish what we started . . ." Jake said.

▪

The second time Jake went up the Brooklyn Bridge was much easier than the first. He was practically racing up the thick cable towards the top. He didn't look back. He didn't stare down. And when his eyes flashed to his feet briefly, his brain wasn't stuck like a long chain of broken pixels. He gazed ahead, towards the precipice. He paced quickly. He was leading Mona. He pursued the target without pause or concern. Rory was right—with the right preparation and tools, anything was possible. It didn't take very long for them to summit the bridge. Jake reached the top first, pulling himself up onto the flat brick surface atop the tower. He helped Mona up.

"Hey," Jake said. "Thanks. I wouldn't be up here without you."

"There we go. That's more like it. You're welcome."

Mona rested against Jake while they sat on the top of the bridge and observed the Freedom Tower like an obelisk blasting to heaven.

"So what's your deal with Rory?" Jake asked.

"What do you mean?"

"I asked what I mean."

"No deal," Mona answered. "I'm not with Rory, if that's your question. We're friends. Sometimes we slip up in that regard, but no one cares. A couple of years ago there was something else. But I was young. I didn't . . ." She turned to look at Jake but couldn't complete the sentence.

"What?"

"I know more about him now," Mona said. "He wise. He's talented. But he's not the best influence. Life isn't so easy to figure out, that's all. Don't worry about Rory."

"Come on. Everyone's telling me to not worry. You can trust me."

"Is that a fact? I'll tell you what I think. I think you came in here hot and heavy. You wanted so bad to be part of Rory's crew, and I'm still not sure why. I don't think it was just me. I hope it wasn't. It's probably because you spent your life trolling the net, catchin' our videos, and aspiring to live the life that we live. You don't tell me anything about your past because there's nothing to tell. Whatever you were doing? It was shit. Shitty friends. You were just existing. Punchin' the card of life. You were nothing before you met us. You're no different than a bunch of other barns that have tried to join our crew. For every Castle, there's five guys that disappear after a few months. How do I know you're not going to become one of them?"

"I'm not going to disappear," Jake said.

"There's no guarantees in life. That's what I've learned."

She was incredibly far off, but she wasn't completely wrong. He needed to tell her more. He needed to tell someone more. He wasn't a cipher—he was a man. There was a reason for everything.

"You want to know why I was afraid of heights?

"Sure."

"I usually just tell people that my dad's dead. He's not. They all live up in Albany . . . Him and my mom. They're normal. Enough. He drank way too much and made my life miserable, but that wasn't the real problem. I was just never what my dad wanted me to be. I didn't like regular stuff. I was like this punk kid who listened to AFI and Rise Against. So he doesn't get me, and I don't like him. Nothing makes a drunk madder than someone walking around their house who's judging them. So he sends me to boarding school . . ."

"Rough," Mona said.

"Guess he thought it would make me a man. But I didn't fit in there, either," Jake reminisced, the memories—*the truth*—flooding through his brain like some long-forgotten horror movie. "Kids would beat me up. But my roommate and I were tight. For the first few weeks. Then I realized he was just like them all. He started stealing from me. Pickin' on me. One night he didn't say anything mean when I went to bed. That's how I knew something was up. The second I fell asleep, he and his buddies pulled me out of the room, start punching me in the face. They stuffed my head in a pillowcase. They dragged me down this hallway, and . . . they held me out the window. First years were at the top of the building. So we're six stories up. I'm hanging. They're holding my feet, but one of them? His hand slips. They lose the foot . . . Now we're all screaming. And I'm starin' down at a brick patio . . . And nothing's going through my brain. Not my dad. Not my mom. I don't miss them. I just hate them. And I hate everything. All I feel is nothing, and for a second the only thing that crosses my mind is that they should just drop me."

"I'm so sorry . . ." Mona put her hand to Jake's neck.

"But then as I'm swinging through the air, I start to think about what I'm going to do if I don't die. And I know exactly what it is. I'm going to do everything in my power to get bigger than those guys, get badder, get cooler than them, so one day I can fight back against the assholes of the world."

"Come here," Mona asked.

Jake didn't move. She pulled him towards her.

"You're good now. You're with me," she said.

She started to kiss him. This time it was deep, romantic.

"And you know something? Now you are that guy. You are cooler. You are the baddest guy in the room."

"I know," Jake said. "But it didn't make me happier."

"That's 'cause you were missing something else."

"What?"

"Me."

Their hands were all over each other now, right there on the top of the bridge. They were two small dark specs, somewhere between lust and love, invisible to the rest of the world but very aware of each other. Their interior world was changing dramatically, but to the outside they were completely indistinguishable from the top of the large brick towers that held up the Brooklyn Bridge. The world moved on without them. The cars and trucks whipped across the span, enabling the commerce of a city. But Jake and Mona didn't care. They weren't part of the hustle and bustle. They were stuck in slow motion—only focused on one another. All that mattered to them in this moment were the tiniest slivers of what was in front of them. The flick of her eye, the crease of her lips. The curl of his mouth, the strength of his shoulders. Her lips on his neck. His hands on the small of her back. It wasn't about what they saw. It was about what they felt.

TWENTY

THE SUN BURNED HIS FACE. Jake cracked one eye open, then the next. Morning light sliced through the open window shades of the room and intersected his eyes. He sat up and took in a view of water tanks and air conditioners lurking over rooftops. He shook his head. Yesterday had been a long blur, but now it was coming back full steam. He expected to find someone else in the bed. But there was no one there.

And it wasn't his bed.

Jake found his clothes from the prior evening in a pile on the floor. He padded down the tiny hallway, following the sound of clacking plates and the smell of bacon. He entered the kitchen to alt-domestic chaos. Mona was manning the stove, frying eggs. Her older sister, Adriana, tended to two little girls struggling to put their backpacks on. One of the little ones, a five-year-old named Mari, stared up at Jake in shock.

"Who's that?" she asked.

"He's my friend, Mari. Now why don't you go with your mommy?" Mona said.

Adriana scooped up Mari and gave her a kiss on the forehead.

Mona turned to Jake. "This is my sister, Adriana. And little Vicki and Mari. My nieces . . ."

Jake shook Mari's hand. "I'm Jake," he said. "What's your favorite subject in school?"

Mari was suddenly shy, not wanting to answer.

"Mine was music. What about you?"

"Lunch!" Mari blurted out. Vicki and Mari started squealing in laughter.

"Nice to meet you, Jake," their mom, Adriana, said. "You must be a good one."

Adriana was finally able to corral the two girls out of the apartment. The door closed.

"That's my morning," Mona exhaled. "And my evenings."

Jake took a seat next to the stove. "What did your sister mean?"

"I'm not so easy to trust people."

"Me either."

"Want some food?"

"I'm starving."

Mona grinned. She headed back to tending the stove, finishing off the eggs with a dash of cheese. She tossed a few pieces of bacon on the plate and placed it in front of Jake.

"So domestic," he said.

"I do my best. Don't tell me you don't like it."

"That wouldn't be true," Jake replied. "I enjoy it." He began to scarf down the food. "So what are you doing today?"

"There's a Friends meeting down by Whale Square. Then our protest before the demolition. Then work."

"Protest. Like, with signs?"

"That's how you do it," she replied.

"Think that's going to work?"

"It's not about the signs. It's the optics. It's all planned out. We'll have the press show up at the right time, and for that hour we'll give 'em our all."

"Impressive," Jake said. "Engineered protest."

"It's very intentional. I live here," Mona put her hands on her hips. "You don't know what we've been going through . . ."

Jake craned his neck to the left. He could make out tops of Whale Square a few blocks down the street.

"He's gonna start there, and then you know where he's coming?"

"Metropolis?" Jake asked.

"Of course."

"Where?"

"Right up this street. He already owns five of the buildings, all except for ours."

"Really?" Jake asked.

"And once he has this one? Whole street's getting the wrecking ball, you can guarantee it. That is . . . before it gets filled up again with a bunch of clones that work in finance and couldn't find culture if it spray-painted them in the face."

All of a sudden, a loud, blaring noise ricocheted through the room—like a headache accelerating to migraine level. Jake glanced at Mona, but she didn't seem panicked. She pointed to a carbon monoxide detector in the apartment.

"So that's been happening too," she said.

"What?"

"We should go outside. Get your stuff," she said.

▪

As they stood outside of Mona's building, the entire building seemed to empty onto the street. About thirty residents of Mona's tower and another twenty-five from next door stood in the chilly morning air, clutching all manner of blankets and jackets to stay warm.

"It'll take about an hour for the city to show up," Mona said. "And by then, there won't be a gas leak anymore."

"This has happened before?"

"A few times a week," she said.

"Weird."

"It's not weird. It's obvious. Metropolis. He wants to make our life difficult, so we start breaking leases so he can buy up the property. Trust me. He's that type of guy."

"I know," Jake said.

Mona chuckled. "You have no idea."

"I . . . Sure. You're right," Jake replied.

They wandered down the street, towards Whale Square. As they passed by wall-wrapped advertisements for new developments, Jake noticed multiple parking lots were filled with all manner of massive construction cranes and vehicles.

"He's getting ready to go."

"Yep," Mona replied glumly. She pointed across the street, towards an under-construction café, one of the lone storefronts in the neighborhood.

"He's building that too. Organic, artisanal breakfast. Who wants their breakfast to look like art? How about just being good? I looked up the menu online. Scrambled eggs are seventeen dollars."

"That's the future," Jake said.

"Then we're the past."

They stopped when they hit the water, holding on to a temporary chain-link fence that separated them from the bay. Everything in this part of the city was old in its bones and bracing itself for the awaiting upheaval. The district had seen the tsunami coming, and the wave wasn't going to arrive lightly like a slow tide. It was going to strike suddenly. And then it would drown everything around it—*including Mona.*

"I just wish I could keep it with me," she said.

"You'll always have the city," Jake replied.

"How so?"

"The riches? They're done for and don't even know it. While they spend their thousand dollars a day for the right to live here, it's still yours."

"There's a lot less space . . ."

"You're right. But that's why I love what you do." Jake restated, "What we do. We get to have this place all to ourselves, 'cause we're willing to look at it differently. That's what I've learned. Look at something from another angle, and maybe you'll see a whole different world."

"Pretty good," Mona grinned.

"What?"

"You sound just like Rory now."

▪

Jake and Mona stepped past the retired creatures of Whale Square. They eventually turned into a tiny speck in the distance. That is—*to the man watching them.* Crouching inside the fourth story of a brick warehouse and gazing through broken window shards, Emanuel Vipa tracked them both.

▪

Stian Ziros sat on the toilet in the opulent bathroom of Arthur's penthouse at the SoHo Modern. He stood and reached the mirror. He slowly rubbed his face with a plush washcloth before staring at his own eyes. He didn't see himself. He only processed his reflection as an image framed by negative space. Ziros viewed the world not as a set of histories, or relationships, but instead as an aesthetic. It was easier that way, and thus better. And he was proud of what he saw. *I mean, just look at the guy.*

Ziros exited the bathroom and padded into the master.

"You're up," a voice whistled over. This was Zazsy. Zazsy was a pure terror of beauty, the type of femme fatale who always figures it out—and ends up convalescing in a twenty-million-dollar mansion later in life. But she was completely naked now as he strode back into the room.

"Work," Ziros replied.

"Yeah. Whatever," Zazsy said. "You got some time?"

"No."

She turned and stared at Stian, smiling with cunning. She turned away from him and slowly sat down on her knees on the carpet in front of him. She leaned forward, her hands riding along the floor. His mouth was agape at the sight in front of him. Zazsy began laughing.

"Still no?" she said.

And—the phone rang. It was Emanuel.

"What do you have?" Ziros asked.

"I got 'em. He's tight with Rory and his crew. But definitely the girl. Her name's Mona Rosas . . ." Emanuel said over the phone.

"So where are they?"

"Uh, they rolled. But I know where she lives now."

Ziros stared at Zazsy ahead of him. He wanted what he saw, and he wasn't going to let anything stop him. The world was at his beck and call. Actually, the world was emptying his balls over and over again—and Arthur Metropolis was paying.

"Good," Ziros said. "Let's meet up."

"When?"

"The second I'm done with this thing."

▪

Jake skirted his Ducati up through Park Slope on the way to I-27, then along the highway. A multitude of thoughts was cascading through his mind, not the least of which was the fast-developing situation with Mona. But Rory was in there as well. Now he had the PIN code for Rory's garage. He was on the inside, so close to cracking this whole thing wide open that he could taste it on his tongue. It was in the middle of this thought that he thought his eyes were flashing. Red? Maybe he was tired. He blinked and refocused. But there it was again, red and blue lights lurking around the periphery of his motorcycle helmet. Jake turned his head towards the side mirror that extended from the handlebars—to catch an unmarked police car on his tail. He glanced down towards his feet as if to fire the accelerator.

"Don't even consider it, Rivett," Tony Villalon's voice blasted over a loudspeaker.

Jake's shoulders slumped. He veered the motorcycle onto the side of the highway as if he'd been pulled over for a traffic stop.

Tony stepped out of the car with his hand on his hip, near his gun. That was unnecessary—but just like Tony. He reached for the back door and swung it open.

"Your presence has been requested," Tony said.

▪

Rivett wasn't particularly surprised to see Susan Herlihy sitting in the back, her thin legs politely folded one over the other. It wasn't just the fact that her outward appearance was such a polar opposite to her interior self; it was that she made no attempt to hide it. Susan didn't even try to become one of the guys—like many of the female cops on the force did for their careers. She had just pranced above them from day one, getting her way with the fierce power of policy.

"Did I ever tell you that the summer before I met my first husband, I dated a cowboy in Galveston, Texas?" Susan asked.

"No. No, Susan, you didn't . . ."

"He was this pompous bastard. Attractive. Good bone structure. But pompous. He pushed too hard to try to be a cowboy when really he was the son of a fat oilman from River Oaks. I knew something was wrong with him. I just couldn't put my finger on it for a while—until the time he took me out for an ATV ride at his ranch. We got stuck two miles into the woods when the sun set. He started crying right then and there and wanted to sleep next to the ATV for the night. Just us, and the mosquitos, and a whole jungle full of predators. I ran back to the house in an hour and seventeen minutes and never spoke to him again. It was my gut that made that decision and my gut was right," she said.

Jake wasn't sure whether to be bemused or frightened.

"He later died. Got eaten by his own crocodile—that he'd imported," Susan said as she beamed a brilliant smile full of dark-red-lipstick and perfect teeth at Jake. "How was your night?"

"Investigation's good."

"Don't even bother," she waved her hand in the air, as if she couldn't be less interested in Jake's response. Jake realized that she was holding a tablet in her hand. She pressed play on a video and turned the iPad so that Jake could observe.

Jake began to watch infrared surveillance footage shot from the point of view of a helicopter across the bay from the Statue of Liberty. It didn't take a rocket scientist to know what he was going to see next. Two small figures—their heat signatures glowing in the footage like video game characters—lowered themselves from the torch of the statue and disappeared into a small door aside Lady Liberty's shoulder.

There was nothing to say.

"Investigation's good. Right?" Susan said. "I put up with you when I knew your head was in the game, Rivett." She manipulated the tablet's feeds, finding one that had been digitally enhanced and zoomed in. One of the two figures turned toward the camera and became unmistakable.

He stared at the slightly blurry but still discernable version of himself.

"Now you're just gallivanting. In my book, that's worse than anything you've ever done to me. That means you and I are breaking up."

"What?"

"The hell do you think?" Susan stared at Jake in order to impart her dead seriousness. But only for about four seconds—as long as she was willing to waste time gazing at him. There were more interesting and pertinent things going on in the world. She pulled her phone out and started to browse emails as she continued to speak under her breath in Jake's direction.

"While you were out with your girlfriend, they hit a yacht across the water. Know anything about that?"

"A yacht?" Jake thought for a moment.

"Do I need to repeat myself?"

"No . . . Wait . . . They picked us up on a boat. I didn't think all the guys would be there. Had a bag full of stuff. Some laptop that they stole."

"A laptop?" Tony said. "Now you're confusing me. First of all, take one guess who owned the boat."

"Arthur Metropolis," Jake said.

"Ding."

"He reported jewelry. Again," Tony said.

"You know that Arthur Metropolis is a complete and utter liar, right?"

"Well, I'm sorry that our victim has failed your morality tests," Susan said.

"It's not that. I—"

"Doesn't matter what you think. Upstairs is pissed. The city bloggers just got hooked into the Metropolis connection to the robberies—which means that in about ten hours, everyone's going to have it. And you? You're not working out. I'm not going to shed one fucking tear thinking about it." Susan shook her pointer finger around Jake's general vicinity.

"What are you going to do without me?"

"I'm simply going to utilize the full resounding power of the police force," Susan continued to scroll on her phone as she spoke, like she couldn't care less that Jake was there anymore. "You're suspended until further notice."

"You don't know what you're doing, Susan." Jake said. He pointed to himself. "I worked hard to get in there. Rory? He likes me. Think about it. It wasn't Emanuel Vipa. He's a nothing. Rory's the one doing this. Rory, Castle, Nik."

"And the girl?" Tony asked.

"No culpability," Jake shook his head.

"It's not whether you know what we all know already. It's your evidence. What's your evidence?" Susan asked.

"I don't have it all. But I've got a lot. I know what they're going to hit next. And last night? That was my in. You get it? The thing at the Statue of Liberty wasn't shits and giggles. It was my initiation. Now they trust me. Give me a week or two. I can tell that Rory's about to tell me everything. The floodgates are opening."

She didn't respond directly. Instead, she beckoned.

"Badge and gun," Susan said. "You'll follow Tony back to the house in

New Rochelle for debrief. I'm stopping rent on the apartment. I'll clear that place out. I heard you're actually living there, so maybe you should think a bit about future accommodations."

"My badge and gun are in the Bronx. At the apartment. Susan, please . . . "

"Okay, enough. Tony will grab it all later," Susan sighed. "I don't have time for this." Susan nodded at Jake then towards the door.

Jake opened the car door and stared down the highway at his bike. It was a warm, beautiful day. But he couldn't feel a bit of sunshine as he stepped out.

"It's okay, you know. I'll keep you on the force," Susan said. "But you're out of the cold. For good. You should look around a little, bask in the sun. Then smile. And don't worry one little bit because believe you me . . . I'm going to kill those jokers." She grinned as she slammed the door shut.

TWENTY-ONE

"THE NEXT PLACE THEY HIT is one of these five locations," Jake said.

He wrote down the list of locations he'd spotted at Rory's apartment and slid the piece of paper towards Villalon. They were sitting outside by the pool, behind the house in New Rochelle.

"I also have his garage door PIN, which might be of use to you," Jake added.

"I'd love that," Tony said. "Thanks. So what about the girl? Is she in on these hits?"

"Who?"

"The person whose bed you slept in last night. The one from social media. Mona."

"She didn't hit the Razor—'cause she was with me. I don't think she really knows."

"That may be," Tony said as he raised an eyebrow, "and if that's true she won't have any problems. Susan wasn't lying. She's planning the full-court press. A couple hundred guys. Head-to-toe surveillance."

"Do me a favor, Tony. Trust me. Mona's not into this stuff."

"You know where she works?"

"She's an art student," Jake said.

"I said where she works . . ."

"The mall, I think?"

"Right . . . Belensky's."

"What's that?"

"Look it up. Might connect a couple more dots. Anyway, time to celebrate the fact that you're still alive." Tony popped open a beer for Jake and pushed it across the table.

"Told you Susan would jack me," Jake said as he took a sip.

"Right in the chest," Tony nodded.

Jake chuckled. "But she wasn't looking me in the eye, unless you count her Blackberry. I guess firing me was about as interesting as revising a Google doc."

"So you know our plan. What's yours?" Tony said.

"Right and wrong doesn't rest on the thin blue line. I am going to bust this open. I am so close—and they trust me. Wanna know what's gonna nail these guys to the wall? Evidence. I'll just become the evidence."

"C'mon . . ."

"What?"

"Why do you gotta say stuff like that? Makes me worried. That doesn't fly with me, Jakey."

"You asked me what I'm going to do . . ."

"No support at all? I gotta cover you, man."

"Not possible," Jake said.

"Just me. Not the force."

"What do you have in mind?" Jake asked.

"Well, you know most of the money they spend on us is useless."

"Yeah? Like the pool?"

"Gotta keep up appearances for the neighbors," Tony replied.

"Oh yeah? In that case . . ." Jake stood up and yanked off his shirt, then went for his belt. Within a moment he was down to his boxer shorts.

"But being SID has some perks too. Like the hand-me-downs the FBI drops on our doorstep every few months," Tony said. "Let me get something for you."

"Whatever you're talking about? That's your bag. Not mine. Me? I'm only here for a few more minutes. I'm going to chug this beer, go for a couple laps, and then I'm outta here, Tony." Jake propelled himself into the air and executed a perfect backflip into the pristine body of water behind him.

▪

Jack Castle didn't wake up when his phone rang the first time. He missed the second call too—finally rousing from his stupor when a text came through.

Nikki was very intent on finding him. Her text read: "*Call me NOW. You need to know something about your 'friend' Jake Easton.*" It didn't take Castle long to remember exactly who Nikki was. He walked up the stairs to the loft bedroom above Rory's living room.

▪

Rory was already up. He was tapping away on his laptop, securing a van rental online and using Tor-anonymizer software to hide his tracks.

"Fun party, eh?" Rory said.

"Listen, we have to talk. About Eastie," Castle said.

"What about him?"

"You know I always got your back, right?"

"Sure . . ." Rory said.

"I put feelers out. Just doing some due diligence. Nothing major. But one came back like a boomerang. We gotta meet this chick," Castle said.

"Who?"

"A girl that knows about Jake. I know you think he's crazy enough to do what we're thinking about . . . But maybe he ain't just broken. Maybe there's a different reason he's game?"

"Fine," Rory said. "Set it up." He turned back to his preparations.

▪

A few hours later, Rory and Castle paced down a Bronx street. A motorcycle bolted past them with a woman seated on the back. Both the female and the driver tipped their heads towards the two men, and then slowed. As Rory and Castle approached, Nikki pulled her helmet off her head. The man on the motorcycle stayed seated.

"Were you expecting two of them?" Rory whispered to Castle.

"No."

"Careful."

Castle shook hands with Nikki. "Hey there," he said. "What's up?"

"Who's he?" Nikki pointed to Rory.

"Everyone has a boss."

"Not me."

"Then who's that guy?" Rory pointed to the man sitting on the motorcycle.

"My fuckin' cowboy," Nikki said.

"You said you've got something. About Jake?" Castle asked.

Nikki glanced back and forth between Rory and Castle. "You got problems, bro," she finally said. "You got a problem with a virus. You're sick and you don't even know it."

Nikki was obviously under the influence of a cocktail of major league drugs. It was tragic, actually, because she was a broken-down beauty. She had the ragged logic of a person who didn't know how far along the sad slide she'd slipped, someone who was accustomed to others doing her bidding and was just on the precipice of that dynamic completely reversing.

"The hell are you talking about?" Rory yelled. "We don't have time for this bullshit," he said, turning to go.

"Hey, homie," the guy on the motorcycle grabbed Rory's shoulder with force. Rory slapped the guy's hand away. But now Hector Trizzo had removed his helmet and stared at Rory and Nikki with snake eyes. "You need to know this. I'm just as interested in Jake as you are. Whatta you do? Your crew. What are they up to?"

"We explore," Rory said.

Hector started cracking up. The laughter rose from his belly and erupted when he couldn't control it anymore. His chuckle was guttural. "I don't know 'bout exploring, homie. Don't know what that means. Let me tell you something, Jake wouldn't be friends with ya unless you were doing something real illegal. And so now I'm a little interested because somehow . . . Your punk asses . . . are like, more of a concern to the po-po than me. Which I find real difficult to believe. But that shit's on the level. I can co-sign with that."

"Don't mess with me, man. Police—why are you using that word?"

"So now you want to know what we know, eh?" Hector cackled.

"Yeah? And who are you?" Rory said.

"I'm a goddamned winning lottery ticket for you, homie. 'Cause your buddy, your pal Jake Easton? I know him. He's the same as my old buddy Jakey, who I ain't seen in a while now. Quite a coincidence. He used to be my best friend . . . Met him a bit ago, and he rolled hard. Not exploring. Thievin'. Then all of a sudden we got busted up by the cops, and Jake rolled on me. I thought it was just the streets for a while, until this finey comes around and tells me something real interesting," Hector nodded to Nikki. "Show him," he said.

Nikki pulled out her cell phone. She scrolled to a photo and flipped the phone around. It was the picture of Jake's badge and gun.

"Jake ain't really our buddy at all. Jake Easton, if that's even his real name?"

"He's . . ." Rory stuttered, the wind actually knocked out of him.

"He's a fuckin' cayp," Hector spat with rage. "And I'm telling you that on the level. There's a couple monsters on the street gonna kill him and everyone he's with. Maybe you included if you still nearby. Not my job anymore. I ain't nothin'. Just a little part in the plan. It's already going down. He screwed with a Leviathan, and he gonna pay the price of a life or three. But maybe you and I, we could do some mutually beneficial work. Together."

▪

Mona exited the Belensky Brothers jewelry store in Manhattan and walked down the sidewalk towards a bus stop. A motorcycle on a side street expelled a guttural roar. She glanced over furtively. When she saw Jake, a smile erupted from her lips. And then concern. Why was he here?

"What are you doing? Thought we were going to meet by the demo."

"I was nearby."

"How'd you know I work here?"

"A little birdie."

"Okay . . ."

"Hey. Can't blame me for looking around. Saw some mail at your place. That's what I always do when I wake up in a strange bed."

"How often does that happen?"

"Never."

"Liar."

"Takes one to know one. Want a ride?" Jake held up a second helmet.

▪

He drove furiously along the Brooklyn Bridge back towards Red Hook. She held onto him tightly. She could feel the nervous energy radiating off him but wasn't sure how to address it.

"What's up, babe?" Mona asked over the radio headset inside her helmet.

"You work at Belensky's? What do you do for them?"

"It pays good," she said.

"I bet."

Mona spied the distinctive red brick structures of Whale Square to the south as Jake guided the motorcycle off the highway. It took another few minutes before the gargantuan parking lot of oversized construction vehicles around Whale Square came into view. The worst of them, like a dragon romping towards a besieged stone castle, was the crane that held the wrecking ball. The machine lumbered slowly down the road, guided by a number of oblivious men in construction helmets. With all of the money flowing into the economy nowadays, and cheap loans available to large and even medium-sized developers, the construction business was booming. What these guys—who were being paid quite well for a few months of history destruction—didn't realize was that the cash wasn't actually going to help them climb the ladder. For every dollar they made, a supplier was making five, a lawyer on the project was making ten, and the developer was making a hundred. The construction workers would never be able to leave Long Island and neither would their own children—the ones they were saving up for. Because they were building value-skyrocketing fortresses for the kids of lawyers and developers. They were marching into the gaping mouths of their own demise, like the slaves who built the pyramids in Egypt. There was no salvation at the top of the pyramid, just a ride back to reality—while their rulers decked themselves in gold and laid down to rest in bunkers designed to withstand Armageddon.

Jake parked the motorcycle, and they headed towards the piers below Whale Square—a vast and rusting oil infrastructure spreading south. Jake was sure that Metropolis would have his eye on this area next. One empty and large lot, the size of a few football fields, had been used as a graveyard for shipping containers. Mona nudged Jake.

"Those will give us a good view," she said.

Jake followed Mona. She climbed up a pyramid of shipping containers. It took a deft combination of leaping, climbing, and shimmying, but Jake was well prepared for the task. They finally found themselves a few hundred feet in the air—sitting atop a pile of steel and aluminum.

Manhattan was glorious and beautiful to their left. Less lovely was the sound of cracking brick and shearing metal to their right. The wrecking ball went through the Whale Square complex without any thought for history or prudence. It was pure destruction. They watched as the walls of the building where they had met were reduced to dust. A huge cloud of debris and detritus clung to the air. Jake had to pull his shirt over his mouth to stop from coughing, but found that he couldn't turn away.

Neither could Mona. Both were enchanted by what was happening—it was a macabre sensation. Mona held her cell phone silently, recording the mess for later use. Jake said nothing, his thoughts already quite dark—and becoming blacker still.

"You're not saying much. What's up?" Mona asked.

Jake scowled.

"Please . . ."

"I can't afford to just . . . do this anymore . . . I need a job," he said.

"What's stopping you?"

"That pisses me off too."

"All you have to do is write your résumé. Start hitting the pavement. That's how normal people do it. That's how I did it," Mona said.

"It's like you think I haven't proven myself yet," Jake replied. "It's obvious that Rory doesn't live the way he does on investments alone. I want in on it. I need in."

Mona absorbed Jake's statement. She stopped recording on her cell phone and put down the device. She stared out over the Whale Square demolition. "You don't want what you're asking for," she finally said.

"Maybe not. But that's where I'm at. And yeah, it pisses me off that you won't give Rory the good word about me." Jake stood up on the container. He began pacing. "I know you're in on this stuff, too. What's up with you? What are you doin' at the jewelry store? You want me to think it's just a coincidence that you work at Belensky's?" Jake grabbed Mona's shoulders and shook her, just a bit harder than she would ever have wanted him to.

Her eyes blew wide—*Jake was frightening.*

"I know he's doing robberies," Jake continued. "I know that's how he makes his bones. Last night they hit another place. A boat. Did you know that was going down? Was I just some sort of diversion?"

"No," Mona replied. Then she doubled back, "I don't know, actually . . ."

"What do you know?"

"I know that . . . I hate him."

"What?" *Unexpected.*

"You don't want to get sucked in," she said.

"Yeah. Actually, I do," he replied. "Tell me. Mona. Please."

"Rory kicked me cash." The truth finally began to erupt. "I don't know where it came from. He knows me too well. We have a history. Mari and Vicki are all I have . . . and he's aware. I just told him about people, and he gave me money for my family.

"People . . . Clients from the store?"

She nodded. "The whales."

"And Rory robs them?"

"Guess so," she said.

"And what about Metropolis? Was he one of your clients?"

"No. Metropolis is all Rory," Mona shook her head. "It doesn't matter, anyway. I'm done with that. Have been for a while. And once I graduate, that's it . . . He doesn't need me. I'm just one of a dozen spokes on his wheel. Rory's got a whole network. Castle takes jobs to learn how places work and get access. They track celebs on Twitter. Nik cracks their emails and schedules. Hit 'em when they're out of town."

"You gotta get away. Today," Jake said.

"I will . . ."

"No. I mean it. Out of town."

Mona nodded tentatively, not sure exactly where Jake was going with this.

"Listen to me." Jake stared at her with deadly serious eyes. "Everything I've told you about me is true. It's all real. But just like you, I left a couple of things out. One thing, actually. I'm the police, Mona."

"What?"

"I'm a cop."

The truth hung like a venomous spider in the air. In that moment, Jake's revelation was definitely more painful than the demolition in front of them. Mona put her hands to her temples, hyperventilating.

"Oh god . . ."

"Rory and everyone around him is goin' down."

"You turned me in?"

Jake shook his head. "They have no evidence when it comes to you. I made sure of that. If you want out, this is your chance. I can save you, save your life—without a scratch. I can end all this. We can. But only if we do it together."

"What do you want me to do?"

"Get me in on Rory's next big thing. Whatever he's planning."

"How am I supposed to do that?"

"Give him the sell. He listens to you."

Mona shrugged without commitment. She stood up and walked to the edge of the container, where she kneeled down and swung off the edge, rolling into a controlled fall on top of the container below.

"Mona!" Jake yelled after her.

Mona wouldn't turn to face him. She had tears in her eyes. As she continued to descend off the pile of shipping containers, the world around her was a blur. Still processing what she had just learned, the cross currents were tremendous. She hated him now. It was easier to hate him once she'd started caring for him. She should do what he said—cooperate. But . . . But no. That wasn't her. It was the opposite of what she stood for. Her interactions with the government had always turned out poorly, and she was positive this time would be no different. Even if he did have a cute face and blond hair and she'd enjoyed sleeping next to him. Even if . . . she loved him.

"Mona!" Jake screamed from above. She was gaining distance, only a few seconds from reaching the surface of the barren oil depot below.

"What?" she yelled without turning.

"Let me help you!"

She finally stopped. "Let's say I get Rory to take you on the heist. Then what? What happens after that?"

"We bust him."

"I can't."

"You just said you hate the man."

"Nothing's black and white, Jake. He might not be good. But he stands for something good. Can you dig it?"

Jake very much did understand that concept. In fact, if there was one criticism leveled at him, it was the same exact one. He tried another tact. "Even if you go down with the ship?" Jake asked.

She shrugged him off, rotating and walking along the piping.

▪

Mona stepped onto the street and began to jog away from Jake, speeding up significantly. She took her first left into a tight alleyway—industrial brick walls on both sides. Her pace had forced them both into a dead sprint at this point.

As Mona raced down the alleyway, a large black blur materialized in front of her. An SUV appeared at the end of the alleyway and stopped. Unsure of the driver's intentions, Mona slowed. The car's backseat window rolled down, and the distinctive features of Stian Ziros glared out. The door opened. Ziros stepped out of the vehicle.

Jake sprinted towards Mona, locking eyes with Stian—who began to raise a pistol into the air. Jake dove forward and pulled Mona out of the way. They fell headfirst onto the cement, protected by a small stoop.

"Who's that?" Mona asked.

"Bad news," Jake replied. Jake glanced back where they'd come from. Another black car was slowly creeping down the alleyway. *Cornered.*

"Hey, Jake! Let her out and I might allow her to live!" Ziros yelled out, his sinister words echoing through the alleyway. "But do know this, sir. If you go to your people? She's dead, man."

Just a few feet from Jake was a sewer cover. He glanced at it. "Can we go in there?" he asked Mona. She nodded nervously, scrambling for a tool in her backpack. She pulled out a manhole cover key and handed it to Jake.

"Elite status," Jake grinned. He inserted the tool into the lid and pulled. The steel manhole cover slowly rose from the ground. The two of them piled in.

Just a moment later, the rapid staccato of semi-automatic gunfire rang out all around the stoop. Two of Ziros' men approached the dumpster in tactical formation, pulling up when they saw that Jake and Mona were no longer there.

"Not here," they yelled. "The sewers!"

Back at the SUV, Ziros opened the back door to his car and barked an order. Within seconds, Emanuel Vipa hopped out of the car—holding his own sewer key.

▪

Mona and Jake pushed through the sewer. It wasn't a main. It was the smaller variety, and they both had to duck and crouch to proceed through the maze. Every once in a while, the loud vibration of a subway car passing made them feel like an earthquake was erupting. They eventually came to the end of the sewer pipe—where it deposited into the main. A small stream of water spilled from a drain at the top of the main, and a ladder led upwards. Jake climbed it. He found the drain's grate could be easily pushed out. He and Mona climbed through the eight feet of bedrock that separated the drain from the subway line and into the dark subway tunnel itself. They began to walk towards the glow of a station entrance, a few hundred yards away.

"I've seen that guy before," Mona said.

"The Nordic one?"

"Yeah."

"Where?"

"Rory had pictures of him."

"His name's Ziros. He works for Metropolis."

"Can you get him arrested?"

"What does he want with you?"

"I don't know . . ." Mona said as she splashed through another puddle on their way to safety.

"They want you. Not me. They're not stupid. With me they have no leverage. Just trouble. With you? They got a hook into me . . . and Rory."

Just then—a rustling behind them. Jake rotated to find Emanuel staring at him with seething eyes, a pistol in his hand.

"The girl's comin' with me," Emanuel said.

Jake knew that in a situation like this, the first strike was critical. It was all about violence of action. Do what the person isn't expecting, faster than they expect it. And what Emanuel wasn't expecting, apparently, was to hold a gun and still become the target of a human torpedo.

Jake launched his body directly at Vipa. He smashed into Emanuel, and the two of them fell against the tracks. The gun instantly dislodged from Emanuel's grip and clattered into the darkness. The third rail of the subway, flowing with electrical juice, sparked behind Emanuel's head. Jake held him down, inches from the current, as he turned to Mona.

"Get outta here!" he yelled.

Mona sprinted down the subway tunnel.

Watching Jake track Mona, Emanuel took advantage of the micro-opening. He kicked Jake directly in the crotch. Once. Again. Jake keeled over, losing his balance and falling on top of Emanuel. He wrestled with Emanuel on the ground. That's when three more men careened through the tunnel. Ziros' goons. They surrounded Jake with rifles at the ready. Emanuel flipped himself on top of Jake, then stood up, keeping his foot positioned directly on Jake's windpipe.

"Where is she?" the goon yelled.

"That way," Emanuel pointed down the tunnel and Mona's shadow.

Jake felt it before he saw it. The vibration. It was another subway train, about to bear down upon them from around the curve. He waited until the lights blew out everyone's irises, then rolled. He placed one hand to the side of the third rail and rotated over it without pause.

Emanuel chased after Jake, but wasn't so cautious. The electricity briefly snagged Emanuel like a thousand stapler shots at once. He was frozen as he mercifully toppled to the ground—still alive, but suffering.

Two of Ziros' men raced towards the station and Mona. The third had his gun trained on Jake rising off the ground. The man slowly squeezed the trigger while Jake stared deeply into the oblivion of the dark barrel.

But in that moment, the train finally swooshed between them. Jake ducked, attempting to locate Ziros' man, or Emanuel, but he couldn't distinguish anything in the dark. The train kept coming—car after car—and there was zero that Rivett could do about it.

And once the train had passed completely, there was no one standing on the other side of the track. Not even Mona. He thought he heard screaming, but maybe it was just the screeching of brakes. He couldn't be sure. All he knew was that the world was falling down around him.

TWENTY-TWO

IT TOOK RIVETT LESS THAN a minute to spot the signals boys. It was just a DHL delivery van parked down the street from Rory's loft, right? *Of course not.* What Jake knew—which perhaps the average citizen did not—was that DHL vans do not sit unprotected on the sides of streets overnight. That is, unless they are an undercover listening post run by the New York Police Department. There was even a solid chance that Tony himself was sitting in that van—which meant that Jake had to be doubly careful. Jake didn't love double dipping, but Stian Ziros had crossed a line that nobody was coming back from. There was no way for Jake to know how deep Metropolis had dug his fingers into the department. And with the mayor sitting on Arthur's lap, Jake didn't actually want to know.

Rivett crossed the street two blocks down from Rory's place then doubled back into an alley. He glanced up, spotting a channel where Rory's building met its neighbor. About two feet apart, it would make a difficult-but-possible shimmy. Jake pressed his body into the crevice. He extended his arms and legs out at ninety-degree angles and slowly began to climb vertically. Luckily, the two buildings were only about three stories high. Jake rose from the ground level and carefully pushed higher, using the tension of his body as leverage. He finally reached the roof. It was a straight shot to Rory's balcony. Jake strode towards the back of Rory's residence. He quietly slid over the edge of the steel roof panels. A ladder connected the roof to the balcony. Jake was about to head down when the glass door to the balcony opened. He stopped in his tracks—just a few feet above Rory Visco's head.

Rory was on the phone, leaving a message. "Mona, we have a huge problem. Where are you?" Rory steamed.

Above Rory, Jake felt his hold on the angled roof slipping. He adjusted his position on the slope in an attempt to maintain inertia, but the inevitable occurred. Jake toppled over and slid down the roof. He crashed into the balcony at Rory's feet.

Rory didn't immediately flee. Instead, he grabbed the patio balcony with both hands and simply jumped off. He fell two stories into a garden below. He sprinted towards the other end of the alley.

Jake couldn't quite bring himself to fling himself over the balcony like Rory. Instead, he carefully hung from the balcony. Then he dropped down ever so slightly, pivoted, and continued the chase.

▪

The apprentice charged his master down the back streets of Williamsburg before turning south. When Rory hit a dead end in front of an MTA fence, he began climbing. Jake sprinted directly at Rory, watching as he rose.

Something tugged at Rory's foot. He glanced down. A piece of chain-link had impaled the sole of his shoe. Rory had to retreat a few feet in order to disengage his shoe.

That's when Jake arrived. Impacting the fence like a meteor, the vibration trampolined Rory backward and to the ground. Jake jumped on top of him, extending his elbows to stop the rain of upward blows emanating from Rory.

It took Rory a few moments before he realized that Jake wasn't going for the kill. No gun. No badge. No threats. When Rory let up for just a moment, Jake furthered his submission hold.

"Will you just listen?" Jake muttered through gritted teeth. "You gonna let up? Or do I have to keep you this way?"

"You're not taking me in," Rory seethed.

Slightly dumbfounded, Jake pulled back. "How'd you know?" Jake asked.

"Why should I tell you anything? Use anything that I say against me, right? Isn't that your rule?" Rory said.

"No," Jake said. He stepped off Rory. Rory scrambled up and stared— quite perturbed. "Would I let you go if I was gonna arrest you?" Jake asked.

"So after all that, you're a blue . . ."

"Tell me how you know."

"Hey dude, she's a fox," Rory said. "You did what every man would. But this one bit you."

"Mona?"

Rory shook his head, "No, of course not. Some other chick. Nikki, I think."

"Nikki?" Jake said, incredulous.

"Is this your way of breaking up with me, too? One more nail for old time's sake, and then the cavalry arrives?"

"No. But they're outside your loft. I guarantee you they've already wrapped up a tailored-access operation and bugged your place. And the five locations you were prepping? They're on those too."

"Why are you telling me all of this?" Rory asked.

"Mona," Jake said. "Metropolis took her."

"So what do you think I can do?" Rory expelled.

"They're gonna use her—to get you to stop. You're the prize, Rory. And I know why. Because you're a nail in that guy's foot, and you've been burrowing for way too long."

Rory didn't say anything.

"But what I don't know . . . is you. What's in your head, man? Why Metropolis? Riskin' it all for that prick?" Jake noticed Rory's mouth opening to rebut. "Don't deny it. Seven hits in a couple months. What's the point? You can annoy him, but you can't actually hurt him that way. And there's a million other people in the city to rob if it's just money . . ."

"He's evil," Rory said.

"So what?"

"He's a murderer."

"Murderer . . . Who'd he murder?" Jake asked.

"My brother."

"I thought he died in the hydra . . ."

"Will didn't break his own rules. Go by himself? Drainsled a route he hadn't spotted? No way."

"You don't have proof . . ." Jake attempted to confirm.

"A few days before Will disappeared, he told me he'd been approached by some of Arthur's thugs on the street. The blond one."

"Ziros."

"They found his body a month later—and now that Will was out of the way? Arthur Metropolis gets his way. Permits start gettin' approved again with no resistance from the community. Clear as day who benefited from my brother's death. Every single dollar that I steal . . ." Rory's voice became heightened as he spoke with passion, "goes to nailing Metropolis."

"Yeah. But how, exactly?" Jake asked.

"The video."

"What video?"

"From Will's GoPro. When they turned his body and belongings over, the GoPro was there. But the card wasn't. Whatever's on that card? It's the smoking gun."

"So the jewels and all that stuff? It was a front."

Rory nodded confirmation.

"But a video? Even if that existed, why would Metropolis keep it?"

"Look, dude. I don't know. I just had to look. Don't even know if it exists. But a guy like that . . . Rumor has it he's got sex tapes. He's a voyeur. Maybe he likes to keep his trophies, not destroy them," Rory said. "What I did find told me more. The city worships Metropolis, but he's actually the devil. The laptop. You saw it, from the yacht . . . You wouldn't believe what we found on there. Nik cracked the encryption and we got the mother lode. Wanna know how Metropolis gets his permits approved so quickly? How he can buy up residential zoned row houses and turn 'em into multi-use in six months?"

"Sure. I'm game."

"This guy is bribing people up and down the East Coast. I'm sure he's been doing it all along, but now it's his full-on business plan. And all the flashy stuff in the news? Like Whale Square and the Modern? He loses money on those. Yet he's got abandoned warehouses up in the Bronx that he's running thirty to forty thousand dollars of profit through a month. If those things are getting rented out for forty thousand dollars a month? Then I'm the Pope almighty. I'll tell you what's happening. He and his buddy Ziros are running a straight-up criminal enterprise," Rory said.

"Leviathan . . ." Rivett muttered to himself.

The loud squeal of rubber burning pavement erupted behind them. Rivett rotated to find Castle driving like a maniac down the street in a Sprinter. The van's window was down—Castle aimed a sawed-off shotgun directly at Jake.

"I knew you were a problem, noob!" Castle screamed.

Jake jacked his hands in the air.

"I gotta go," Rory said.

Castle kept his gun trained on Jake as Rory scrambled away from the fence.

"Please," Jake begged. "Mona's in trouble. I need your help, Rory."

"If a chick's AWOL, probably best to call the police, right?"

At that very moment, Rory's phone began to vibrate. He pulled it out of his pocket and caller ID lit up: "Mona." He answered on speaker. "Mona?"

A filtered voice responded. It certainly wasn't female. "Rory Visco—you step on another Metropolis property in the next forty-eight hours, and we kill the girl. We'll contact you in two days."

"Where is she?" Jake jumped in unrestrained.

A long pause greeted them, then . . . "Do what we say and maybe she'll still be alive."

"Put her on. I need to know you have her," Jake said.

Click. The anonymous caller hung up.

"Holy lord," Rory said to Jake.

"I told you. But . . . I don't understand the demand. They just want you to 'not' do anything?"

"Makes perfect sense. They know I have the laptop. That means they know I know about the handoff."

"The handoff?"

"If my place is off limits, where can we keep talking?" Rory asked.

"I was evicted. Me and my superiors aren't on the best terms right now. But I got another spot," Jake replied. "As long as you tell your number one fan to put down the fire stick."

Rory nodded at Castle, who exhaled angrily through his nose but tucked the shotgun into his jacket.

▪

Say what you will about Susan Herlihy, she was true to her word. The safe house had been cleared out. At least she hadn't changed the locks yet. Jake didn't worry about surveillance. He knew Tony was running thin already, so the chances were low. But he'd still had Rory and Castle park a quarter mile away.

The inside of the apartment where he'd spent the last year was bare and tragic—just wooden floors, white walls, and memories. And it was covered in orange spraypaint. Unsure what to make of the paint job, Rivett held his breath when he approached the area where his desk used to stand. He kneeled down and pulled out the fake wooden panel. The safe he'd installed was still there. He breathed a sigh of relief.

▪

Schaub was deep in slumber when the knocking began. He wasn't happy to be woken. But after he'd shaken off the cobwebs and gazed through his peephole, his discontent turned to absolute acid. It was just like Jake Rivett to appear like this. Two weeks of silence, and then all of a sudden he shows—with two unknown dudes. But Schaub opened the door. He always did and always would.

"You don't show up for practice. Don't answer my calls. And it doesn't even look like you brought breakfast," Schaub said. "Who are they?"

"I need your computer, Schaub."

"Oh, okay, I'll just go screw myself . . ."

"Boys. This is Schaub. He's my best friend. We're in a band. Schaub—some work friends. I need a favor . . . or two or three. I need it bad."

Schaub took another look at the three men. "I'm going back to bed," he said.

▪

Sitting in front of Schaub's computer, Jake pulled the pile of SD cards from his pocket. "I believe you were looking for these," Jake said. "I took the privilege of liberating them myself. Should we start watching?"

Jake, Rory, and Castle began to go through the videos. After about a hundred sexual encounters, they were quite discouraged. They'd started to fast forward through the video files, scrubbing as quickly as they could to establish the content. Castle smoked a cigarette. Rory was the most fascinated—glued to the screen while Jake controlled the playback. They were nearing the end of the cards and still hadn't found anything of interest.

"Tell me about this . . . handoff," Jake said.

"Metropolis is scheduled to give one million dollars, cash, to the mayor."

"To Ronald Berg?"

"Indeed," Rory said.

"Insane."

"You don't have to believe it. It's the truth. They know we know. She's their insurance policy. Make sure it all goes down smooth."

"We gotta find her. Now. Insurance ain't worth anything after the expiration date . . ." Jake trailed off.

"I know that," Rory agreed. "But it's a big city, Jake. I'm not omnipotent. I can't just divine her location."

"With the laptop, you're not just a story. You're a fact. Here's what we can do. You turn state's evidence," Jake said. "Come in with me. I'll do my best to protect you. We'll make you a CI . . . get them to take Metropolis down the right way."

Rory's laughter echoed all the way into Schaub's dreams. "By that time? She'll be dead. And the money? Gone."

Jake angrily jammed the last SD card into the computer and hit play.

"What other option is there?"

"We take the fight right to them. Take the money. Then we make a trade. Mona for their cash back."

"Think that would fly?" Jake asked.

"You're the cop," Rory replied.

But before Jake could answer, both of their eyes were drawn directly to the computer screen as if by an electromagnetic pulse. Wide across the monitor were the excited eyes of an urban explorer. Jake had never seen this explorer's face before, but he didn't need to be told who it was. He glanced at Rory for confirmation. Rory was white as a sheet, words barely emoting from his dry and quivering lips.

"Will."

TWENTY-THREE

WILL VISCO'S FACE FILLED THE screen. His smile was wide and open with features that mirrored Rory's. Wearing a helmet, he grinned from ear to ear, culminating in a long microphone-blowing scream powered by pure adrenaline.

"Sleddin' the hydra!" Will yelled, his face still too close to the camera for any observers to make out his surroundings. "It's really goin' down!"

The camera suddenly whipped around 180 degrees and was secured into a bracket on Will's helmet. Now gazing forward, it was much easier to make out Will's environment. To the left and right, the curved steel walls of an old sewer system filtered past. Will's two feet—and the tops of his hands—were visible ahead. He was holding onto a small sled as if he were an Olympic luger. But instead of ice for a surface, Will's track was the slick inside channel of the small descending drain. He whipped around each curve screaming at the top of his lungs while the force of physics mixed with the gyrations of the track and attempted to tear him from his sled. Will held extremely tight, fluidly adjusting his body in the exact rhythm necessary to not lose his balance.

After one final curve, the drain dropped precipitously. Will fell along with it. He flew almost vertically through the air with his head in the lead

—down a thirty-foot section of pipe. His sled reached the bottom of the vertical portion and ripped forward through a small elbow into a straightaway.

The tunnel finally stabilized, flattened, and began to grow wider. Will careened down the straightaway, gradually slowing and losing speed from friction. Midway down the route, the inch of water that had collected became half a foot deep. When his sled hit the pooling water, it caused giant fans of water molecules to explode on each side of his small sled, like tires ripping through a puddle on a dreary afternoon. The water proved the final obstacle—slowing Will down almost completely until his sled came to a stop.

Will reached for the camera on his helmet, yanked it out of the bracket, and aimed back towards himself.

"Holy crap." He breathed heavily from the exertion. "Incredible. Sometimes you scout for two months and get two minutes out of it. But it was all worth it. Best thrill ride of my life. If the water hadn't stopped me up . . ." Will angled the camera towards the end of the tunnel. It was a large brick room consisting of multiple drain inputs and outputs leading to further depths. This was one of the multi-jointed vertices that brought together the disparate elements of the first sewer system in the city. That fact was also evidenced by the elegant creatures chiseled into the keystone of each tunnel ahead of him. Will shined his flashlight through each of the channels. The drains below Will's feet were almost completely open and rusted through, in very bad condition due to decades of water flow without maintenance.

"Well, I'm not gonna go any farther today," Will said to the camera. "It'll take me a few hours to climb back out. Lates."

The camera was secured to Will's helmet again. He reached into muddy water at the bottom of the tunnel to pick up his sled when another voice could be heard in the background.

"Visco," the mysterious voice said.

Will's view straightened and whipped, searching through the dark for the source of the words. Then a man emerged from the open sewer channel to Will's left. Will's spotlight caught the man's gaunt face as he entered. Wearing waterproof pants with a respirator hanging around his neck, Stian Ziros glared at Will.

"Funny seeing you here," Ziros said. He held up a pistol, aimed directly at the camera.

"Uh . . ." Will stammered.

"Don't move," Ziros said.

Two more men surrounded Will on both sides.

It was at that moment the camera began to frantically spasm. Will was running the other direction, heading back down the narrowing tunnel that he'd emerged from.

Freedom ahead—or at least a shot at it.

But no.

A destructive crunch crackled—

Will's perspective dove to the floor—then aimed upwards.

Ziros jumped on top of Will. With a bloodthirsty expression dominating his face, the plastic surgery-enhanced thug hit Will repeatedly. Alternating between his left and right hands like a UFC fighter, the camera wobbled back and forth with each hit until the man was done.

"Should we finish him off, sir?" one of the henchmen asked.

"Not with the gun," Ziros replied as he stood. "But make sure he's a goner." Ziros leaned in quizzically until his face encompassed the entire screen of the video. Ziros' fingers gripped the camera and yanked it off Will's helmet. "And . . . cut," he said.

TWENTY-FOUR

THE SILENCE WAS DEAFENING. NONE of the three of them had been prepared for the raw delivery of this particular video. Rory was clearly the one affected most by the haunting and horrible memorialization of his brother's death. His eyes glistened. But he wasn't crying. He was contemplative, lost somewhere else, eyes focused on nothing.

Castle, however, was bawling on the bed—much more willing to externalize his feelings.

"I'll take it in," Jake finally said.

"I'm sorry. I'm so sorry. That's disgusting," Castle said between gasps.

"It was worse in my mind," Rory finally said.

"Ror . . ." Castle said.

"It's okay," Rory replied.

"I can't imagine . . ." Jake said.

"I've seen it for years. Up here," Rory tapped his skull. "To be honest? It helps to know. It really does."

"I'll bring this in to Tony. My partner."

"No," Rory said after another long pause.

"Really?" Jake asked.

"That video doesn't have Arthur Metropolis in it. I don't win if the ghost gets a first-class ticket to the electric chair. I want Arthur's head on a pitchfork."

"Think about this like a cop," Jake said. "Some cases—most, actually— reach a point when you're just slogging along. You're draggin' mud, and you hit a wall that you just can't climb. But there's a little birdie sitting there—it's something, and it's good. Sometimes you gotta take the bird in hand. You want justice? We'll get it. We'll nail Stian Ziros and the other two. They won't see freedom for the rest of their pathetic-ass lives."

"Nah, Jake. I told you a long time ago, I do what I want. I access all areas. What I want is Arthur Metropolis. It's not enough to break a couple windows. I am going to take his life down to the studs and then melt the frame. The whole thing—the whole organization."

"What about Mona?"

"Her too. All of it. Get the handoff on video, get the cash, get Mona, then release the footage. Understand? The preparations have been made. Whaddya think, noob?"

The whole room knew where Rivett was going before he opened his mouth.

"Of course," Jake said. "I'm absolutely in."

▪

The gray stone of Fifteen Central Park West, an imposing residential building on the west side of Manhattan, rose into the air with geometric precision. This building was notable for many reasons, but the wealth of its inhabitants was definitely its most remarkable factor. It was also important to Tony Villalon because it was one of Rory's five possible targets. Jake's information had arrived at exactly the right time. While Susan Herlihy was making plans to physically locate Rory and the rest of his crew, Tony had presented another idea: "We know the five places that they're going to hit, right? Conduct a grade-A stakeout and nab them while committing the crime itself." That would lock Rory right on up, and the police wouldn't have to rely on the testimony of an unreliable undercover or overcomplicated surveillance data.

Fifteen Central Park West's regal central courtyard reflected a bygone era—one in which a building in Manhattan could afford to sacrifice open-air building opportunities for the sake of residents' comfort. But considering that the inhabitants of this building's total net worth would add up to a sum greater than the value of many countries, it wasn't that out of the ordinary. What was unusual was the boxy, gray NERV truck parked just a few feet from the entrance to the building. A Networked Emergency Response Vehicle, it housed multiple live feeds and formed a virtual "command station" for Villalon. Other techs connected and booted up various surveillance systems within the truck as Tony stood outside and sampled from a tray of catering the building's manager had brought out for them.

"We'll need to tread very carefully," the manager told Tony.

"Agreed."

"The residents of this building are not accustomed overt police presence."

"Let me tell you what your people really won't like," Tony said bluntly. "Having all of their jewelry and documents swiped by a bunch of cat burglars who've never been caught." Tony finished up a scrumptious croissant then turned as another NYPD car arrived in the driveway.

Susan emerged from the vehicle completely poised, as usual. She was wearing a large, wide-brimmed hat as if her next stop was the Preakness. She tilted the chapeau up just enough to read Tony.

"Isn't this exciting?" she asked. Then she nodded her head towards the NERV and took the stairs in her high heels.

▪

When they were both inside the truck, Tony quickly briefed Susan on the coordination between various elements of the NYPD's counterterror, SWAT, surveillance, and technical units.

"We've contacted the managers, and in some case the owners, of the remaining four places. That's the Trump, Time Warner Center right down the street, Eighteen Gramercy and the Millennium building. You see the moving truck right there?" Tony pointed through the one-directional glass of the NERV truck and past the wrought-iron gates of Fifteen's motor court towards a large eighteen-wheeler parked innocuously on the street.

"Is that where my boys are?"

"Indeed," Tony said. "Markle and some of the most terrifying men that SWAT has on payroll are in there prepping their gear as we speak. We have smaller units at the other buildings, but given how close Fifteen and the Time Warner Center are, we figured this was the best place for the main squad."

"Fine," Susan said. "So now what?"

"Now? We wait."

"I was never good at that."

Tony chuckled.

"What?" she asked.

"You and Rivett. You bicker like cats and dogs. But you're more similar than anything else."

"Rivett. Where is he?"

Tony could only shrug. "Don't know about Jake. Lickin' his wounds, I bet."

TWENTY-FIVE

JAKE HAD A SIXTH SENSE for sniffing tails and he didn't like what he was smelling.

"You prepared?" Castle asked Rory—who was now driving the three of them away from Schaub's apartment inside Schaub's old Toyota Corolla. They had left the Sprinter parked on the street.

Rory's hand emerged from the side pocket of his jacket holding a pistol. "I am," Rory said.

"What the hell?" Jake asked. "What's the gun for, dude?"

"Oh, this? Not for the cops. Not your boys. It's for my main man."

"You didn't say anything about firearms."

"Well, you didn't say you were a pig, but that didn't stop you from being one, did it? I don't care. Why should I? You saw the video."

"You know that everything's coming down on you, right? Half of anti-terror's doing waterfall surveillance on you. There's so many people out there we won't see a single repeated face if they're onto us. Whole borough's on tactical alert, and there's a SWAT team at each one of those five places you prepped for." Jake glanced back through the back window of the car. A good distance away, a beat-up Saab followed them, the two headlights of the vehicle only barely visible about four hundred feet back.

"You see that car back there?"

"I see the Saab, yes."

"We can't go anywhere near your five buildings. Right? Would be suicide."

"I'm well aware, noob. You also forgot to mention our cell phones."

"Well, we need to get rid of them too—ASAP," Jake responded.

"We still good, Jack?" Rory asked Castle, avoiding Jake's statement.

"A-okay," Castle replied.

Jake looked over Castle's shoulder. Castle was browsing an Instagram profile on his phone. But Jake couldn't quite make out who it was.

"If it isn't one of those five buildings, then what's the target?"

"Hold your horses. First we need to deal with the hippie."

▪

Back inside the NERV truck at Fifteen Central Park West, Tony Villalon observed a cluster of two cell phone signals moving in unison onscreen. Jake was right about the Saab, and Rory was right about the cell phones. Tony was indeed tracking Rory's location dynamically via signals intelligence.

Tony, Susan, and various other police and special situations commanders all stood in the truck, focused on the data scrolling across the screen in front of them. The place hummed with op-speed adrenaline. It was a drug that all of them were addicted to but could never admit and might not even know—at least until the doldrums of retirement hit them like a sledgehammer.

"I can taste it," Susan said while she turned towards Villalon. "Can you? Just like, on the tip of your tongue? Just a little bit?"

"What?"

"Blood."

Tony chuckled nervously. The location dots were now heading towards one of the massive new parking lots that had emerged around the new Brooklyn Nets stadium at Flatbush and Atlantic.

▪

Whipping down Flatbush Avenue, the Toyota skidded around a left turn and raced with breakneck speed into the large parking complex.

Following just a few moments later, the Saab arrived and turned on its blinkers across the street from the entrance to the parking garage. It wasn't thirty seconds before another car, a blue BMW, slowly passed by the Saab. The professionals inside the Saab nodded to those inside the Beemer—three men from major crimes and expert human trackers. The trackers entered the garage in pursuit.

▪

On the second story of the garage, Castle turned to Jake. He was holding a large plastic Ziploc that already contained his own and Rory's cell phones.

"Ready to give them up?" Castle asked.

"Sure." Jake pulled out his two cell phones. He placed them into the bag.

Rory focused his attention forward. He gunned the accelerator, ripping up the circular parking ramp in the middle of the complex. They finally crunched into a stop on the third level.

Rory turned back to Jake. "It's now or never."

"Now," Jake replied.

"What I like to hear," Rory grinned.

All three men opened the doors simultaneously. Jake didn't even bother glancing back. He didn't want to know or see. He could hear the screeching of another car racing up the circular parking ramp behind them. They only had seconds to spare—and no time to think. The three of them sprinted forward through the third level of the parking garage, like a slalom run through the other parked cars. The edge of the parking lot was a four-foot wall of cement. Beyond that, just the city ahead and a four-story drop to the ground. Placing both hands on the concrete wall ahead, they each jumped over the barrier. And within a split second, all three men had disappeared completely.

▪

The tracking professionals careened up the last turn of the ramp and onto the third level, eyes on the lookout for their intended targets. The driver slammed his brakes down just a foot from the Toyota—still cooling down in its parking spot. The trackers jumped out, anxious expressions drawn across their faces. No one was in the car. Their anxiety turned to confusion as their heads whipsawed around the parking structure, looking for signs. But there were none. Just silence, and the ghosts of targets they'd missed by the hair of a millisecond.

▪

On the outside cladding of the parking structure, a few hundred feet from the aggressive trackers, Jake, Rory, and Castle were descending the building in silence. The back flank of the parking structure was composed of metal panels. Each panel was about three feet tall, forming a scaled-up ladder that the explorers were painstakingly climbing down. Within a few moments, they hit the ground. They raced across the street, where another Sprinter van was waiting. The three of them piled into the van, driven by Nikolai, who ripped the hell outta there.

▪

Villalon wiped a sweaty hand across his brow while Susan and Markle hovered over the tracking screens inside the vehicle. The dots had completely stopped moving. According to their viewpoint, the robbers were still located directly inside the parking garage.

"They're right there!" Markle yelled into the radio in the truck.

They waited for a response from their surveillance team.

▪

Back in the third story of the parking garage, the tracker whispered into his earbud microphone, "No one's here. Car's empty. Think they're on foot."

The pro gestured to one of his colleagues who stood behind him. He was holding a crowbar in his hands. The man jammed it into the front door of Schaub's Toyota, wrenching it open. The alarm began to blare, but the door eventually gave way with the window breaking first. Now they could clearly see the bag loaded with cell phones on the floor.

The tracker got back onto his microphone. "We do not have eyes on them. Repeat. We do not have eyes. They slipped us. Sorry. Dammit."

▪

The mood in the NERV truck quickly transformed into a depressive and melancholy standby. The tracking coordinates glowed ominously in Brooklyn, apparently guilty of tracking nothing at all. In the meantime, all of the screens that were pulling visual feeds from Rory's five "targets" showed normal patterns of high-end condo life. Nothing wrong. Nothing unusual. If a heist was occurring right now, it wasn't anywhere near Tony's or Susan's radar.

Noticing that Susan was involved in a close conversation with Markle, Tony moved to the other end of the NERV truck. He tapped his lead tech, Fong, on the shoulder.

"If Susan asks, tell her I got sick. Need to clear my head."

"Seriously, boss? Where are you going? Now?"

"Just for a second."

"She won't believe you."

"Then I'm going out for a smoke," Tony said.

"Didn't you quit?"

"Pretty sure e-cigs are just as bad as the real ones," Tony said as he headed down the steps.

Another tech glanced over at Fong after Tony had stepped out, raising his eyebrow as if to inquire, "What was that?"

Fonger pantomimed smoking a cigarette, complete with a gasping and deadly cough. Both techs laughed.

▪

Standing outside the trailer, Tony Villalon glanced at the coffee and cookie tray. But he didn't go for a bite, nor reach for his battery-powered addiction machine. Instead he pulled out his cell phone. Another location tracker blinked over a map of Manhattan. This blinking was emanating from Brooklyn, just a few blocks from the parking garage. It was moving quickly away from the Toyota's location. Tony took another long glance and watched the trajectory of the dot.

Tony pushed his hands through his hair and paced back and forth hyperactively. Jake Rivett was going to be the end of him, but he could never turn on the guy. Rivett wasn't the problem—he was the solution. Jake was busy doing the same thing he always did: cracking the case. But that didn't mean that Tony wasn't worried. The stakes were massive now, and worse, the knives were out. Susan was expecting to season her steak, eat it, and have it too. And Tony knew that no matter how hard he tried to protect Jake, both of them would be cut loose if this ended badly. Tony stood outside of the most expensive apartment building in the entire world, and he worried. What the hell should he do? Keep hoping on a dream? Or go back in there and tell Susan what he knew? It wasn't much. But it was certainly more than he was telling her now.

▪

Jake was also experiencing the discomfort that accompanies a distinct lack of information. Now "safely" ensconced in the van, he was finally able to peer over Castle's shoulder and figure out what profile Jack had been incessantly browsing: Cassandra Berg's Instagram. The mayor's wife. Her account memorialized the gilded and ultra-connected world that she and her husband occupied on a daily basis. It was a smorgasbord of elegant galas attended, speeches delivered, and close-ups of outrageously expensive flower arrangements. Every once in a while she'd turn the camera on herself for a selfie, just saucy enough to keep her followers interested—but with a distinctly socially correct flavor that said, "I'm one of the exciting ones, but I'm still a politician's wife." Jake watched with interest as Castle used his thumb to scroll to the top of the feed. Her most recent picture was the framed molding of a hotel window overlooking

New York. She'd written a comment: "Home away from home! #Staycation" Jake could make out the location tag as well: the Waldorf Astoria.

Meanwhile, Nik had navigated the van into Manhattan, where the rabid LED-scape of Times Square whipped past like a screensaver on crack.

"We still good?" Rory asked Castle.

"Think so, boss."

Jake couldn't resist popping in. "We're not going to any of those five buildings, are we? Metropolis and Berg. The handoff . . . It's at the Waldorf. That's where we're going."

"I'm going to show those people. There's nowhere I can't touch in their city," Rory replied.

TWENTY-SIX

THE WALDORF ASTORIA HOTEL ROSE regally into the air at the bottom of Park Avenue. Forty-seven stories of art deco brilliance, the Waldorf was considered one of the most luxurious hotels in the world. An oasis of calm in the city, it offered more than peace. It was a place for the kings and queens of society to feel at home, a natural resting zone for multitudes of United States presidents and Middle Eastern sheiks—and every billionaire in between.

As the Sprinter van raced along Park Avenue, it stopped just a few blocks from the Waldorf. Jake realized that Castle was exiting the van, completely decked out in a Waldorf Astoria uniform. Castle walked around to the back door. He rolled out a large hotel hamper. He pushed the hamper along the sidewalk, and headed towards one of the hotel's loading docks as the Sprinter accelerated away.

"Four weeks on the job. Knows the place like the back of his hand," Rory said.

"Impressive," Jake replied.

"How does it feel to not be in control?"

"I can flip a one-eighty at any time and take you down."

"And Mona?"

"She's the reason I won't."

"I don't want you out of the loop, Jake. Trust me. It's the opposite. I need you. You need to take Mona's place in our plan. And you can. You're good and you know it now. But I'm also helping you, 'cause the less you're aware of? The better. Just in case those bosses of yours start to get real pissy. Right?"

"Sure," Jake replied, gritting his teeth.

The Sprinter slowed down again. Jake and Rory jumped out of the van and padded into a small alleyway. As they dipped down a set of service stairs leading past the entrances to a couple of small businesses, including a Chinese restaurant, Jake began to feel a sense of déjà vu.

"Brilliant," Jake said.

Rory turned and smiled. He didn't have to say anything else.

"The secret subway station, right?"

"You're gettin' good, noob."

▪

Castle pushed his laundry hamper through the basement washroom of the Waldorf. Two ladies from Honduras folded towels across a long metal table. As he passed, one of them attempted to take the hamper from him. But Castle angrily tugged it out of her grip. She was slightly taken aback, but mostly entertained. The other lady leaned in conspiratorially and whispered in Spanish, "Beautiful face, but head's as empty as the hamper he's pushin'!" The two ladies started to crack up, causing a chain reaction of laughter throughout the entire laundry room.

Except for one maid. She stared at Castle with suspicion as he pushed through the back exit of the laundry room into another service hallway.

The hallway behind the industrial washroom led to a bank of service elevators. Castle pressed a button and waited nervously, watching the elevator tick down floors until finally reaching his level. The doors creaked open. He pushed the hamper into the elevator. He hastily scanned the floor options and dashed the PH1 button for the penthouse. With a long scrape and groan, the elevator began to ascend. It was clear to Castle, from the lack of velvet walls and neatly shined gold plating, that these service elevators did not receive the same high level of inspection that the guest elevators did. But that made perfect sense in the grand scheme of things—one side was paying the bills and the other taking the meager scraps.

▪

Nikolai raced the Sprinter through the traffic of Times Square, now heading back in the direction of the Waldorf. He almost barreled over multiple bikers, honking as he careened past. Moving a touch too fast, Nik glanced at his watch. They were a few minutes behind schedule already. Even though he wasn't going up into the hotel, his role was critical. Without him, his best friends would be stuck at the top of an ivory tower with no escape.

▪

Rory and Jake walked through the abandoned-but-beautiful subway station, complete with mosaic tiling, that Jake had been introduced to during his first official night of urban exploration. But instead of exiting there, they continued through the station, staying on the old tracks and walking farther into the heart of darkness. As they moved through the eerie blackness, Jake eyed another old entrance to the hydra.

"You know about this one?" Jake asked.

"I know almost everything about the hydra."

"So, the next stop is the Waldorf?"

"Yep."

"And we're going to use Roosevelt's car elevator?" Jake asked.

"Close. Did you know that when the Waldorf was built, it defined the American cosmopolitan experience and became the basis of all modern hospitality?"

"No. I didn't know that, Rory. Don't you think it's a little late for another history lesson?"

Rory shook his head as if to say, "*You don't get it.*"

The two explorers finally reached their destination. Multiple sub-basements underneath the Waldorf, their flashlights captured the end of the tracks. The terminus was a huge station platform, glazed in the familiar rusted brown of metal meeting its own half-life. Jake and Rory climbed off the tracks and onto the station platform, which was centered around a giant column the size of a car. The structure had a roll-up portal, similar to a garage door, and it led to an old hydraulic system connected directly to the tracks.

"So they would literally drive cars off the train and into the hotel?"

"Yessir," Rory answered.

"Who got to do that?"

"Presidents." Rory pulled his backpack off and tossed it on the floor. He rummaged through various devices inside before pulling out a gas-powered climbing ascender. About the size of a leaf blower, it was designed to help someone automatically rise on a rope. He also pulled out a large crowbar.

"You're going to make the elevator work . . . with that?" Jake asked incredulously.

"Like I said, we're going up. But not exactly how you think," Rory replied. He stepped towards the control booth behind the elevator. It was protected by an old, rusted-over lock. Rory gripped the crowbar and smacked the lock. While pieces of rusted detritus flew off it, the lock held.

"Let me have that," Jake said. Seeing Rory's eyebrow rise, he continued, "Crowbars are my specialty."

Rory handed Jake the crowbar and stood back. Jake held it with both hands and delivered a single, fatal blow to the lock. It flung itself open like a succulent accepting water. Jake tried the door. It was still tight and unwilling to open. He found an exposed air gap along the doorjamb and pounded the crowbar's thin end into it then reared back his shoulders with a mighty yell.

"*YAYAYAAAAAAA!*" Jake screamed.

The door popped open abruptly.

Rory and Jake walked inside the abandoned office.

"Most important lesson about history is that it repeats itself," Rory said as they disrupted the resting dust of the past. There was a corkboard on the wall with long-yellowed papers and work orders pinned all over it. "Just because you board up something doesn't mean it's gone forever." In a sudden motion, Rory lifted the corkboard off the wall. Behind it were two wood-paneled doors. He opened the doors wide in each direction. "Ever heard of a dumbwaiter?"

Jake could only smile in expectation as his mind filled with new possibilities regarding Rory's planned infiltration.

"In the early 1900s, if one was operating a fine institution, which the Waldorf undoubtedly was, one had a dumbwaiter on the premises."

▪

Castle loitered in the utility hallway of the penthouse level. When he was sure that no other staffers were nearby, he eyed a rack of linens in a back closet. Placing his two paws on the shelving, he dragged it out of the way. Behind the shelves were the familiar doors of another old dumbwaiter opening. Castle opened the doors, reached in, and affixed a large carabiner to the bolted steel at the top of the shaft. Then he rolled the laundry basket—the one he'd been escorting through the building for the last hour—into the closet. He pulled four towels off the top of the laundry basket, and his ultimate cargo was revealed. Underneath the towels was a long climbing rope. It was tightly coiled and just fit inside the vessel chosen to transport it. This wasn't just a few feet of rope. It was hundreds upon hundreds of feet in length—and thick. Castle attached the rope to the carabiner at the top of the dumbwaiter. He secured a large lead weight to the other end of the rope and began to carefully guide the rope down the dumbwaiter shaft itself.

The rope fell through the air, aided by the force of gravity. Whenever it hit a snag, Castle would pull up a few feet, allowing the lead to swing free—and then drop it again. The rope continued to career down all forty-seven stories of the Waldorf's dumbwaiter channel. For a largely forgotten relic of the past, the dumbwaiter channel was proving to be quite useful in current day.

■

In the abandoned subway station's office, Rory and Jake could hear a light clanging before they saw anything. Then the weight emerged, thudding against the floor at the bottom of the dumbwaiter. Rory reached for it and affixed the gas-powered ascending machine to the rope.

"Now it's real," Rory said. He slowly pulled his body into the dumbwaiter's opening. He hooked himself onto the device. Rory ignited the ascender and gingerly rolled the throttle on the device forward, quickly rising six feet and disappearing into the channel. Rory dropped an auxiliary rope that was secured to his own harness. Jake latched his carabiner in. Now they were both attached to one another and operating as a single entity; an entity secured to a thousand-foot rope that was about to jerk them vertically through the bloodline of the old hotel. Rory took control of the ascender again, and before there was time for a prayer or even a breath—up they went.

The two men flew vertical like Superman, with only fragmented slices of light to illuminate their way. It wasn't unlike riding the rollercoaster at Space Mountain. At any moment, an errant beam or incongruent piece of metal could rip them to shreds. But they had to cede control to fate—and the guidance of Castle above. They flew vertical towards the penthouse at the top of the hotel like two angels heading towards Mount Olympus. But these two weren't actually angels. They were justice incarnate, one official and the other never anything of the sort, moving ever closer to their final goal.

■

Jake and Rory safely reached the top of the dumbwaiter channel where Castle awaited. Jake reached for the ledge to pull himself into the service closet on the penthouse level, but Rory shook his head.

"We're staying in here," Rory said.

"Really?"

Castle had now outfitted himself with a harness. He secured a strap to the inside of the dumbwaiter but didn't step in. "All set for the gas?" Castle asked Rory.

Jake rotated to see what Rory was doing.

Rory had secured a series of carabiners to the steel girders at the top of the dumbwaiter's ceiling. Rory addressed Castle through the door. "Ready."

Castle disappeared from the entrance for just a moment before returning with a giant gas tank—about four feet tall and eighteen inches in diameter. The tank had been smuggled into the hotel, by Castle, a few days earlier. As Castle tilted the gas canister into the dumbwaiter's opening, Rory attached carabiners to closed steel loops that had been welded to its sides. A few hard pulls later, and the canister was also hanging in the dumbwaiter channel.

"Where'd you get that?" Jake asked.

"Stole it, obviously," Rory replied.

"From who?"

"Who do you think?"

Without any further ado, Castle pulled the shelving as close as he could to the entrance. He climbed into the dumbwaiter channel and closed the doors. The small area, now extremely so, turned pitch black.

"If that was the maintenance closet . . . where's the penthouse?" Jake asked.

"Right here," Rory said. Rory folded his hand into a fist and knocked quietly on the wall closest to him.

"It's walled over," Jake said.

"Right, in the early eighties. Two major renovations ago."

"How are we gettin' in?"

"First, we drill our holes."

Rory pulled out a small drill. He took a few measurements against the wall and compared them to a schematic he'd loaded on his phone. He checked the bit then began to slowly and carefully drill a tiny hole into the boarded-up side of the channel.

"How do we know they're not in there?" Jake asked.

"Castle, tell him," Rory said.

"They're all at the opera right now. Instagram is a helluva social network," Castle said. He held his cell phone towards Jake, who was greeted with a giant selfie of not only Mayor Berg and his wife but also Arthur Metropolis and his model-of-the-moment, Isabelle.

Rory finished drilling the hole. He placed his eye to the opening, confirming a good field of view into the room. Then Rory inserted a tiny camera through the hole. Only the lens entered. Rory taped the unit's battery pack and small monitor to the backside of the wall. He confirmed the device was recording.

While Jake and Castle settled in for a long wait, Rory began drilling a second, slightly larger, hole at the other end of the dumbwaiter opening . . .

▪

Sitting—or rather, *hanging*—from the rafters inside a hotel for a few hours while in close proximity to two other large men wasn't the easiest task to accomplish. But the three of them succeeded, their peace of mind aided by the fact that Cassandra Berg seemed to update her Instagram every half an hour. Finally, the group appeared to be headed back from the theater.

And just a few minutes after that, the camera began to track movement inside the Waldorf's penthouse suite . . .

TWENTY-SEVEN

ARTHUR METROPOLIS GRUNTED AS ISABELLE removed his Ermenegildo Zegna suit and hung it from a chair by the door.

"What is it with those things? Always feel like a million dollars when you're in the changing room, and then within two months you can't fit into them anymore."

"It's not the suit, honey," Isabelle answered.

"Enjoy the show, Arthur?" Ronald Berg asked while preparing a cocktail.

"Can't pay attention in those things . . ." Arthur replied.

"How come? Too intellectual?"

"I dunno. Just me. The way I am. ADD or something."

"Undiagnosed," Isabelle popped in.

"It's like when my parents forced me to go to church down south. I daydream. Can't help myself. Honestly? I spent a lot of the time thinking about glass."

"Whale Square?"

"Yeah. The tower."

"All you can think of is your buildings—probably why you're always winning, Arthur. Hey. I'm just here to make it nice and easy for ya," Berg announced. He sipped his martini with haste.

"That's what friends are for."

"But I am a little nervous about the heat . . ."

"The robberies?"

Berg nodded.

"You don't need to worry," Arthur said. "They're on ice. I'm making sure of it."

"Making sure or made?"

"Ronald, this is not your problem. It's not really even my problem. Who cares about a bunch of burglars?"

"I do," Berg said.

"You only need to worry about one thing. And it's a beautiful thing. That is—what you're gonna buy with all the greenbacks I'm about to place in your possession."

"Don't be obtuse," Berg said.

"And also, C1-7."

"I'll try."

"No try," Arthur said. "The property must be full-on mixed use, with air rights. C1-7. Can you do it?"

"Absolutely. Ralphie used to do numbers at Disneyworld 'til I came into office."

"Literally?" Arthur asked.

"I saved him from the mosquitos and fatties, and now all he has to deal with is a bunch of pricks. At least those ones come in nice suits and give sweet presents."

"All right. And . . . I still haven't forgotten about the big one . . ."

"The subway," Berg nodded. "I'm sure I don't have to tell you that ain't a simple ask. It's infrastructure . . . Billions. Has to make sense from every direction."

"I get it," Arthur said. "I'm prepared to start a nonprofit. A couple of them. Whatever. My name won't be anywhere. It's all about the people in the community who need public transportation. That's your message. You sure could help. The people that live there need to get to work quickly. That's important to them, which means it's crucial to me. I think, like, 20, 30 percent upside on units if we get the station."

"I'll do what I can . . ."

Arthur chuckled a little. He patted the seat next to him. Berg took a sip of his drink and sat down. Arthur wrapped his arm around Berg's shoulders, physically dominating the man. "You do what you can, and then you do more. Pretty please. You do everything you need to do to get me that subway station, and I'll do everything I can to make sure that no one knows about the three-point-four-seven million in cash that I've handed to you over the years."

"Yes," the mayor grimaced.

"Wonderful," Arthur's face broke into a huge smile. "Because even though you might think I'm obtuse, I'm a good counter."

▪

A few minutes later, there was a knock on the penthouse door. Cassandra Berg walked over and opened it. Ziros paced in. He handed a large suitcase to Metropolis, who unzipped it. Arthur tilted the bag towards Berg—it was stuffed with cash.

The sight of all that green mixed with the fresh scent of money recently emerged from a bank vault made the mayor very, very happy. He did his best to restrain the urge to touch it. He was definitely the bitch in this situation, but that didn't mean anyone was going to see him slobbering like a dog.

"I'll just leave it right here," Arthur said. He placed the bag behind the couch.

"Thanks, Arthur," Berg grinned.

"Stian, get yourself a drink," Arthur commanded.

"Can't drink too much. Need to take the trash out later," Ziros said as he poured a few gulps of bourbon into a small glass.

"Ah yes, of course," Arthur said. "Well, cheers . . . to our happy little family."

All three men, along with Isabelle and Cassandra, raised their glasses into the air. The crystal edges kissed, and then fell away. The first glass hit the ground directly on the bottom. It didn't shatter, but the sound was loud enough to shock them all. They were unable to respond. They couldn't move. They couldn't do anything—except stare at one another in dumfounded silence.

Something was happening—*a very bad thing.*

An evil substance was gripping their nervous systems with a vice-lock grip. The two women fell to the floor first, followed by the mayor. Within milliseconds of resting their heads on the wooden floor, they were out. *Unconscious.*

"The money . . ." Arthur muttered as he fell.

As Ziros hit the ground, he was holding his breath. His vision was blurry, and the simple process of moving his arms felt like Olympic weightlifting. But at least he was still conscious. He could smell the stuff all around him and he knew exactly what it was. He dragged himself along the hotel room floor towards the bag of cash. He held the bag in his hands as he rotated towards the door. He lifted his left knee. It was an arduous process, like the end of an Everest ascent. He managed. His body was running out of oxygen, but the door was just four bounds away. Ziros stumbled ahead, against all the odds—an experimental rat not responding as intended to stimuli. The rodent raged forward. The doorknob was this close . . .

TWENTY-EIGHT

NITROUS OXIDE IS A HELL of a drug. It didn't take a genius to know this. But witnessing the effects of the gas firsthand, Jake was definitely worried about the future of civilization. If more criminals got their hands on it? Chaos on the streets.

"It's not taking Ziros," Castle said, watching the surveillance feed.

They watched Stian Ziros struggle in slow motion to reach the door.

"Patience. It will," Rory replied.

But there was clearly something within Ziros' Scandinavian DNA that was not cooperating. Now he was just a few feet from the doorway and gaining on the doorknob.

"We gotta stop him . . . now," Rory said.

Castle groaned. Pushing the dumbwaiter doors open, he fell back into the small supply closet. Rory hastily turned off the gas, stopping the flow of nitrous oxide into the penthouse. There was no time to pull the camera or drop the ropes, but as they left, Jake made sure to fasten the cabinet and pull the shelving back over the entrance.

■

Castle barreled out of the service entrance and into penthouse's entrance hall—a transformation akin to portal-ing from the Third World to a land of alien luxury. The entire hallway was decorated in various levels of velvet, from the richly luxurious purple beneath their feet to the slick tan wallpaper coating the vertical surfaces. Castle took the hallway like a linebacker inside the slot, and he reached the penthouse door just as it opened.

Ziros stared at Castle with wide, curious eyes. He couldn't comprehend exactly what was going on around him, nor even 20 percent of such. He held out the bag of money for Castle—he wasn't even sure why.

But the intent on Castle's eyes was pure fury. Castle leaned through the impact, his shoulders colliding directly with Ziros' center mass. Both men flew back into the room. The bag of cash arced through the air and thudded on the other end of the living room, near massive windows overlooking the city.

▪

Just a few seconds later, the service elevator to the penthouse floor opened. A maid—the same one who had spotted Castle in the laundry room—emerged. She was pushing her own laundry cart. She stared quizzically at the empty cart positioned directly in front of her.

▪

Tony Villalon glanced nervously at his watch while he drove through the city. He didn't have long before Susan would pick up on his absence. He peered at his cell phone as he drove, attempting to track the blinking dot that appeared on the map of Manhattan in front of him. He pulled up to a curb and placed his flashers on. He was right on top of the blinking dot, but Jake was nowhere. All he could see, quite unmistakably, was the towering mass of the Waldorf Astoria hotel just ahead of him. Tony shook his head. That wasn't one of the five locations. But . . .

Tony stepped out of the car and stared into the sky, wondering where Jake was right now.

▪

Ziros mumbled on the ground. He was immobilized but trying to roll over. The other four were completely out cold. Jake raced to the mayor and checked his pulse.

"What're you doing, noob?" Castle asked.

"I'm not here to murder anyone."

"They'll wake up in a few minutes. We need to hurry up and make it look like a robbery."

"Aren't we way past that?" Jake asked.

"No one wants this cash to exist," Rory said and pointed to the black duffel bag. "Not us, and not them. So we have to give the esteemed mayor and Arthur something to complain to the police about, right?"

At that point, a complete and utter marauding of the room took place.

Castle paced to the master bedroom. He picked up piles of Cassandra Berg's hastily arranged jewelry and dumped the spoils into a small go-bag.

Rory stared down at the mayor on the floor. After a few moments, he kneeled down and pulled a gold Rolex off the Mayor's wrist. He looked up at Jake as he rose. "For my brother," Rory said.

Jake nodded in agreement. He didn't feel comfortable participating. But he did feel accepted. The irony was deep and unfunny. Being involved, like this, was exactly what he had been seeking all along. Not only that—it was his mission. No one could take that away from him. Susan's greatest expectations couldn't hold a candle to what he'd accomplished. But Jake was well aware that he might not have the canopy of the law above him. It wasn't all clear in the fog of war. He was ready for a break, but it wasn't around the corner. He just knew that he needed to get Mona back safe, and perhaps then he could relax.

▪

The suspicious maid walked along the penthouse hallway, pushing her hamper full of towels. Hearing major commotion on the other side of the door, she stood quizzically in front of the penthouse. She took a breath then stepped towards the door and knocked. Once. Twice. A few more times.

"Maid service!" she yelled loud and clear.

All of the noise emanating from inside the chamber ceased suddenly, but no one responded to her command. The woman keyed into the door.

▪

She took one step into the room and became a witness. She stared at them. They stared at her. She opened her mouth and hers was a wild scream, a berserk one, filled with fear. She sprinted out of the room and down the hallway to the service elevators before Jake, Castle, or Rory could even respond.

"Guess that's our sign," Rory announced.

Castle angled a chair against the suite's door handle. Then he approached the region of the wall where the dumbwaiter opening had been covered years ago. He kneeled down to inspect the two holes Rory had drilled earlier. Castle reached into his pocket. His hand emerged with a small container of fast-dry spackle—the size of a small tube of toothpaste. Castle squeezed the spackle over the two holes and rubbed it in with his gloved hands. Jake glanced at the repair job—not perfect but impressive. It was very likely that CSI would miss the holes later.

Jake walked with the two men onto the penthouse's outdoor patio.

Behind them, Stian Ziros had recovered and was kneeling on the floor. He stared at the men on the balcony but decided against heading that direction. Instead, he stumbled out a back entrance and into the service stairs.

▪

At the exact same instant, the maid's emergency call reached the security room on the second floor of the hotel. The Waldorf's head of security, an Irishman named Alastair Albany, rose while still holding the phone against his right ear. He motioned towards three burly security guards who were sitting at various monitors and desks throughout the room. Able to read the sense of panic on Alastair's normally ultra-zen face, they all stood. Alastair addressed his troops. "There's a smash 'n' grab in

Penthouse A. Let's git up there lickety-split. And somebody call 911!"

Alastair crouched down to the personal safe underneath his desk. His finger tapped a scanner, and the vault opened. He pulled out a pistol. Then the four men—in black suits, black shirts, and black ties—sprinted out of the security room and towards the elevator bank.

▪

Nikolai skidded the Sprinter van to a stop on the side of Park Avenue. He ducked down and hustled through the center aisle to the back of the van, stepping to the side of an enormous roll of cable as he did. He reached forward and opened the back doors as wide as they would rotate. Nik stared across the street. Framed above him—about a football field away—was the grand Waldorf Astoria.

▪

Inside the NERV truck at Fifteen Central Park West—a mile and a half northwest of the Waldorf—Susan, Markle, Fong, and the other techs were focused on a small radio system replaying a 911 call. It was one of Alastair's men from the hotel. As the call continued, the entire place blasted to attention. Susan looked around.

"Where's Tony?"

"I . . . dunno," Fong replied. "I think he went to get some food."

"Find out . . . and drive me to the Waldorf, big guy."

▪

Villalon approached the front desk of the Waldorf Astoria. A rotund and sunburned man was complaining loudly about the volume of liquor bottles in his fridge. Tony glanced at his cell phone again. As before, he was right on top of the location dot. He couldn't bear listening to this filthy roll of lard—a modern Jabba the Hut—in front of him any longer. He reached for his wallet and flipped his badge out as he stepped up to the desk himself. The desk attendant instantly became alert.

"Sir . . . it's the penthouse."

"What is?" Tony asked.

"The penthouse. We're supposed to bring you guys up there."

"Who?"

"Huh? You. The cops."

■

Jake heard the sirens before he saw them. It took only one brief lean over the penthouse's railing to notice three police cars churning down Park with sirens blazing.

"We got problems," Jake said.

"Not really," Rory replied.

"How are we gettin' off here, Rory?"

"That's not your concern, noob," Rory said.

Jake's eyebrow jacked up.

"You're not coming with us," Rory finally said.

"I didn't rock the boat . . ." Jake said.

Jake heard a loud buzzing behind Rory's head. It was the Phantom drone. Operated by Nik below, the flying robot careened through the air, directly towards the three men standing on the balcony.

"He's gonna kill her," Jake said.

"Nope. I don't think so."

"You don't know that . . ."

"Mona's not really my . . . first priority, noob. That's where you got everything wrong. That girl, bless her heart, but she has caused me so much consternation. You were the biggest mistake I ever made. And she was the reason for it!" Rory yelled.

As the drone finally came out of the afternoon shadows, it was illuminated by the glorious sconces on the side of the hotel. Jake finally noticed that the drone seemed to be dragging something through the air with it. He couldn't believe his eyes. The drone was lifting a long cable from the ground. Unspooling out from the back of Nik's van, the drone was actually a delivery system. The drone collapsed onto the balcony. Rory fastened the cable to the stone building with a huge fish-eye loop secured by saddle clamps to an I-bolt.

▪

At the other end of the line, Nikolai was hard at work. A small motor rotated the cable along a spool in the van until it was taut. Nik's muscles erupted in agony as he tightened the cable further using a one-directional winch.

▪

"All that bullshit about your crew. You don't care about her. You're going to let her die!" Jake screamed.

"I'm not an animal," Rory glanced back at Jake. "That's why I made a side deal for Mona already . . ."

"The hell?" Jake's confusion accelerated into overdrive.

"I'm just saving you from yourself, noob. See, I know the guy who's got Mona. Met him a couple days ago. Hector's his name. You two have a history. I don't think you like each other very much . . . Anyway, turns out Metropolis called upon him for a favor. But Hector's done with favors. Our priorities aligned."

"And what about me? The cops are on the way up!"

"That's exactly why you're here, Jake," Rory said calmly and succinctly. He held his pistol casually by his side, keeping Jake at bay. "Did you think I brought you on for your skills? We didn't need you. You're our insurance policy. I know you're good at telling stories. You're about to tell the story of your life. It goes something like this. You were suspicious of Ziros. You followed him up here, where he incapacitated his boss and the mayor. Then he robbed the place—God knows why—and fled. If you tell the right story, you'll be back in the solid with your people, and Mona will live a long and prosperous life. But if not? If I feel so much as one degree of heat from this day forward? Who knows? Mona might find herself at the bottom of a drain . . . The sewers are a dangerous place . . . She should never have gone alone."

And without any further ado, Rory jumped off the top of the Waldorf's tower. His harness was attached to the taut zip-line that had been formed between the penthouse and the van below. He raced through the air, only slowing his descent ever so slightly with a brake block.

Jake watched as Castle attached his own brake block to the cord. He could hear the Waldorf's security force going after the door with an axe. Jake turned back to Castle, who was fiddling with his harness. Jake took this momentary respite to dive at Castle, smacking both of them to the ground. But Castle held onto Jake's head, crunching Jake's face into the stone balcony. Castle rolled over on top of him and flipped him into a submission hold, whaling on Rivett with his fists.

Jake saw stars—little dots of light flickering across his corneas—and then the pressure released.

Castle sprinted to the line. He reached for the brake block and jumped off the edge of the building.

Jake shook his head. The banging on the door was becoming more vital, more insistent. He glanced back inside. A large hole had been blasted through the wood. A hand was pushing at the levered chair . . .

In between Jake and the door was Metropolis, still on the ground of the living room—but stirring. Jake paced back into the penthouse, towards Arthur. "Arthur!" Jake screamed. Metropolis' consciousness was not fully complete. Jake smacked him directly on the face, three times in quick succession. Arthur finally focused on the angry eyes above him.

"Where's Mona?"

"Screw you," Arthur finally muttered.

"I'll kill you if anything happens to her," Jake spit out.

"Wait . . . Detective . . ."

But Jake didn't wait. He pulled his backpack off his back. He wrapped his right hand around one of the straps. It would do. He exited towards the balcony. He flipped the backpack over the wire and secured his left hand to the other strap as best he could. He pulled himself up, orienting his feet on the balcony's railing.

Jake Rivett took a deep breath—and jumped over the precipice of nothing.

TWENTY-NINE

THE TIERED ART DECO FAÇADE of the Waldorf gave way to the steel and glass cliffs of Park Avenue as Jake ripped through the middle of the city. It only took a few seconds for Jake to make out Nik's van—the point of conclusion for his impromptu zip-line ride. Just avoiding a power wire's potential garrote to his neck, Jake saw the Sprinter growing in stature ahead of him.

■

Rory glanced upwards as he disentangled himself from the steel cable. He saw Jake, halfway down the wire and just a handful of seconds behind.

"Cut it!" Rory screamed at Nik.

Nik quickly pivoted, reaching for a huge pair of wire cutters. The seconds ticked as he gripped the cutters' teeth onto the cable.

■

Jake careened past a streetlamp—now milliseconds to arrival. He'd stopped braking because his hands could barely handle the tension on the backpack. Now his two feet aimed ahead, bracing for the impact of the van ahead.

Nik didn't cut the wire in time. Jake smashed through Nikolai feet first. The van shuddered from the impact, rolling forward. Rory was thrown out, the pistol he'd tucked into the small of his back rolling into a small geranium garden.

Castle scrambled towards Rory, gripping the large duffel of cash. He helped Rory to his feet, and the two of them sprinted away from the van.

Jake moved his legs gingerly. He could feel the impact working its way up his body in slow motion—feet to ankles to knees to core—like a tsunami of pain. He dragged himself out of the van, which had fully impaled a small car parked ahead. Jake saw Nikolai passed out on the sidewalk. But Rory and Castle where nowhere to be seen.

Jake peered past the van. He noticed two small specks running away from him—holding a bag. *Rory and Castle.* He took a deep breath and doubled down.

▪

Tony Villalon stared over the balcony of the Waldorf's penthouse, watching the steel cable flopping in the wind against the building. He was in awe. He glanced at his phone. Sure enough, the dot was finally moving again. It was progressing west of Park and towards Lexington. He turned around, passing the hotel's security as he departed.

"Where you goin', detective? Where's your troops?" Alastair asked him.

"They're . . ." To be perfectly frank, Tony had no idea where his people were. He was afraid of calling Susan, who he was sure was steaming from her nostrils. At that very moment, the elevator doors opened, and four cops raced inside. *Saved by the bell.* "Right here," Tony said. He nodded politely at the officers and hopped onto the elevator, jamming the lobby button incessantly.

▪

After watching Rory and Castle round a corner a few hundred feet away, Rivett breathlessly reached the same nexus point and turned—to encounter nothing. He stood on a quiet and tree-lined street framed by brownstones on each side. Bewildered, Jake jogged slowly down the street.

He gazed into each alleyway, trash nook, and stairwell. But he couldn't locate them anywhere. Jake doubled back across the street, a panic now rising within his chest. He couldn't lose those two. Not when he was so close. Not with Mona on the hook. As he glanced up at one brownstone, Jake suddenly stopped.

He bounded up the stairs. It was only when he was a few feet from the front door of the house that he realized what he was looking at. The small golden plaque had seemed slightly out of place, if only because it was attached directly to the front door. But this was no embassy or law office. He read the words transcribed on the plaque: "*NYC TRANSIT - EXIT NO. 3.*"

"Exit three," Jake said to himself. Jake vaguely remembered Rory referring to something like this—weeks ago. Rory's "favorite." *The fake brownstones.* Here was one of them. Jake tried the door. The lock had been pried open.

▪

Tony Villalon drove alone through the city, peering at his cell phone as he did. He was now right on top of the blinking GPS dot for the second time today, and like clockwork, his undercover was nowhere to be seen. As he craned his neck to stare out the windows, he was greeted by nothing. Just a row of brownstones standing idle and watching him—judging him with the weight of their beauty and stature. All of a sudden, the dot simply disappeared from Tony's phone.

"Shit!" He slammed his hand on the dashboard. Ahead was the East River. He approached, still not sure what he was looking for. A yellow reflection caught his eye, emerging from the edge of an old brick aqueduct built into the bottom of the East River's retaining wall. Tony screeched his car to a stop.

It was a large drain entrance. That was for sure. But where did it lead? Tony had no clue. He shined a flashlight inside the drain, attempting to figure out what he'd just seen a moment earlier. His flashlight beam eventually rested on two bright yellow-and-green motorcycles. A very odd location to park bikes. Tony reached for his radio.

"This is Detective Tony Villalon . . . I'm on the east side of the FDR. Just south of the Queensboro. I need backup, 10-45, 10-45." Tony thought for a moment. "I, uh, Susan . . . I don't think they're in the hotel. They're not at the hotel. They're in the pipes."

He pulled his gun and cautiously entered the drain.

▪

Susan Herlihy stood in front of the Waldorf, listening to the radio.

"Well, I guess he wasn't getting food, was he? Send SWAT. Send everyone," she said. "And me. Make sure I've got a gat, too."

Fong nodded and escorted her back to the car.

▪

A grand-and-moneyed foyer did not greet Jake Rivett inside the brownstone. Instead, he finally understood what Rory had been talking about. The brownstone was a complete and utter façade. A fake. It had been designed by the city as an access point into the subterranean jungle that lay below the streets. The entrance hall was small, cement-lined, and industrial. It was lit by a bare bulb, and led to another door ahead. This one was marked clearly: "Electrical Distribution Room." Rivett pushed through the door and descended stairs into the depths of the city.

THIRTY

THE ELECTRICAL DISTRIBUTION ROOM WAS a huge subterranean space filled with high-voltage switch boxes. The few lights that illuminated the room were quite low, casting the entire location in a murky darkness. Jake stalked through the room, careful to remain in the shadows. He couldn't hear Rory and Castle—or anyone—ahead of him. That had him worried. Time was of the essence now. As he walked through the room, Jake saw an old chalkboard positioned atop an office table. He grabbed a piece of chalk and swiftly drew an arrow pointing the direction he was going. He stepped through the portico to another service stairway and began jumping down the steps, two at a time.

.

Tony Villalon soon found himself inside a massive aqueduct sewer and deep underneath Manhattan. He padded slowly down the pipe, heading towards a loud male voice that echoed throughout the chambers. As Tony neared the end of a long, curving pipe, he could see a light slowly growing. He flicked off his own phone flashlight and slowed to listen further, making sure to step out of the pooling water so his footsteps didn't cause a disturbance. Tony situated himself behind a large vertical buttress to the tunnel, then slowly peered around the edge.

Mona Rosas sat in handcuffs, staring glumly at the ground. Hector Trizzo and Emanuel Vipa sat on either side of her, drinking beers, while Stian Ziros paced back and forth in front of them.

"What are you doin' here, homie? I don't need you to take care of her. You don't trust me?" Hector asked Ziros.

"I gotta call Arthur again," Ziros responded.

"Where is he?" Hector asked.

"That's not your problem . . ."

"You guys don't know what the hell you're doing, do you?" Mona asked.

"Shut up, woman. You can drown in one inch of water. Did you know that? Is a fact! I done it before!" Hector screamed into her face.

"Fuck you!"

"That ain't your decision, *puta*," Hector pretended to pull down his zipper.

"Stop it. I'm going back up top to get a signal," Ziros announced. He turned and headed down the pipe.

He was pacing directly towards the position where Villalon was holed up. Tony suddenly stepped into the middle of the drain.

"Put your hands up!" Tony yelled, the front sights of his sidearm trained directly upon Ziros.

The first thing that happened was nothing—a brief, shocked silence.

Then all hell broke loose, like a rat in a bridal suite. Ziros dove to the side of the tunnel and into the water. Tony kept his pistol trained on Ziros but caught Hector in the corner of his eye. Hector was reaching into the back of his pants. His weapon glinted as it rotated towards Tony.

Bam. Bam. Two holes drilled into Hector's chest. Hector stared down at the abyss that was his heart, as his own blood erupted like a volcano. Then he dropped directly to the ground, doornail dead.

Tony trained his gun back on Ziros before realizing that Emanuel had disappeared.

"Where'd the other one go?" Tony asked Mona.

"That way," Mona pointed into the catacombs behind her.

Ziros used the moment to his advantage. He launched himself at Villalon, tackling Tony onto the ground. The two men struggled for dominance, with Stian slowly gaining an advantage over the detective.

Ziros' eyes were wide, his pupils blown out with adrenaline, as he held his thumbs into Tony's neck. Tony felt the room getting darker and murkier than it already was. He thought he could hear Jake yelling for him, but he realized it wasn't Rivett. It was his husband. It was his friends, his family, and every single person he knew. They were all calling out, telling him to come back from wherever he was going. And where was that? At least it wouldn't be straight to Hell, like the man on top of him.

In his last second of consciousness, Tony heard an explosion. He blinked. The light came streaming back. Ziros was slumping over him. Tony glanced over Ziros' shoulder to find Mona, holding Hector's gun, smoke articulating from the muzzle. Tony shook his head while the oxygen returned to his brain. Ziros moaned on the floor while Mona repeatedly kicked him. Tony realized that Ziros wasn't dead—but he was certainly headed in that direction.

"You're the girl. Jake's girl," Tony finally said.

"I'm myself, actually."

"Let's get the hell out of here," Tony said as he rose from the ground. "I think it's this way. Come on!"

Ziros watched the light of Tony's cell phone fade away in the darkness.

▪

Making his way down from the electrical distribution room, Rivett emerged onto an older brick pathway. This hallway seemed to access the steampunk-esque world of original copper and stone sewers underneath Manhattan. Above Jake's head passed a keystone. A mystical creature, the hydra, stared back at him. Jake worked his way through the aqueduct sewer, making sure to denote his path with chalk at every turn. Jake realized that the sewer was getting wider, not narrowing. Strange. Where was it going? He realized that he'd reached a large abandoned room inside the hydra, no longer used for Manhattan's sanitation or water.

As Jake stepped around one of the ancient brick columns, he caught a blur of motion behind him. A shape flung through the air—towards him. Jack Castle piledrove Jake into the ground, but before Jake could pull himself back onto all fours, Castle was holding him down. Rory appeared and bent towards Jake's face . . .

"You made a big mistake following us . . ."

All of a sudden, Jake caught sight of a pistol flying through the air towards Rory. Rory's neck snapped all the way back and ricocheted almost 180 degrees as he was pistol whipped. Tony stood behind Rory, who fell to the ground.

But Castle had regained his footing and jumped Tony. They fought for the gun, which spun out directly in front of Jake. Jake held the pistol with both hands and used his back to push himself up against a wall.

"Don't make me!" Jake screamed at Castle, who slowly rose, his hands in surrender.

Tony used the moment to push Castle face-first into the muck below, a knee in his back while the handcuffs jangled from Tony's pocket and headed directly for his perp's wrists.

Jake realized that Rory was splashing through the large dark room and away from them.

Mona stumbled over to Jake.

"Where's Hector?" he asked.

"Dead," Mona said, pointing to Tony. "It wasn't me," she added. "I didn't tell them who you were. They already knew . . ."

"I know. You're one of the good guys . . ."

"And so are you." She hugged him, holding him tight. She could tell Jake was tensing for more action. She gazed in the same direction as Jake —where Rory had gone. "I'll go with you," she said.

"No. Stick with Tony or else you'll never get out of here." He pointed to the wall behind him and one of the white chalk arrows he'd drawn. "I was prepared. Follow the arrows in reverse."

Jake raced down the dark tunnel in pursuit of Rory.

▪

Not so far away, Emanuel shined his flashlight down a dark and empty tunnel. It looked innocuous. Emanuel's flashlight began to flicker. He shook the batteries inside, and the light grew powerful again but quickly began to fade a second time. As Emanuel passed through the entrance to the tunnel, his weak flashlight missed a spray-painted message on the wall: "*NO ZONE . . . NO O2!*"

After about thirty more steps, Emanuel's face turned ugly. He couldn't smell it. He couldn't see it. But his brain could certainly feel it. He stopped in his tracks, turning back in the direction he'd come from. Emanuel sprinted towards the end of the tunnel—but his motor functions began to fail him. He ran at an angle, adjacent to the wall, before tripping over his own legs and falling to the ground. He sat up, a bewildered expression across his face. His lungs and chest began to heave horribly. He dropped to the ground, and his flashlight fell into the sewer water below him, extinguishing.

Then Emanuel lay down to rest.

▪

At the aqueduct drain entrance underneath the FDR, at the base of the Queensboro Bridge, Stian Ziros crawled through mud. He'd managed to work his way out with a bullet hole in him. He reached Hector's motorcycle. He dragged himself on top of the bike using all of his effort.

A blinding light shined directly at him—

A man's loudspeaker-enhanced voice pierced deeply through Ziros' eardrums. "Arms out! On the ground!"

▪

A ring of cop cars was situated around the entrance to the hydra. Susan Herlihy stood behind one of the cars, holding a massive black shotgun about two times larger than her own forearm. She cradled the weapon of doom with menace, proving her worth in the land of the copman.

But Ziros wasn't one for following orders. He didn't put his arms out. Instead, he smiled. The skin of his face curled up unnaturally. He revved the motorcycle and he rocketed out of the entrance, careening directly towards the cops.

Susan watched the bike approaching. She dropped her arm a few inches and pulled the trigger. The shotgun bucked in her arms. The blast ricocheted in a deadly cone towards Ziros.

Their reflexes triggered by Susan's shot, all of the other cops opened up as well.

And Stian Ziros smashed into a police car in a hail of gunfire.

▪

In the belly of the beast, Jake Rivett pushed through the darkness until he emerged into another atrium-like zone. A massive, three-story-high aqueduct loomed above him. Jake couldn't find Rory anywhere. He raced around the border of the room before returning to the columns that held the aqueduct above. He finally noticed an old tunnel entrance with a wooden door—an ancient hydra carved into the door.

Jake pulled the small door open, fiddling with the lock. He reached down and grabbed some pebbles from the ground. He stuffed the natural detritus into the lock—to prevent it from latching behind him—and he stepped inside.

Jake could hear splashing ahead. He turned on his flashlight to see Rory running away from him.

"Rory, stop!" Jake yelled. Rory did not. Jake pulled the trigger on his pistol. The shot echoed through the tunnel, just missing Rory.

He crept slowly through the small chamber. He finally spied Rory twisting open an old rusted iron grate, one of the final outflow channels to the East River. "No Zone" graffiti was visible all around the pipe.

"Not another step!" Jake yelled. He trained his gun on Rory, who seemed nonplussed. "You got nowhere to go!" he screamed.

"Is that a fact? Because I know a little differently . . ."

"Don't move, dude. You don't have to do this. Come in with me."

Rory straightened. He placed the bag of cash on the ground and addressed Jake. "I'm not going back with you. If you want to stop me, you'll have to shoot me."

"You don't think I'll do my job?"

"I dunno. Is that what you were doing when you were out exploring with us every night? Is that what you're doing with Mona? She's just your job?"

Jake's gun hand quivered. "Maybe I did some things wrong. But you're a hypocrite too. You don't stand for exploring . . . Or friendship. You stand for yourself."

Rory shrugged. "I tried, Jake. I really did. Everyone thinks they're the hero of their own story. At least I'm going to be remembered." He held up the item he'd pulled from the mayor at the Waldorf. It was the shiny golden Rolex watch. "When Ronald Berg shook my hand and told me I'd never see my brother again, he was wearing this watch . . ." Rory slowly wrapped the watch around his own wrist. "I told you there's nothing in their city that I can't touch. It was right here, you know," Rory pointed towards the drain. "Down there. That's where they killed him."

"Step towards me," Jake said.

Rory obeyed and slowly took one step forward.

"Good. Keep coming."

"I do have a question," Rory asked. "How was that cop able to find us so fast?"

"Just some covert preparation for an overt operation," Jake said. He pulled out a small moist towelette from his back pocket. It was ripped halfway open. Inside was an electronic location transmitter about the size of a quarter. Jake grinned. "You were right. Always gotta have towelettes. They'll save your life."

Rory sighed. His body posture slouched as if he was giving up. But he suddenly crouched down and picked up an aluminum sled that had been sitting on the floor between the two men. "I told you I was gonna be remembered," Rory said. He stepped back, holding the sled. "I'm going to finish what Will started. Drainsled the hydra. All the way to the river . . ."

"Don't move! Don't! You don't have to become him in every single way!"

"I'm past that. I've transcended it all. I'm better now than Will ever was."

"No, Rory. You'll bust epic."

"I can beat it. I'll beat the hydra, and that's all anyone will ever talk about when they talk about me." Rory shook his head with a final smile. "Explore or die, noob."

Rory turned and dove into the tunnel. A loud and long shriek of adrenaline cascaded out of the hole and slowly faded to nothing.

"No!" Jake screamed. He raced to the entrance of the pipe, shining his flashlight as far as it would go. But Rory was already gone, drainsledding down the hydra.

■

It was like luge—in the dark. Only fragments and flickers of light were visible to Rory. The old tunnel twisted like a serpent scaled in oxidized copper. Without knowing exactly when they were coming, Rory managed to navigate one turn then another. The tunnel became quite narrow before descending into an almost vertical pitch. Rory picked up speed. He was now flying along at a hundred miles per hour. The extreme velocity reduced his vision to a transcendental blur.

A white light appeared ahead of Rory. It was a glowing pixel at first, but it expanded rapidly. It felt warm. It pulled him in like a magnet. It was somewhere between oblivion and destiny. This was his home. This was where he was supposed to be.

Rory disappeared into the pure whiteness—

THIRTY-ONE

JAKE RIVETT STUMBLED OUT OF the hydra and into the underpass where Ziros had met his demise. The entire street was crowded with cops and authorities of every possible stripe and denomination. It was like a convention of lawmen and lawwomen, all led by their conductor: Susan Herlihy. He approached her and Tony, holding the dusty black bag filled with cash. Susan stood up. She stepped so close to Jake that he swore that he could hear her heartbeat.

"What's that?" she asked.

"Listen, Susan . . ." Jake said. "You're the boss and ultimately it's your choice. But I'm telling you right now, Arthur Metropolis has Berg in his pocket. This is the proof. One million dollars in cash."

"I'm just looking at a bunch of money. Where's the connection?" Susan said.

"My testimony will hold up . . ."

"No way, Jake. You're not dead, but you're buried."

"The hell does that mean?"

"You're holding some cards now. I respect that. But we're still not putting you up on the stand. You get to come back into the office—after a nice long break."

"So you're not going to pursue Metropolis?"

Susan shrugged. "Police department is a million bucks richer, but I still don't have evidence that's irrefutable—that ain't from an Internal Affairs gold mine on a bender. It's not that we're not going to . . . It's that we cannot. Not yet. Not unless you can sweeten the pot or I find something down in those caves. Okay?" Susan leaned even closer to Jake. Her lips practically brushed against his ear. "You did a good job, Rivett. You should be thrilled. I hear you're in a band. Maybe I'll come to one of your shows one day." Susan clicked her heels and turned on a dime, heading back towards the crime scene investigators suiting up to go into the sewer system and begin to systematically collect evidence.

Jake glanced at Tony, who shrugged back.

"Thanks. For everything," Jake said as he handed the bag over to Tony, who held it with gloved hands like a precious jewel.

"As long as you let me keep track of you, kid, I'll keep doing it," Tony replied.

"You saved her. Not me."

"Everybody played a part. That's why it helps to be on a team . . ."

"Where's Mona?"

"There," Tony pointed. "I've never seen you stick your neck out for a lady like that before. Maybe you should take her home?"

Jake glanced over Tony's shoulder. Mona was sitting in the back of an ambulance, a few scrapes on her knees. "If she'll let me," Rivett replied.

"So you gonna stick with us? Or is this your fork in the road?"

"Can't let it go . . ." Jake said.

"Which side of the blue line?" Tony asked.

Jake thought about his response for a long time. It was an excellent question—prescient, even. "Both," Jake finally replied. "I'll be back, Tony. But I gotta take care of a few things first."

"You know where to find me."

Jake clapped Tony's shoulder as he passed and headed towards Mona.

"You okay?" he asked her.

She looked up at him, then away. "I'm alive," she said. "What's going to happen to Metropolis?" Mona asked.

"He'll go down."

"When?"

"I dunno . . . Whenever I'm done with him," Jake said.

"You're still in it to win it?"

"I'm a survivor," Jake said.

"Me too," Mona replied. "And thanks. As much as I fucking hate you right now and want to murder you in your sleep, I guess you're the reason I'm alive. But you know what I can't believe?"

"What?"

"How well you fit in with all of them."

"I am a cop," Jake said.

"Thought you were something different. Something special."

"I can't be both?"

"I don't know . . ."

"This isn't goodbye," Jake said. "Right?"

Mona didn't reply. Jake reached for her hand, which she did not offer. So he grabbed it. She gave him five seconds before she pulled away and jumped off the ambulance.

"I'll see you around, Eastie," she said.

THIRTY-TWO

HE WASN'T THE EYE OF the storm—he was the rage powering it. His anger crushed the stage. It came from mother and father. It came from Albany, from boarding school, from not fitting in—with anyone. He was too good for the criminals and too bad for the squares.

His spit flew across the dotted planet of the microphone. His purest state was now—always had been and always would be. The stage could take many forms, but Jake was a chameleon. He was just like Jack Castle. He was just like Hector Trizzo. He was just like Arthur Metropolis. He was just like Stian Ziros. He was just like . . . Susan. He was the ultimate cipher, only happy when not representing himself. Sometimes he didn't know if he knew himself either. He saw the outline, on occasion, but only when he was buried in the bright lights. Like right now.

The whole band was having the greatest night of their lives. It was an epic performance. He knew that scouts were in the audience—Schaub had informed him—but he couldn't spend any time worrying about it. He'd only truly mastered the words to "Out of the Mist" two nights before, but that didn't matter either. He was focused on his feelings alone—on what the lines meant as they spilled out. Every few lines, on the downbeat of the rhythm, he was able to lift his eyelids and gaze out into the crowd. He wanted to take them all in and understand what they were going through. He needed to make sure the ride was as good for them as it was for him. He saw the crowd rolling up and down like a gigantic Turkish rug under Aladdin—success. They were hypnotized. By him. By Jake Rivett.

The unsaid truth, the elephant on the stage, was that the band always knew where Jake's first priority lay. Jake was justice. He was the man who stood the line against evil—and dealt out retribution. Jake would never want to be anything except justice. It was his calling, and perhaps one of the main reasons that the band still remained on the billing of back burner venues like this instead of Madison Square Garden. Jake thrived onstage. But he *lived* undercover—where the ramifications were real, where the excitement was the difference between life and death. That's why he didn't look for the scouts. He didn't care who they were or what they had to say. This was his vacation; his life was on the streets. His life was formed by the experiences of each case, and his music would be nothing if it weren't for that.

As the song reached its crescendo, towards the end, Jake thought about where he was going next. Susan was going to rotate his world. A desk job.

The notion brought him down. Just for a moment—

Until he saw her face.

She was right there. Clear as day. He hadn't been looking for her, but his brain immediately locked onto her like a guided missile.

Mona stood in the middle of the crowd. He hadn't seen her in over a month, since the hydra. In all that time, she hadn't returned any of his calls or answered his texts. She no longer replied or commented on UrbEx. Her sister had slammed the door on Jake's face a handful of times. But after all that—she had come. She was there.

The song was ending. It was now or never. Jake finished off with an insane scream, his trademark: "YAYAYAYAAA." Then he grabbed the mic stand and vaulted directly into the surprised crowd—who half split and half tried to break his fall.

He regained his balance as the music died down. He pushed through the crowd to Mona. He'd worry about the rest later. For now, he had her.

THIRTY-THREE

IF MONA COULD TURN THE other cheek, maybe he could too. That's why he was in Albany—one of the reasons, at least. It had been almost five years since he'd seen them. But sometimes people who won't help you still need help from you. His father was still drinking. And his mother was still apologizing without saying a word. But they were also undeniably happy to see him. He appreciated it. It didn't wipe away the horrible remnants of the past, but their sincerity did mollify his hatred.

Their conversation that evening did not dive deep. He wasn't sure if it ever would, or could. Deep down inside, his mother and father were busy celebrating his return. But they couldn't mention that fact. They were the original Rivetts, after all—kings and queens of not saying what is felt. He knew his mom would never go there, and while his dad might at some point, Jake didn't necessarily want to know what Senior had to say. Dinner was fine. Jake regaled them with tales from his life—and boy, had he lived. He told them about making detective and his past cases. They'd seen him in the news, for the flash crash case a year before, and he described the ins and outs of that investigation. He even told them about the urban explorers and Metropolis, with certain details excluded. And he pitched his future to them. With Tony's support, he'd accepted Susan's "suggestion" and taken the desk job. He was still a detective, but when he returned he'd start reporting to One Police Plaza again. He was out of the rain.

At the end of dinner, as his mother was clearing the dishes, she cleared her throat and spoke. "I called you, because I loved you," she said.

"I know."

"But you never answered."

"I didn't know what to say. Can we just move on?"

"It did make me sad. But I also understood. I lived through it with you too," she said seriously and then brightened. "I knew this day would come. You had to fall into the darkness in order to see the light. We all did. I'm just happy you came out of it in the end."

"Me too," Jake said after a long pause. "But have you?"

She said nothing.

The truth was, while he was doing the right thing by visiting Albany, a feel-good reunion was not the primary reason he was there. Later that evening, once his mother was in bed and his father started snoring while seated on the chair in front of the television, Jake rose. He pulled a large package out of his weekender. He quietly exited the house and entered the garage. He found the keys to his father's pickup truck inside the exposed beams of the garage—where they always hung. He drove out into the night.

▪

Unbeknownst to anyone else in the entire world except for Mona, a few days earlier Jake had paid a visit to Midtown Manhattan. The Waldorf, to be exact. Of course they hadn't walked in the front door. He and Mona had entered in the only way they knew how—via infiltration. While Mona had remained at the subway level to ensure that Jake was covered, he'd risen up through the dumbwaiter channel. It was a three-hour climb. But sure enough, once he'd reached the penthouse level, the camera was still there. Jake had grabbed the device and descended as fast as possible.

He didn't need to spend any more time in the Waldorf than absolutely necessary. It was true that the criminal world held very little esteem for

Jake. He was done with it on both sides of his life. But he was also finished with the opposite—a gilded existence was not what he desired either. He didn't care about being the baddest guy in the room, nor the richest. He actually—finally—knew exactly what he wanted. It was standing at the bottom of the Waldorf's dumbwaiter channel, in the dark, with only a small headlamp to illuminate the surrounding environs. What he wanted was *her*.

▪

In his father's pickup in Albany, Jake drove through the sleepy city and kept going. He drove west—to the tiny town of Berne, New York. He didn't know Berne very well, but he had verified two specific facts regarding the small municipality. He'd spent some time researching the state police's surveillance systems in upstate New York. Their apparatus was spotty at best, and he was quite confident there were no networked cameras anywhere near Berne. Second, Berne had a post office.

He reached the tiny little hamlet. Just a main street, really. After he'd exited the pickup, he pulled his hat over his head and hustled towards a blue mailbox sitting placidly outside the post office. He pushed the package he'd brought from the city—addressed to the *New York Times*—into the mailbox. It landed in the empty box with a thud. Jake pivoted and rubbed his hands together in the cold. For once in his life, just for a moment, he was actually happy about the prospect of returning to the warm hearth of his family home.

He was there in Berne—and then he wasn't. No one saw him. No one heard him. No one even passed him on the road. When he arrived back home, his father was still asleep and unaware of his truck's role in Jake's mission. Not a soul except for Jake Rivett actually knew that in this moment, at this time, Jake Rivett was happy.

THIRTY-FOUR

ARTHUR METROPOLIS STOOD ON THE sixtieth floor of his unfinished skyscraper, consulting with his new head engineer. The last firm he'd hired had quit a week prior, citing the recent *New York Times* exposé.

The article had blown a ragged hole through Arthur's heart. Talk about a midlife crisis. For the first time in his life, Arthur Metropolis didn't know exactly what to say. His cell phone had thousands of missed calls from unknown numbers—but they weren't really unknown. They were members of the press, literally the world round, all attempting to get their claws into him on the record. It wasn't the well-researched, eloquent, and logical writing in the article that had damaged Arthur so much. It wasn't the fact that the weasel-ass hack had hidden behind an "anonymous" source and only jammed a warning down Arthur's throat at the last minute before he could defend himself at all. No. The worst part was the *photos*. The still frames. Right there—plastered across the front page of the newspaper—a huge bag of cash sitting between him and the mayor. It went without saying that Ronald Berg wasn't returning Arthur's calls either. Berg had his own personal cavalcade of horrors to weather at this moment. But New York was a tornado, and Arthur was twisting aimlessly in the center of it. At this point he was in survival mode. He was just trying to keep his head above water. But now he had lenders, subcontractors, and suppliers questioning his reputation and worse, his credit.

The Greeks were right. Reality has moments of comedy but is always a tragedy in the end. The last twenty years had taught Arthur that cash was king. Especially in New York, and specifically in real estate, there was nothing like a crisp dollar bill to get what you wanted. But all of the money in the world wasn't helping Arthur now. Because while cash could buy a reputation, that reputation could be sunk by an infinite number of other issues—like an article in the *New York Times* that positioned Arthur as a slumlord and corruptive influence on regional politics with employees running numerous criminal enterprises throughout the five boroughs. That's ultimately why Arthur was dealing with a second-rate engineer, gazing at a new budget 30 percent higher than the last one, and had heard from his counsel that all of the Whale Square permits had been retroactively yanked in favor of a community center. What a disgrace.

Arthur still had a lot of money in his bank accounts, but he felt like he did when he was a janitor. He felt poor. He felt helpless—he was very, very unhappy about his station in life. Actually, it was worse than when he was young and had nothing. Building something from nothing feels a hell of a lot better than watching one's empire tumble down to zilch. A person on the way up can climb incrementally—feeling their new muscles form. A soul on the way down is simply deflating, wildly, with no idea what they're going to look like when it's all finished.

Arthur stared out over the beast of Manhattan. "It's beautiful," he said.

"Excuse me, sir?" asked Anton, his new engineer.

"The view."

"I agree with you. Wholeheartedly. I just got word on the radio . . ."

"Yes?"

"Guess the city's here."

"Did you forget something?" Arthur asked, his face growing red and indignant.

"Don't think so. Truly. We'll just talk it out . . ."

"They want to ruin me," Arthur said.

"I'm sure it's just the inspectors. Let me talk to them."

Ahead of the two men, the yellow elevator rose and clanked as it locked into place. Arthur stared at the cage. Yes, it was filled with men from the "city." But they sure weren't inspectors. That was clear from the badge hanging from Dennis Fong's dress shirt—and the five cops standing behind him.

Fong stepped out of the elevator. "Hi there, Mr. Metropolis. I'd like to chat."

"Surely," Arthur said.

"At the station, sir . . ."

Arthur didn't step towards Fong. Instead, he coyly stepped back across the construction site. He tripped on a cage of rebar emerging from the cement pad of the floor and fell. His hands landed roughly on the surface. He pushed himself up. He saw the cops jogging towards him. He knew they weren't there to help. One of them was holding handcuffs, hard metal reflecting off the beautiful sunlight. He could hear something. It entered his eardrums, but his brain did not process it. He could not comprehend it.

"You're under arrest," they were saying.

But Arthur wasn't listening. He dusted off his Zegna suit. He kept retreating as the cops raced towards him. They were only a few feet away when he reached the end. A revelation washed over Arthur. No one was going to care about what happened next. Stian Ziros had been his best friend, and he was dead. The ladies—hey, at least Isabelle would come to the funeral. But she didn't really care. She didn't actually know him. He had made sure of that. They'd all found him at the top of the heap and they'd used him to keep themselves there too. Now they'd have to fight for their own food, shelter, and reputation. He didn't even have a will. The girls, the city, the banks, the tenants, the contractors—they'd probably rip themselves to shreds figuring out how to take all of his money.

When Arthur Metropolis stepped off the back of his tower, the last thing he thought about was how much effort he'd put into the suit he was wearing. It had taken approximately five fittings to master. He'd made sure to test out the fabric by hand before it was cut. The suit was fully canvassed, of course. It was an elegant and bespoke garment. It made him feel different than he really was. All of it had, and that was what this came down to. He'd used his money to hide reality, instead of building a new one. A man can hide, but one can never truly avoid his true self. Now, after all that work, his suit was going to be ruined. And so was he.

Arthur Metropolis floated through the air on the way down, a loud scream erupting from the inside of his lungs as he fell. It was supposed to be a fast descent, like a rollercoaster, but it felt like forever to him. And then it was over.

▪

At One Police Plaza, Jake sat at his new desk and kicked his feet up. Sick beats rolled through his headphones as he zoned out. There had been a few major benefits to reporting back to the main office for the first time in a year. The first was the view. The second was the fact that no one seemed to bother him. He wasn't sure if they'd forgotten what he could do —or were just afraid of him? He didn't know. But it didn't particularly bother Jake that they were treating him with kid gloves. Tony wouldn't be able to resist consulting with him soon. Maybe in a couple weeks, Susan might even return his phone calls. In the meantime, he would enjoy his sabbatical.

Jake didn't hear the knock on the door, but he caught the motion from the corner of his eye. Tony Villalon stood in the middle of Jake's office. His mouth was moving, which meant he was talking. But Jake still couldn't comprehend a word coming out because the music blaring into his eardrums was so loud. He slowly reduced the volume while continuing to nod at Tony.

"Crazy, isn't it," Tony was saying. "Case starts with a selfie. Got everyone else involved, but we never did find that selfie . . ."

"Sometimes where you think you're going? It's way different from where you end up," Jake replied.

"Yeah. Like in the *New York Times.*"

Classic Tony. Both his best friend on the force, even though neither of them would ever say that out loud, and the guy that most exasperated him. They each had a little of what the other one wanted. And right now, Jake realized, Tony wasn't there to talk about selfies. What Tony wanted was a confession.

"You know who I hate?" Tony continued. "Reporters. Been swattin' them away for three weeks now . . ."

"Agreed," Jake replied.

"That's what I thought. I mean, I figured if there was anyone in the world who'd agree with me, it'd be you. And that's not just because you hate on everyone. It's because they don't help. They just get in the way. Of course, they don't think so."

"Couldn't agree more," Jake grinned back.

"Fong's taking Arthur to the pen right now."

"Great," Jake replied.

"'Cause of the article . . ."

Jake nodded.

"It's . . ." Tony struggled to choose his words. "It's a real nice coincidence those letters came from a mailbox in Albany. Isn't that where your pops is?"

"I thought you hated reporters. Not sources."

"You're neither. You're a cop."

"And so are you, Tony. So why are you spending your time worrying about fuckin' over some little guy . . . who exposed a big bad who was screwing everyone?"

"Pretty eloquent."

"Answer the question."

"You first," Tony replied.

"You didn't ask me anything . . ."

"Did you leak the Metropolis video?" Tony asked Jake.

He really, really didn't want to lie to Tony. But another certitude of Rivett's existence was that his worldview was his constitution. Everyone who knew him knew that. Even Villalon. That's why Tony probably knew that Jake was about to lie to him, and he'd forgive Jake for it eventually. Jake did not always obey the law, and he didn't always uphold the law. What Jake Rivett did—which was the bravest stance of all—was do the right thing.

"I didn't leak it, Tony. That all?"

Tony stewed. "Just remember what I do for a paycheck," he finally said.

"Bust perps," Jake said. "Same as moi. What's up with Berg, by the way?"

"Susan's over there right now."

"Arresting him?"

"She wasn't exactly clear about that . . ."

"Why does she always need to be right in the center of everything?"

"Now that question, my dear Jake, is way above my pay grade . . ." Tony replied as he reached into his pocket. His cell phone was vibrating. He pulled it out, and his face immediately contracted into a pained expression.

"What?" Jake asked.

"Metropolis. He . . . he's dead." Tony read through his text. "He jumped, man. The bastard jumped off his own building."

THIRTY-FIVE

SUSAN HERLIHY SAT ACROSS FROM the mayor. Ronald Berg's personal lawyer, Mr. Rosen, was next to him.

"We were under the impression that this was just a conversation," Berg said.

"That's why you've got Rosen?" Susan replied.

"If you're planning on arresting the mayor, we'd like to do it in private. He can turn himself in during the middle of the night. I hope you'll consider that, for the sake of the stability . . . of the city," Rosen said.

"So you're the grim reaper? Where's Marks?" Berg asked her.

"Tom's in Washington. He's got an important meeting on a golf course with some conglomerate and its squids. Harris—or Northrop—or Carlyle. I forget. Listen, Ronald. I don't think you're a bad guy. But you can't be the mayor anymore," Susan said.

"I'm not going to the pen?" Berg asked.

"First, I'm going to ask your lapdog to leave."

"Excuse me, Mrs. Herlihy? That's entirely inappropriate," Rosen said.

"Okay," Susan proclaimed. She stood up and tapped her heels together. She yanked a pair of handcuffs out of her pocketbook and dangled them in front of Berg. "Then you can turn around, sir."

Berg glanced at his lawyer. "Leave," he commanded Rosen.

Rosen acquiesced.

"Tell me what I can do," Berg said. He peered up at Susan. He'd found her quite attractive when he first met her, but he was staring at a wraith now. None of her curves mattered. But the part he could not see—what was in her brain—was critical to his survival. Susan had that effect on most people. No one knew what they were dealing with. By the time they did, they were sprawled out on a couch, gazing up at her in submission and begging for mercy.

"If you resign today, I won't arrest you."

"How can you guarantee that?"

"I've run it past the DA . . . Now those photos are bullshit. Unbelievable. But besides that, we're not so solid. Can't connect all the dots. Can't prove the whole spider's web. You know the old phrase: 'If you're going to shoot the king, make sure you kill him.' So we're not ready to shoot yet. But if you don't resign? You can bet your ass we'll keep digging your grave."

"And you'll do this . . . just out of civic duty?"

"You're not the only one retiring. Marks is too. That's why he's in Washington. He's pitching his golden parachute. Here's what happens. You leave and make everyone happy. That means that your boy Green, the public advocate, gets to become mayor. And a few weeks later, the chief of police will be up for nomination."

"You want to be the commissioner. What if Green doesn't listen to me?"

"That's your problem. Let me put it this way. If I don't become chief? Every little last piece of evidence that I can possibly scrounge up is going directly to the DA's office with my strongest recommendation for prosecution . . ."

Berg grinned all silly at Susan. "It's not just police, is it, with you?"

"Excuse me?"

"You think this could be your office one day," Berg pronounced.

"Don't shortchange me," Susan Herlihy remarked. "Mayor's just the beginning. So, do we have a deal?"

THIRTY-SIX

SUNLIGHT BLASTED ACROSS THE NEON-blue sky—perfection. A large crowd was milling at Whale Square, complete with the requisite media presence. All the flacks were out in grand display, probably a bit resentful that their colleagues were racing across the city in rabid pursuit of the facts regarding Arthur Metropolis' untimely death. But here, now, was the community center's first shovel. That's what was happening at Whale Square this morning—why all of the custom suits were encircling a group of community organizers, local politicians and their aides, nonprofit regulars, well-meaning Manhattanites, and yes, even actual residents.

Jake drove a dark sedan to the ceremony. He still had the Ducati. The machine was a part of him. But he was in transition. In some ways, he was mourning his past life. He had been forced by the coffin of his work assignment and the love of one woman to say goodbye to a particular lifestyle, but that didn't mean it was all done. It just meant that he now showed up in a black Ford with a V8 under the hood. He parked in front of a set of police barriers and nodded at the two cops assigned to the event. They knew exactly who he was. For a guy with very few friends, Jake Rivett was more than household name. He was a legend.

Jake walked through the crowd in search of a particular group.

Eventually he found Adriana, Mona's sister—and her little nieces, Mari and Vicki. They locked eyes, and they hugged.

"I like your suit," Adriana said.

"Thanks. Still getting used to it. She's not here yet?" Jake asked.

"She's coming. She texted me."

A few moments later, Mona appeared in front of them, stepping through the crowd. She let loose a huge, ebullient smile when she saw Jake, and pulled him in for a hug and kiss.

"You're here!" she said.

"C'mon. You think I was going to miss it? Most exciting thing I'm going to do today . . ."

"Oh yeah?" Mona was scrambling through her purse for something, reaching into the crevices. "Take some pictures for me, babe? My camera's in there," she said as she handed her bag to Jake.

"You got it."

"I gotta go!" Mona ran towards the stage.

Jake reached into her bag and pulled out Mona's small digital camera.

"Can't believe my sister's gonna be up there with all the bigwigs," Adriana said.

"She's a special one," Jake said.

Jake's view was blocked by the football field of heads in front of him. He gazed around, searching for an acceptable vantage point. He quickly spotted a makeshift TV tower that had been erected in the back. Jake headed towards the tower. A lone cameraman sat atop, doing his duty. Jake climbed a ladder and pulled himself onto the platform.

"Ain't for spectators, buddy."

Jake flashed the badge attached his belt. "We can share."

The cameraman shut up.

Ahead of them, the ceremony was just beginning. A state representative presented at the microphone while two nonprofit executives and Mona stood with their hands sharing a giant shovel.

"Today is about the future. It is about the people of this neighborhood taking control of the place they call home—and helping everyone rise together."

Just a few seconds to go. Jake looked down at Mona's camera. He turned on the device but encountered an error: "No Memory Card." *Uh-oh*. He could hear the congresswoman wrapping her speech up. The groundbreaking was about to occur. Still holding Mona's purse, he scrambled through the pockets looking for a card.

"In just about two years, you will be looking at a climbing gym and basketball court on the east side of this property, multiple conference rooms and classrooms to the west—and a library in the middle. I must add one thing. Holding this shovel are three exceptional women. None of this would have been possible without the cooperation of our community leaders . . . "

Jake finally found what he was looking for—two small memory cards at the bottom of Mona's purse. He grabbed one and jammed it into the camera. The card's photos folder popped up immediately. There were a bunch of pictures of himself and Mona. Jake couldn't help himself. He quickly scanned backwards, checking out all of the images. At the end of the memory card was another folder labeled: "Imported Archive." Jake selected that folder.

A photograph displayed. It was Mona. She stood on top of a crane. A penthouse was below her, and she was flashing the upside down V sign at the camera—

The selfie.

He was staring at the selfie. The truth hit Jake like a sledgehammer. He was looking at the original sin. *Mona* was the explorer on the video surveillance. His mind was full of shock—and truthfully—awe.

"And to my left, we have Nancy Sloane, Rhonda Smith and . . . Mona Rosas representing the Friends of Unincorporated Brooklyn!"

Applause erupted. Jake scrambled to get the camera ready. *Click. Click. Click.* He snapped photos of Mona as she moved the shovel into the ground with the two other women. Then she released the shovel and waved at the crowd.

Jake zoomed in. A small diamond necklace glistened on Mona's neck. The diamonds formed the letter "M." He hadn't noticed it earlier. He definitely hadn't given it to her.

▪

Half an hour later, Rivett found Mona chatting with Adriana and the little girls.

"I'm really proud of you," Jake said.

"Ready to go to lunch?"

"Definitely," he answered.

They turned and walked across the lot. Jake pulled Mona closer to him. They kissed. "We've each done wrong," he said. "And that's okay. I just want to tell you that. I forgive you, because you forgave me—"

"Babe, what are you talking about?"

"Oh nothing." Jake paused for a long moment. "Just one question. Where'd you get that necklace?"

THE END

ENJOY *NEVER GO ALONE?*

Dear Reader:

More RIVETT is coming fast. Next time, he will be catapulted into events on the international stage. As usual, each book in the *Rivett* series is a thrilling standalone, but reading them all pays the most dividends. To stay up to date, sign up for my mailing list: **DenisonHatch.com/signup/**

Reviews are the lifeblood of an independent author. If you enjoyed *Never Go Alone* or *Flash Crash*, I would be grateful if you would post your review on Amazon, Goodreads, or any preferred site.

And most importantly, **thank you for reading** from Lookout Press and Denison Hatch!

GET THE **JAKE RIVETT** SERIES ON **AMAZON!**

Stay up-to-date with Denison's latest musings and news: **DenisonHatch.com/signup/**

ABOUT THE AUTHOR

Denison Hatch is a screenwriter and novelist based in Los Angeles. Although he lives in the proverbial desert now, he is originally from Delaware—land of rolling hills and DuPont gunpowder.

Denison has a number of feature and television projects in development, including his original screenplay, *Vanish Man*, which is set up at Lionsgate. A graduate of Cornell University, Denison lives with his wife and big dog in a little house in Hollywood.

Never Go Alone is the second novel in the *Jake Rivett* series.

GET THE **JAKE RIVETT** SERIES ON **AMAZON!**

Stay up-to-date with Denison's book announcements:
DenisonHatch.com/signup/